# HEART OF THE WORLD

## Cecelia Holland

Eric Flint's Ring of Fire PRESS

Sharing stories around the campfire since 1632

Cecelia Holland
Visit my website at www.thefiredrake.com

Printed in the United States of America

First Printing: Sep 2020
1632, Inc. Eric Flint's Ring of Fire Press

eBook ISBN-13 978-1-953034-05-2
Trade paperback ISBN-13 978-1-953034-06-9

# CONTENTS

Cecelia Holland

# CHAPTER 1

## Baghdad

Rikart braced his hands on the rail of the balcony, looking out. The City of Peace spread away before him in its orderly array, green with orchards and gardens. The blue stripe of the Great Canal crossed it like a sash. Among the packed houses a hundred minarets pointed up into the sky. A fringe of palm trees hid the walls of the Round City, on its hilltop at the center of Baghdad, but above the fronds the gold dome of the House of Wisdom shone like a rising sun, and beyond that the green dome of the Palace. The people moving through the streets seemed all one being, slowly flowing along through the markets and alleys, in and out of the buildings, the lifeblood of the city.

Rikart loved Baghdad. His mother had brought him here when he was ten years old, after his father died. He had grown up here, the greatest city in the world. Now a shadow was creeping over it. The sunlight still shone down clear and bright, but out beyond, where the city ended, the air churned with yellow dust. This had begun that morning in the north and the dust cloud was moving swiftly west and south and now stretched almost to the river on the southwest, turning the sun pale.

"You were right," the old man said, behind him. "They're here, after all."

Rikart kept back the anger in his throat. He said, "You've got to come with me. Now, before sundown."

"I can't." The Reb shook his head. His hands went to the sash of his robe. "I am too old. But you go. And you must take Dinah."

"You have to come," Rikart said. "You're why I came back here." He cast another look out over the city toward the dust. "You don't know what's going to happen next. The Caliph can't stop them. Nobody can stop them."

The old man said, "Swear to me you will save my daughter." He was untying his belt.

Rikart faced him, thinking he might carry the Reb away in his arms. He would bring Dinah to help him. He looked past the old man, the little room with all its books, the table in the middle piled with scrolls and papers, with maps and pens. This place of peace. "I'll talk to her. Get ready." He went in two long strides to the curtained door, and through to the next room.

This room was the highest in the house. On the stairs below the landing, two of the servants huddled, muttering. He went by them, going down, but before he came to the bottom of the stairs, Dinah had come out to meet him.

She was a tall girl, not pretty, with thick dark hair. Younger than Rikart was, maybe 17, she had managed her father's household since her mother died and she seemed older. She wore a married woman's headcloth and lately she had taken to holding her hand over her lower face when she talked to him, which he thought was ridiculous. She did it now, veiling herself, and she said, "What is this? Where is my father?"

"It's what I told you yesterday," he said. "The Mongols have come. We have to get out, now."

Behind him, on the stairs, the women wailed. Dinah said, "Look what you've done," and went by him to them.

He followed, ready to argue, but she was sending the two women off on chores. This made them happy and they left. Rikart caught her elbow. "Listen. Reb Moseh is refusing to go. We may have to force him."

She frowned at him. "How little you know my father." But then she turned her head, as if she heard something, and her face flattened. She went on up the stairs.

Rikart followed her. On the landing, he looked out the window toward the east, and saw there more of the dust boiling into the sky. He wondered if they had waited too long. Then from the next room Dinah let out a wail like a stab to the heart.

He went into the old man's room. The table was overturned. Where it had been, Reb Moseh was hanging from the beam, the sash of his robe wrapped around his neck. Dinah was clutching him, trying desperately to lift him up, off the pressure of the sash. She turned to Rikart. "Help me! Help me!" But the old man was dead.

* *

He said, "The river is our best chance. Meet me at the quay on the canal. I have a boat."

Dinah's face was slobbered with tears. He put an arm around her, holding her up on her feet. "He wanted you to escape. You have to try. Pack what you need. I'll be back." He hugged her against him; she smelled of lilac. Her body was slack against him. What would happen to her if they took her? He went on down the stairs to the door and out onto the little street.

He had not been here for years but this place was baked into his bones. He remembered everything, the warmth of the air, the peeling wall, the paving stones underfoot. The city was oddly quiet. He walked down to the canal. A boat full of watermelons was tied up at the quay. The sweet-seller who usually perched on this corner was gone. Someone called out from a house across the way and a shutter banged closed. He went down along the canal, past the edge of the Caliph's gardens, toward the Tigris. A dozen speckled peahens were pecking in the grass under the palm trees. He smelled jasmine and oranges.

He was planning this out as he went; they could go south on the river to Maniyyurah where he knew people. There were Jews in Maniyyurah who would take in Dinah. Where the canal came down to the river, he stood a moment, watching the boats as they went back and forth. The water shone in the afternoon light. A flat-bottomed riverboat slid out of the canal, wobbling in the tangled current, and started south. Down there, the bridge crawled with people crossing toward the west.

He went upstream a little way. Days before, when he first came back, he had hidden a riverboat on the bank, pulled it up high out of the water and buried it under palm fronds. He hauled it down to the river, fit the scull into its socket, and climbed in. The current took the boat down toward the canal again. Across the city, first one voice and then another and another took up the midafternoon call to prayer.

"God is greeeaat—" The long syllables quavered out.

Just above where the canal came boiling into the river he steered the boat to the bank, got out, and wading along the edge of the canal towed the boat up against the flow.

The call to prayer still hung in the air but somewhere far off, a thin whistle sounded. His hackles rose. A moment later he heard a distant crash. He did not see where what was struck. He bent to the work of pulling the boat against the river's flow.

The quay was just ahead. In the western sky, the dust and smoke climbed up over the setting sun; the light was yellow as sulfur. Dark against that, Dinah stood, with a crowd of other people. He had not reckoned for that. He should have known she would try to save them all. He turned to look over the boat. Maybe it could carry four people. He wrestled the long narrow boat into the lee of the quay.

At once Dinah was pushing people into it, two children, an old woman. Rikart held the gunwale to keep the boat from tipping under their weight. "They can't all go—there isn't enough room!"

She ignored him. She was handing in another child. Two more women waited—her maids. Rikart pulled his shirt off; it was warm for a winter's day. He tossed the shirt aside. The people sat in a line down the center of the boat, knees up, the children on laps, and Dinah got in.

Rikart climbed over the stern, took the scull, and pushed them out into the flow of the canal. Other boats rowed past them, pulling hard. Rikart held his boat in near the bank, where the rip would be less, and nudged them out through the mouth of the canal. With the scull he held the boat steady, feeling for the edge of the wave.

The Tigris was running full and the rip current caught them at once. The long narrow boat creaked. One of the women wailed, and they all clutched for the gunwales. Dinah began to sing, a high cheerful note, which calmed them. Rikart eased the boat along, riding the high side of the wave, steering out of the way of a big barge paddling hard for the east bank. All along the river between them and the bridge, boats thrashed along. Most were moving east. He thought that would not help them. He let the current take them on south. The sun had disappeared into the smeared dust of the sky. An early darkness came. The bridge spanned the river on its seven piers. Rikart steered them toward the space in the middle and leaned on the scull, holding the boat at the edge of the standing wave there, and they swooped on through the momentary darkness under the arch.

The old woman at the bow with Dinah let out a scream, but Dinah cheered, and so they all cheered. Rikart moved them back toward the west bank, where the river ran slower. The river curved to his right. Up there he saw the top of the old Al-Shams mosque, gold against the last light.

Now they were coming to the al-Mansur bridge. Beyond the long arched span, he knew, the river ran broader, out past the walls, past the mouth of the New Canal, out across the plain between the fields and gardens. He thought if they passed through this bridge, they would escape.

The bridge crawled with people. He steered the boat down toward the second arch. In the dark he could just make out the women and children huddled in the boat, clutching each other. Downriver a sudden burst of light shone. For an instant the bridge, outlined against the red light, was a creeping black line across the river.

Thin and far away, but coming closer, a thin shriek like a flock of piping birds reached his ears. He clenched his jaw. Too late. They were sweeping down toward the archway through the bridge, and then a roaring torrent of rocks hammered down out of the sky.

Almost overhead, the center span of the bridge collapsed, flinging people down as it went, and the river heaved and churned and the boat swung around. Rikart fell out. People bobbed in the water around him, dead, alive. He swam hard after the boat, which was drifting off sideways toward the bank; against the last pale sky he saw Dinah in the bow, the old woman hunched at her feet. The scull swung idle. The boat rocked in the violent water.

Rising out of the water ahead of him, a long arm seized hold of the boat. The old woman struck wildly at it and the boat tipped and rolled over.

The wash broke over Rikart and he swallowed greasy water. The current was dragging him off. He kicked out and his feet struck something floating behind him, something wooden. Not the boat. He could not see the boat. Heads floated in the water around him. He looked for Dinah. A canal opened in the bank here and in the back eddy above it, the boat was wallowing upside down. He swam to it, searching the water around him for Dinah. People screamed. A corpse floated beside the boat, the shirt full of air like a bubble over the water.

He pushed the boat ahead of him into the shallows. High overhead, the shrill shriek sounded again, high and coming closer. He sank down deeper into the water and a blazing red ball flew out of the dark and plunged into the middle of the Tigris. For an instant he saw nothing but the wash of light. Then the river out there began to burn and the whole sky turned blood red.

He smelled the hot oily smoke, the smell of sea coal. They were firing naftun. He thought, Baghdad is gone. He cast another broad look around him for Dinah, and then heard the whimpering under the boat.

He dove down, and came up beneath the overturned hull, into a pocket of air, dark as pitch. "Dinah," he said.

Then something leapt on him and clutched him, sobbing, wrapped itself around him. He pulled himself loose enough to grope over this body. Not Dinah, too small. He wrapped the screaming child in one arm and dove again, out and up to the surface of the river.

This was not wholly dark. Red flickering light streaked across the river, glittered on the waves, glowed in the rolling smoke just overhead. His feet struck the riverbed here, and he stood to his shoulders in the water and fought through the churning water his way up to the canal gate. In his arms the child was gagging and coughing. He heaved the body up on the bank beside the canal and pounded on its back to knock out the water. He could smell the fire burning on the scummy water. Another thunderous crash echoed out.

He went along the shore, looking out at the filthy, churning river. Cupping his hands around his mouth he screamed her name. Twenty feet off shore in a red patch of fire a body floated, burning. Not Dinah. Other things bobbed in the glow. The catapults whistled again, and he backed away, and down out of the sky came a rain of stuff that hit the water and burst into flames.

The child had followed him—a scrawny boy. Rikart said, "We have to get out of here." He put his hand on the boy's shoulder, pushing him back the way they had come. At the canal gate a stone stair went up the bank. "What's your name?"

The boy whispered, "Daud." He was shivering.

"Come with me. I know some people here." Rikart with a hand on his shoulder steered him into the city.

* *

Daud was nine, small for his age. He had no father. He had worked in Reb Moseh's house, carrying water, hauling wood, because his mother was the cook. Now his mother was gone. Everything was gone, except Rikart the Frank beside him in the dark.

He ran to keep up. They went on away from the burning river, along the street by the canal. The light from the river flickered around them, ahead of them. Rikart got him by the arm and pulled him back under the palm trees. Three horses galloped by them; the riders carried spears. Daud was wet to the bone, and cold. He thought of his mother. He had been reaching for her when the boat went over. He tore his mind away from that. They moved through the trees. In the square beyond that lots of people crowded around a mosque and the high drone of prayers sounded. Rikart went around the edge of the square, and down a lane. At a door in the stone wall he knocked.

His teeth chattering, Daud went in close against him, to the shelter of the wall. The door opened, letting out a shadowy lantern beam. A deep voice said, "Rik! I thought you had gone. Come in. Quick."

The Frank pushed Daud on ahead through the door. In the warmth and the light, he stood blinking. The men talked over his head.

"I thought you had escaped."

"I tried," Rikart's voice said. "They're sealing the city off, even on the river."

"Then you can join us. The Caliph has ordered me to gather the city guard. Tomorrow, by the will of God, we will save Baghdad."

"So the old fool has finally realized what this is that's happening." Rikart's voice cut.

"Yes, you were right. But now we have to save Baghdad, somehow."

That man was tall, stocky. Daud knew that the jewel on his turban meant something important: he was an amir, a soldier.

Rikart said, "There are a hundred thousand of them, Ra'is. They have machines. They have greasebombs. They won't let anybody live."

"If you're with me," the stocky man said steadily, "I can give you a sword. Otherwise, get out of my house."

Rikart flung his hands up. Daud saw he was angry. Rikart said, "Very well. Give me the sword."

The soldier struck him across the shoulder. "I knew you would stand up." He went across the room, and Rikart followed him, and Daud got up and went after. Through an archway they went into another room, smaller, where on the walls hung swords and shields.

"Nothing matters but the will of God," the soldier said. "Here, arm yourself."

Rikart took a sword from the wall, held it a moment, and put it down and took another. He looked around for Daud. The soldier had gone out.

"You can stay here."

"No," Daud said.

"They'll take care of you." Rikart balanced this sword a moment and laid it aside also, and looked back at the wall full of blades. "Better than I can."

"No, please," the boy said. He imagined another ripping away of everything, this time all. "I want to go with you."

The Frank turned and knelt down and put his hands on Daud's shoulders. "Boy. Listen to me. This is as far as you can go with me. Tomorrow we will go out to fight. You are too young to do that. You have to stay here." He gave the boy a little shake, his eyes fixed on Daud's. "You're lucky, little brother. Stay that way."

Another shake, and his tone changed. "You need some dry clothes," he said. He stood up, turning back to the arms on the wall. His gaze sharpened; he reached down into a chest below the swords, and took out a tunic of fine white cloth. He laid this on top of the chest and smoothed it with his hands; on the breast was a red cross, like a splash of blood. Rikart stroked his hands over it. Without looking up from it, he said, "Go ask for Umm Maryam, she will take care of you." Daud turned, wooden, and walked back to the next room.

* *

Rikart went into the garden, into the back where no one would see him, and standing with his face toward the wall, his feet apart, he stretched his arms straight out to either side like a cross. He did not pray. He had no one to pray to. His God had failed. The Muslims had won that war, and now in turn the Muslims would lose. He saw no sense in this. His arms began to ache but he held them outstretched. He thought of the old man hanging from the beam, of the bodies floating in the river. The boy, clinging to him, whom he could not save. The thin shriek of the catapults. His muscles were burning, his body shaking with the effort of holding his arms out. Some order in it teased the corner of his mind but he could not grasp it. Maybe he was unworthy of it. He lowered his arms to his sides.

\* \*

Something pounded in the distance, not coming closer, just a steady far off thud. Daud, leaning on the palm tree, thought he could feel the shudder of it through the tree's skin. Smoke drifted in the air even here at the heart of the Round City. He began to climb the tree, his hands on the boll, his feet walking up the slender trunk.

As he climbed higher he rose above the level of the wall around the palace, and he could see the hundreds of mounted men lined up on the pavement there. Rikart was one of them, somewhere. He looked for the white coat with its cross, in a sea of white coats. He swallowed a bitter taste in his mouth. Rikart had said he would take care of him and then had abandoned him. He climbed higher.

Now he could see the porch of the Caliph's Palace. On the balcony there a man in a big white turban was waving his arms and speaking. Now and then the crowd watching gave off spurts of loud noise. They thrust their arms into the air. The horses reared and danced. There were very many of them, he could not pick Rikart out among them.

His eyes stung. Rikart had cast him off.

Now a great shout went up from the army—"God is God! God is great—!"

All around the city, behind Daud and on either side and all over, other voices rose. "God is great!" as if the whole of Baghdad cheered. His heart swelled, part of this great power.

He put his cheek against the palm tree. God would save them. Rikart would come back a hero and Daud would go to him and they would be friends again. Brothers, as Rikart had said.

Now they were turning, the whole army, swiveling in place, still in their lines, and riding toward the gateway. In his plumed turban the amir led the way. "God is great!" all the people shouted, and Daud scurried down from the palm tree and ran around the side of the palace, toward the great street there.

Crowds packed the side of the street; he had to worm his way through them to get to where he could see. He squeezed in between two men shouting God's name. Down the broad pavement the mounted horsemen rode in their ranks, and the ground trembled under them. Daud let out a cheer. He saw Rikart, there in the first row, and waved, and ran along the edge of the street, keeping up. The roar of the crowd rolled like thunder. The horsemen waved their hands, and their horses capered, dancing, their eyes flashing. A girl darted out of the crowd and cast an armful of flowers in the way of the army. Daud cheered again, exalted. Ahead was the gate; he worked his way off through the crowd again, down to the wall, and up the stair along the wall to the parapet.

A boardwalk ran along the wall just below the top of the parapet and from here he could see, out there on the plain beyond the Canal, the whole long dusty mass of the enemy, an indistinct shifting cloud. People crowded in around him, so close he had trouble keeping his feet. The walk groaned under their weight. Everybody was jumping up and down, shouting and waving their fists. He leaned on the wall to keep his place. Below, the broad brown water of the New Canal flowed by, pent between the city wall and the high earthen dike.

The Southern Gate opened out here, leading over a bridge across the canal. As the army came out the gate they had to slow, narrow their ranks to four abreast, edge their way onto the bridge. The howling crowd urged them on.

And out there, even the enemy quailed at their approach. The dusty cloud was backing away, giving up the broad plain beyond the canal. They were afraid. Daud yelled and could not hear his own voice in the uproar. He beat his fists on the wall. The Caliph's army was crossing the bridge, was forming up its ranks on the far side. The Amir with his feathered turban held his arm up. In the screaming of the crowd Daud could hear nothing, but then the Amir dropped his arm.

The army charged forward, the front rank stretching out to either side, broad as a blade. Behind that the rest of the horsemen pushed up to fill the gaps. Their cloaks fluttered. The manes of their horses rippled like banners. They swung their lances down to level, and bolted across the level ground at the enemy, which was shrinking back, retreating.

Under Daud's feet the ground shook, slightly, and a low boom reached his ears.

He leaned across the wall, trying to pick Rikart out of the mass of charging men. Then someone near him wailed, and pointed, and he swung around—they all swung around—and saw, up beyond the bridge, the dike of the New Canal collapsing, and the water gushing through onto the plain.

The charging army wavered. Daud called out, sobbing. It was too late. The tide of water was sweeping down along the plain, flooding the low ground, cutting the horsemen off from the city. And now the cloud of the enemy was wheeling back, closing in. From all sides they pushed in against the Caliph's army, a dusty horde, a whirlwind, a storm. They filled the air with their arrows. The Caliph's army broke into bits, running men, running horses, and the enemy swarmed over them, and they were gone.

Around Daud the people sank down, their voices failed. A low moan rose from them. Daud was gasping for breath. A prickle of terror ran down his back. He wheeled around, and ran.

He kept running, his breath a fire in his lungs. He could hear screaming somewhere. Dust and smoke drifted in the air. He slowed, at last, exhausted, by the Caliph's Garden, and realized he was two streets down from Reb Moseh's house.

That steadied him, to know where he was. He ran down an alleyway and across a little bridge and came to the street, and there was the house where his mother worked. The high gate was closed, but he knew how to open it—push the bar there, then lean on the little wooden door set in the side of the barrier. He went into the courtyard, panting.

It was quiet. It was as if nothing had ever happened, except he saw no one else. He crossed the empty courtyard to the kitchen house, where his mother would be. She was not there. The kitchen maids were not there. The long room silent, cool, empty. Smelling of bad milk. The oven was cold. He went along the table; beneath that were baskets of fruit, of vegetables, and he took an apple and ate it. He could stay here. There was food here, and his mother would come back. He went out of the kitchen, across the courtyard again, to the main house.

That door was open. He went in. On the threshold he started to call out, but his own voice choked him.

He walked through the front room, the carpets neatly laid, the tables with their embroidered cloths. Nobody was there, but they would come back. The house was all ready for them. The silence was just for now. He would stay here and wait. At the foot of the steps he looked up. He had never been allowed to go there. He trembled to think of it. But he climbed the stair. The air grew warmer as he climbed. He could still smell smoke but only a little. He went up to the landing. The rooms opening off were empty. In one a loom stood, the beater still in the threads. A jug was turned over on the floor.

He went on, up the last flight, to Reb Moseh's room.

Before he pulled back the curtain a bad smell reached him. He stood on the threshold, and saw there on the floor the old man stretched out on his back, his hands folded on his chest. Flies buzzed around him. Daud's stomach clenched. He could not move. The old man's eyes were closed but if Daud moved surely the lids would fly open, Reb Moseh would look at him, would scold him. He whined in his throat. He could not stay. He had to go, he had to get out of here fast.

He went back downstairs, and back to the kitchen. Outside, as he was crossing the courtyard he could hear, again, the pound and crash of the catapults. In the kitchen he found one of his mother's marketing baskets and went around filling it with food, figs and apples, some flatbread, a cheese. He ate cheese as he went around, looking for anything else. He took a knife from the wall. In a jug he found water and washed down the last of the cheese.

He hauled the heavy basket back to the gate. He had to find somewhere to hide. To keep his stock of food. He would come back for a blanket. As he went out the gate to the street, a dozen boys pounced down on him.

He shouted. Went to his knees. They tore the basket out of his hands and knocked him flat. He dropped the knife. Someone kicked him. He bounded up to his feet, and they swung fists at him and battered him down again. While they were doing that one grabbed the basket and ran off, and the others chased him. He crept off a little on hands and knees. The knife lay before him on the pavement and he snatched it up. Getting to his feet, he raced away down the street.

* *

He walked, going nowhere, through an empty bazaar, the beggars gone, the rugs taken up and the displays, the shop doors shut. Beyond that, the rutted back street led him through orchards, between high walls. In a gateway a man with a sword leaned against the wall. When Daud came by, and slowed, the guard reached down for a stone at his feet, and Daud hurried off.

He saw a band of boys coming around the corner, and went the other way.

His stomach hurt with hunger. He was tired but if he tried to stop his legs soon drove him on again, urgent. The distant bang and crash of the war faded into the back of his mind. He thought of nothing but getting something to eat. He should have eaten more when he had had the chance. He trudged along, dreaming of food.

There were people in the street; as he passed, he looked, but he saw no face he knew.

A wavering voice called out overhead, and he twitched all over. Yearning, he turned that way. Old words came to him, blessing Mohammed who was calling him to God. He forgot most of the prayer, the words were always strange, not ordinary talk. He went in a gate. Other people everywhere, and he hung back. At the water fountain he waited for a chance to wash. Women and children were pushing one way, to the side of the courtyard, to another door into the mosque. He went in a tide of men through the main door.

The call to prayer went on above him. He thought, Mohammed, Prophet of God, blessings to you, give me something to eat.

They were calling the men to line up, inside the mosque. He sidled in along the doorway. There was no room, already hundreds of men filled the wide space, and now they were kneeling, all at once, a wave descending. He knelt down where he was, back in a corner.

Like a thunder, the voices rose, begging for salvation. He huddled against the wall, tired. The men around him bent and banged their foreheads on the floor and rose with their faces dripping blood. His stomach turned. He drew back as far as he could, and shut his eyes, and the giant voices rolled over him.

Then he was waking up, climbing up through sleep, a soft voice calling him.

"Daud. Daud."

He opened his eyes. The prayers were a rumble in his ears. Before him, smiling, was the long pale face of his master's daughter Dinah.

He sat up, making his obeisance, and she touched his face. "No need. How glad I am to see you. Here." She pressed a wooden cup into his hands. Warm. He lifted it to his lips and drank the hot meaty broth. She was looking into his eyes, still smiling. She said, "Be well, little man. Here." She leaned forward and kissed his forehead. "Be blessed." She went away, carrying more cups, a big jug.

He finished the broth before he ended his hunger. But he sat up now. He looked around for Dinah and saw her across the mosque, giving food to people. He took heart; he got up, went out to the courtyard, washed his hands and face in the fountain.

Out in the street, several men stood in a clump, talking in low voices. Their eyes followed him, suspicious. Daud went on down toward the canal and walked along the street there. The day before, it had been running nearly full but now it was only knee deep. At the foot of the next bridge was a man selling from a wagon, strings of onions and fruit and herbs. On either side a big man held a sword across his body. Several people stood before the wagon, ready to buy, and more coming all the time.

Daud hung back. No one seemed to notice him. He had nothing to buy with. Quickly he looked back at the canal. His mother had given him treats for catching fish. If he caught some fish, or turtles even, he might trade them. He went to the edge of the canal and slid down the side.

Made of fitted stones, the bank sloped easily at first but then turned steep, and he slipped and slid most of the way, grabbing for handholds on the rough wall. Halfway down the dry stone vanished under slick wet green weed, crusted with sand and shells. Yesterday that had been under water. He skidded through it, down into the ditch, his feet sinking into the muck and stones of the bottom. He began to work his way up the current, watching the water, looking for anything he could catch.

Ahead of him, something plopped into the water. Maybe he could sell frogs. Nobody ate frogs. The dark water flowed slowly along, bending over the waving floating carpet of the weedy bottom. A patch of scum floated toward him, evil smelling. He drew back, his stomach gripped. Looking up he saw the sky above him, a blue arch between the high walls of the canal, and then far off, up in the air, there came a sound that stood his hair on end, a thin distant shriek coming closer.

He scrambled toward the far wall. A little way down, a round hole opened in it, a culvert through to the next canal, and he made for that, struggling through the thigh-deep water. A crash of rocks shattered the air above him. The sound rocketed eerily around in the canal and another thundering downpour came and another, not into the canal, but striking just beyond, into the street. A few rocks bounced down into the canal and Daud reached the culvert and dove into it.

The sound boomed inside this space, stuffed his ears. He clutched his knees to his chest. A horrible smell reached him. Halfway down the tunnel a body lay on its back. His stomach rolled. He had to get away from that, and inched toward the opening, but then another barrage struck just outside the tunnel. Dust sprayed him. He shrank down. Whatever that was, behind him in the tunnel, it was dead. It wouldn't hurt him. Another crash and boom of rocks. He buried his face against his knees.

The rolling crash went on and on, long after, he thought, the stones stood falling. He went up to the edge of the tunnel and looked out. A heap of stones lay along the foot of the far wall. He sat there a long while, waiting for more, but no more happened.

He was thirsty. He crept down out of the tunnel and out along the canal. The water was murky, littered with new stones. Where the water ran clear he knelt to drink but before he could even dip his hand into the stream he saw a dead man lying face down a few feet away and he lurched backward, his heart racing.

He staggered on, crossed the canal beneath the bridge, and climbed up on the pier. At the top, he stood still for a moment, unable to move. The main barrage had struck here. The air was filmy with dust. Two men lay on the ground in front of him, battered to bloody rags. The wagon that had sold figs was half buried under rocks. He bolted, running as fast as he could past the bodies, dodging past another in the street. The screaming kept going on. He ran into the courtyard of the mosque, where the fountain had been.

The fountain was gone, lost under a pile of rocks, although the water still bubbled up through the rubble. Other dead people lay around the courtyard. A woman knelt by the gate sobbing a prayer. Dazed, Daud looked for the mosque, and could not find that either. Finally he realized that the wall still stood, but the dome was broken in like an eggshell.

Dinah, he thought, and for a moment could not think at all. He knelt down at the fountain, and drank the water. His hands were shaking and his stomach hurt. He went off again to the street, toward Reb Moseh's house. Little groups of people stood around the street, muttering ton each other. There was no litter of stones in the street here, so far inside the wall, Daud thought, this was out of range. He wound his way quickly through the thin crowds. Going by the Caliph's garden he smelled smoke and saw fires, back under the trees.

He found Reb Moseh's house, but someone else lived there, now. The gate was barred, the windows shuttered tight, even the balcony covered up. He walked back up the canal street. Night was coming. He could not stop shaking. There were people ahead of him at the bridge, already groping through the rubble for the vendor's goods, rummaging around the dead. They gave him piercing looks as he went by them.

He crossed over the bridge in the dark, going toward the wall. The streets here were battered with rocks but there were no people. He found a place out of the wind and slept. Every few moments, he woke, his body clenched like a fist.

* *

In the morning, going in close under the city wall, he climbed over a locked gate and into an enclosed courtyard. The whole compound had been bombarded and bits of rock strewed the courtyard and the roofs of the buildings were crushed in. He saw no bodies. These people had run away when the barrage started. He looked for a kitchen house, found a hall with ovens and tables, but no food. Somebody had already taken everything. An ewer, empty, on the floor.

Across the way was a bedroom, opening onto the courtyard. The roof had come down inside, burying most of it, but he uncovered cushions, finely stitched, and a blanket. He dragged these into an angle of the courtyard wall—he wanted to be outside, where he could run—and made a bed. His stomach ached with hunger. He took the ewer and went out through the ruins, over the gate again, to the canal, and filled the ewer with water. The canal was only a shallow stream here. Maybe the water was going away all over Baghdad. He had not thought of that. He remembered the dike breaking. Maybe soon even the canals would be empty. Sitting, exhausted, hungry, on his new bed, he faced the far wall, where there were rows of shelves, like Reb Moseh's book shelves. Some bits of pottery still on the shelves. He lay down, but he did not sleep; he fell to brooding.

After a long while he saw a huge rat crawl along the bottom shelf, pick its way through the debris of pots and stones to a hole in the wall, and go through.

Daud thought about that a while, and then he went over to the shelves. These were boards, held up on the wall with metal braces poked into the seams of the bricks. He felt over the shelf the rat had traveled. Some of the braces were loose and he worried the holes wider with his knife, so that the braces sagged. He loosened the braces on the shelf above that one. Taking out a board higher on the wall, he cut pieces of that and braced up the bottom shelf with them, where the rat had run, so it wouldn't come down too soon. Then he went around the courtyard and gathered all the stones he could, and piled them on the upper shelf until it groaned.

He went off, morose. It would not work, it was too obvious, the rat would see. He wandered off into the broken rooms. Under the dust the floors were tiled. In a tiny back room he found a lamp full of oil and a striker to light it. He thought these people had been rich, even more than Reb Moseh. In a corner there was a chest, full of clothes. The smallest thobe was too big for him. He fingered the embroidery around the neck, the fine shell buttons. Finally he cut off the bottom and put the garment on over his head, rolling up the sleeves.

Beside an overturned bed he found a little wooden boat. Some boy had lived here, a boy like him. He wondered where that boy was now. His stomach hurt from hunger. Dark was coming. He had found nothing to eat for days. Finally he went back to his space, curled up against the wall, and went to sleep.

The crash brought him up out of his sleep like a shocked bird. It was dark. The moon shone down into the courtyard in a silver flood but the far wall was in a pit of shadow. Something was shrieking, across the way, venting tiny screams. He pulled out his knife and went toward the noise, which got higher, the thing knowing he was coming. In the dark he plunged the knife down toward the noise. The blade skidded on something hard and down into something soft, and he twisted and hauled at it, both hands on the hilt, until the tiny screaming had stopped.

He dug the great furry stinking body up out of the rocks and carried it out to the moonlight. He would make a fire. He had the lamp, with the striker, and there was plenty of wood. He cut the rat open, the warm, smoking coils of its guts spilling silvery as fish into the moonlight. Without thinking he knew what he was going for. He had seen his mother cut up chickens. He knew the heart, the nugget of blood and meat, at the middle of this. He found that, and put it into his mouth, still hot with life, and gnashed it down, delicious, before he skinned the rest of the rat and cooked the flesh over his fire.

* *

The city wall made the back wall of his compound, and climbing up onto the roof he could see all the way to the Basra Gate with its two towers. He sat there a while, watching. The Mongol army was off on the far side of the plain. Between them and the wall the flood from the dike had drained away into glassy puddles. On this mucky groundsat monstrous wooden frames, like horrible birds, with necks that craned back and forth, and spat rocks. The rocks were crashing into the Basra Gate. He could see people swarming all over the top of the gate, but now someone was running toward him along the parapet, wailing.

"Lost! Lost, we're lost—

Up there, the near gate tower suddenly swayed like a dancer. Daud drew in a hard breath. Dust rose all around the tower, and the stonework collapsed into the dust.

Then from the great churning mass of the Mongol army, on the plain outside the wall, there went up such a howl that Daud himself yelled out. They were charging in toward the new gap in the wall, a raging torrent, as if the whole plain dissolved into horsemen. He wheeled around and jumped down to the courtyard.

Outside, on the street, people streamed by him, running, a woman with children clinging to her, a man pushing a two-wheeled cart. Boys raced past. A tiny child stumbled along, alone, its face twisted with sobs. He went to the edge of the canal. People rushed along the street on the far side, too, but down at the bridge he saw a knot of men.

Pushing against the current of the fleeing crowd, he went on down the street and across the bridge. On the far side some people were throwing up a barricade across it; they had already hauled a boat up to block the bridge's mouth. Daud jumped over it. "I'll help—Let me help—" They were piling on chunks of rock and he hauled stones, and with two other men found a wagon abandoned down the street, all together lifted it, and heaved it on top, to make a  wall as high as his head.

The man on the far side of the wagon gave him a quick, hard look and a nod and a wave. Daud followed him across the street, where a big woman in an apron was chopping with an axe at a wooden gate in the wall.

More people ran to join them. The uproar at the Basra Gate was swelling toward them like a rolling wave. They heaved up chunks of wood onto the barricade and the first of the Mongols appeared at the far end of the bridge, small men on little horses.

The woman with the axe let out a scream. She wore no headcloth, no veil. Her great breasts swelled the cloth above her apron. The rest of them surged up beside her, Daud one of them, his hands full of rocks. He scrambled up onto the wagon on top of the wall. The Mongols charged across the narrow bridge, and everybody at the barricade hurled rocks.

One of the horses went down. Daud screamed in triumph, waving his arms in the air, and then the woman was shoving him down into the shelter of the barricade. The air whistled. Something struck the broken gate right before him, and the tip of an arrow like a wicked snake head poked through, still shivering. The woman, panting beside him, said, "Watch out for that."

She reared up again, the axe canted back over her shoulder, and he rose beside her. Just over the barricade three horses were scrambling up on the boat part of the wall, smashing the thin hull strakes with their hoofs. The little horse closest to Daud, lunging forward, drove one foreleg through the boat, and hung there, stuck. The rider jumped off. Under the round metal cap of his helmet the slits of eyes looked out from a flat inhuman face, dark as leather. The woman struck his knees out from under him with her axe. On Daud's other side an old man swung a long Mameluke sword and blood sprayed across the barricade. Daud could reach nothing with his club and the horsemen were falling back now. He shrank down away from another wave of arrows. The woman flung an arm around him.

"Noble boy! Noble boy!"

The ground under them shook. He pushed himself up to see a dozen horsemen charge toward the barricade. He reared up to meet them. With the chunk of wood he laid around him as they surged onto the broken wood. Something struck him from behind and he fell.

*  *  *  *

He struggled awake. He was dead, he thought. He could not move and around him was only darkness. His neck hurt. He turned his head a little, to ease that. He was not dead, he was pinned down under something. Under a body, he thought, still warm, spread above him like a blanket. He could hear screaming, but there was always screaming. He slept again.

He woke when the weight above him suddenly shifted away, and the light shone in, and someone grabbed him. He struck out with his fists. Above him a face goggled, a thin Baghdadi face, not Mongol. "This one's alive!" he backed away, his hands up. "I didn't mean—I didn't—" He went away, quickly, following some others down the street.

Daud sat up, still heavy with sleep. Beside him lay the woman with the axe, her face sliced in half, her apron sodden with blood. He felt the ground shake under him and flung himself down again into the shelter of the body.

A stream of horsemen galloped by him. He heard a whoop; they had caught the looters. Daud lifted his head slightly, looking around.

Down the street a tight knot of horsemen was striking down with swords at something in their midst. Closer, three dead people lay on their backs. Across the canal, he heard a crash, and twisted to see; a string of Mongols rode along the row of gated houses there, and at each gate, two men with axes smashed it in.

Another band of horsemen raced across the bridge, carrying torches. They passed within arm's length of him and galloped off down the street.

Daud crept back down among the bodies and the wreckage of the barricade. He knew where he was; the bridge was just below him, its footing only a few yards away. He had hidden there before. He wormed his way along, sliding past the woman with the axe. She still had the axe clutched in her hand and he thought of taking it. It belonged to her. He crawled under a section of the broken gate to the edge of the bridge, and waited there a long while. He could see most of the two streets here, one on either side of the canal, and they were full of people and horses. Two buildings were on fire. Just across the way from him, a man on the rooftop flung a body over the edge, which twisted and screamed down into the canal. Down the way, smoke began to rise from the roof of a house.

The canal had run dry, but down the middle of it now a little stream began to flow, a dark trickle. He had a momentary idea of the whole city bleeding. The air smelled bitter.

Shimmering red, the sun was sinking down into a haze of smoke and dust. He lowered himself feet first down the side of the bridge platform, got a foothold on the structure underneath, and swung down into the close space between the span and the bank of the canal. The bridge shook overhead, more people passing over it, they stopped in a pounding of hoofs and a sharp exchange of orders, and then suddenly the rest of the barricade was showering down over the side of the bridge into the canal. The bloody woman fell by him, splayed out, the axe still in her hand.

He huddled in the dark, his arms around his knees, all the long night. Up and down the canal, fires bloomed. The coppery light flickered along the canal wall, now and then dimmed in rolling dark smoke. The smoke made him gag, reeking of burnt meat.

In the morning, he went along under the bridge and along the side of the canal. There was no water in the stream bed but there were puddles of blood . He went through another culvert and into the canal that went by Reb Moseh's street. Even before he came up to the street he saw smoke and the flicker of a fire and heard the flames crackle. The Caliph's garden was burning. In the street before him a woman's body lay, stripped naked. A sword stuck up between her legs. He went quickly along the side of the street, keeping close to the wall. The clatter of hoofbeats behind him warned him to duck into a gateway. A stream of horsemen went by him; they rode right over the body in the street. One of them in passing pulled out the sword.

Pressed to the wall of the gateway arch, he turned to look inside. The house was still smoking, inside its brick walls. Its hollow windows gaped, its door only a hole to a black emptiness. His stomach heaved. In the burnt ash and char that lay thick as a blanket on the courtyard he saw the outlines of bodies.

Somewhere a woman screamed, "No—Please, no—"

He went on through the street. The flames from the big trees in the Caliph's garden were crinkling the air and embers and ash floated by him. He stepped over things in the street that he did not look at. He did not look into the gateways. At the corner he stood and looked across at the wreckage of Reb Moseh's house and knew it only by the wall, the last thing standing.

In the next street he heard a crash, and a howl of voices, and he walked the other way.

There was no water. The canals dry, the fountains dry. He went toward the Tigris. In a little garden tucked behind a wall, where rocks had smashed the trees, he found water in a basin. He rummaged through the broken trees and found oranges. He heard someone coming and went back over the wall again, and down a long narrow arcade into a bazaar. On the far side of the little courtyard, while he was eating the oranges, he noticed the arcade he had just come through, a stretch of shelf along the wall. The roof beyond was tilted, and all the fallen rocks had rolled down onto the top of the arcade, which groaned on its buckling wooden posts.

He went along this, looking at it. Picking up a chunk of wood he swung it at a post, and the wood cracked and part of the roof sagged abruptly.

He went back out to the canal street again. The smoke was rolling thick along the street, and he had to go a good way along the street to find any Mongols. He heard the howling ahead, and looking in a gateway saw three or four men inside, still on their horses, hammering at a door with poles.

He picked up a rock and threw it at them, threw another when they turned, and took off running back the way he had come. They came whooping after him. In the smoke he slowed a little, to make sure he did not lose them, and they came charging after him, yipping like dogs. He dodged into the arcade and they followed. In the narrow space the horses collided, grunting, only a few yards behind him. He ran along. Not caring if he fell, he shoved at the columns as he passed and smashed into the last one shoulder first, drove it out into the courtyard, and the roof came down with a long rumbling roar.

He got to his feet in the courtyard. The falling roof and the rocks on top were burying the three horsemen. He could heard whimpering, and under the heap of stones something thrashed and more stones fell and then the crying stopped. He went closer. He saw, among the dusty stones, a horse's tail, a limp hand. He went on down the arcade toward the gate.

The last rider had nearly escaped. At the end of the arcade he sat to his waist in a pile of rocks, his back to the wall, his horse crumpled under him. Dust covered him, his skin and hair grey as a tombstone. Blood leaked from his head, from his ears and his mouth and nose, bright against the grey dust. His eyes glistened. He looked across the narrow distance at Daud, and their eyes met. Daud did nothing, said nothing. He watched the shining eyes dull into stones. After a while, Daud went back out to the street, toward the little garden, to gather more nuts, but the Mongols had been there in the meantime and the place was torched.

* *

He stood on the roof of his compound, a while later, and looked out over Baghdad. The air was grimy. In columns like trees, in long filmy veils, the smoke lay all over the city. There were no real trees. There was nothing green left. The wreckage of the houses stretched out before him like a desert. Above the broken roofs the smoke gathered, and the wind caught it and blew it away.

Where he had walked on the roof his footprints showed black in the pale ash.

The Caliph's palace still stood, out in the middle of the city, but the domes were broken in. The House of Wisdom was a blackened husk. Nothing moved in Baghdad. It was dead, it was empty.

In the distance, the yellow dust cloud of the Mongols was drifting away. They had been marching out all morning. They hadn't even wanted Baghdad, only to destroy it, and now they were going somewhere else.

He got down off the wall. Crossing the bridge, he went to the Basra Gate. One of the towers had come down in a tumble of rock and the other leaned like an old woman. As Daud got nearer, birds rose up from the ruin in a cloud. The guards had defended Baghdad until they all died, and they remained, rotting in the new sun, already half-eaten. The stench made his stomach heave. He walked among the dead and out to the road, and crossed over to the plain beyond. One foot after the other, he walked along the road.

* *

He was lying on his face in the road. He could not remember falling. The heat on his back. His eyes were full of dust. His mouth. The ground under him trembled. Something was coming. He could not move out of the way.

Something touched him. He could not open his eyes. He was lifted up. A cool wet rag passed over his face, he gasped, trying to lap at the wetness, and he blinked his eyes open, saw a beard, two dark eyes. Smiling. A flask came to his lips. He gulped at the taste, sweet and mild, of milk. He opened his throat and let it pour down into him and flood him. The man lifted him up again. He sank down into a close space with woven sides. A basket. The warm rank shaggy smell of an animal enveloped him. A moment later the basket was rocking along, carrying him along. He slept.

Cecelia Holland

# CHAPTER 2

## In The Ordu of the Il-Khan

Dinah ached, her whole body a single burning pain, her bottom half ripped and ruined. Lying on the hard ground in the dark she shivered, thinking she might be pregnant. Some horror growing in her.

No matter. They would kill her soon. They would kill them all soon.

She had always been the one to care for others. She had always had that power. Now she needed care and no one. No one.

She cried, lying on the ground. Around her, the others cried. On the far side of the room a woman called out, "No—No—"

It was not happening now. It had happened before, outside. They would kill them all soon. She had seen them killing all the people, even the children. The babies. Broken like loaves of bread.

She had lost her mind then, gone mad, or partway died, she remembered nothing, only waking, here in the dark among so many others. Her body throbbed. Torn open. No seed could flourish there. Pray to God no seed would take there.

She cried again, hopeless, wanting to die.

Instead they came and made her stand up. Short men, stocky, narrow eyes. Skin like leather. One nudged her. "Hey. Christian? Christian?" He poked her breast, laughing. "Christian?" She plodded on, uncaring now, it was not her body now.

Then hands pushed a cup of water into her hands. She grunted. The inside of her mouth puckered. She had not known how thirsty she was. She lifted the cup and drank.

She was outside, in a street. Smoke drifted by her. The wall before her was broken in. With a dozen other women she stood on the pavement, with horsemen all around her.

The hands took the cup. The man behind them gave her a bowl full of a tasteless gruel.

They were all eating. The other women. She saw their rags and clutched at her own dress, torn from the waist down. Stiff with dried blood against her legs. Their hair wild and frizzy, and she lifted her hand to her hair, matted and crusted with dirt.

A short brown man on a horse rode in among them. "Listen to me! All you women. You are spared because you are Christian. The Khatun Dokaz herself has gone before her lord the Khan and begged for your lives. Thank God for this."

Dinah shivered. He was looking straight at her as he said this. She said, "I am not Christian."

The horsemen were moving them all toward the gate, herding them along like sheep. The man before her shifted his horse to block Dinah's way. "Someone said you were, or you would not be here." He spoke stilted Arabic. In his broad dark face his teeth suddenly gleamed. "Maybe better you are, so?"

She said, "I am not a Christian." She was crying again. That was all she had left. She would not lie to save her life. She said, "I am a Jew."

He said something under his breath in his own language. The horse sidestepped, restless, the other women were filing off, and the countless riders all around them, out the broken gate. She thought, I will not leave Baghdad. Die here. She felt comfort in that.

The Mongol rider said, "I'm tired of killing people. I say you are a Christian. Go with them." He reined his horse around and rode away.

* *

They trudged on after the army, their little band of women among hundreds moving, masses of people and animals going on across the plain. There were seventeen of them, a few young girls, one old woman, the rest of middle years. The horses ahead of them kicked up a dust that yellowed the sun. After them came a train of carts. Dinah thought they were crossing fields, put under for the winter, but nothing grew here now. The ground beaten to flour. They came to a canal and had to wade it. The carts took longer to get across and fell behind them. Horsemen trotted busily up and down, swerving past them, but paid no heed to them, except to bring water and food.

The other women watched her. One said, "She's not one of us. You heard her."

"Jew."

She pretended not to hear them but the skin crawled on the back of her neck. The Mongols brought them bowls and a jug, and she licked her lips, hungry.

"Jew."

She stood back. They were passing the jug, full of the thin clear stuff the Mongols drank, that tasted like sour milk. She waited until they were all done, and sipped up the little left in the bottom.

That night they slept on the ground. Before dawn the horsemen roused them up and started them off again. Soon after the old woman sat down where she stood, and they all walked on and left her there.

Dinah turned to look over her shoulder; in the dust the woman was a disappearing lump on the plain behind them. She thought, I could do that. Escape like that.

The Mongols fed them all more of the sour milk, bread, a handful of figs. She thought of Persephone, but she ate it all.

The days blended together. A horseman brought her a blanket—she thought he might be the same man who had talked to her in the ruins, young, a round face, high cheekbones, slits for eyes. The other women would not let her eat with them. One shoved her away and another threw stones at her.

The flat ground was rising, and ahead, hills lifted from it, long ridges like waves  they walked along the valley between them. During the day she wrapped her blanket around her like a skirt and at night she curled up beneath it. The other women spat at her. They tried to keep her from getting any food at all.

They came out of the valley onto a broad grassland, stretching off long to the horizon. From the height of the pass she looked out to what seemed the edge of the world. Great herds of horses grazed on it but the enormous sky made them seem little. There were no clouds. The wind ruffled along the hillsides, turning over the grass in waves.

A dozen riders came up to the women, and with their horses herded them all together, as if they were sheep. Dinah hung back, wary of the other women, until a horse struck her from behind and bumped her forward into their midst.

The tall woman wheeled and slapped her. She turned to the horsemen and shouted in Arabic, "Take her away! She is not one of us, you heard her—the dirty Jew! Take her away!"

The horse behind her brushed up against her again. She turned, trying to escape, and the rider got her by the arm and hoisted her like a child up in front of him. He slung her across his saddlebows, face down. She clutched at the air, at the horse, at the stirrup by her shoulder, and the horse bounded forward and she was sailing off along with it, the grass sweeping by her, a foot from her nose.

They stopped, abruptly, in front of a round tent. The Mongol lifted Dinah by the arms and slid her down feet first to the ground. He shouted something; his horse backed a few steps away from her. It was that same boy, she thought, who had first spoken to her in the church.

In front of the tent was a two-wheeled cart. Three women stood there, their arms full of cloth and boxes, staring at them. When the Mongol boy shouted again, one turned, set her load of boxes down, and came up toward Dinah.

Dinah backed away; she could not stop herself. The woman stopped. She spoke to the Mongol, who answered her with a shrug and some words. Turning back to Dinah, she said something in another language, and then, suddenly, in Arabic, "You want water? To wash."

Dinah's mouth fell open. She said, "Yes, please."

The Mongol boy galloped off. The woman—lanky, a lean face, a gap between her front teeth—brought out a basin of water. The other two were younger, maybe her daughters. They stood watching her; when she looked up one smiled and nodded and made sweeping motions toward her face. Dinah set the basin on the tail of the cart. Bending over it, she washed her face, and the water turned to mud.

They brought more. She washed down through a crust of dirt, to the sunburnt skin of face and arms, and then—with a glance at the women watching her—she peeled off the rags of her dress. Her underthings were gone. She washed her body, her legs.

They brought more water, and some cloths. She washed between her legs, the blood caked on her thighs, everything still sore.

They brought her leggings of thin leather, and a long coat, blue, with a front that crossed one side over the other and buttoned on the shoulder. The gap-toothed woman said, "Sit down, here," and sat behind her and took a comb to Dinah's hair.

The comb stuck in her hair. One of the daughters murmured. The mother muttered to herself. Dinah could see the comb full of broken hair. Finally the woman got up and went to the cart.

She came back with shears, and Dinah cried out, "No!" and put her hands to her head. Under her fingers a mass of filthy straw. One daughter seized her wrists and held them out in front of her, and the other gripped her head by the ears.

It was terrible; it was like the other time, when they held her, and she thrashed and screamed and wept. They kept her fast. They cut her hair off, and let her go, and she sat there panting.

The gap-toothed woman said, "You are done, now. Be calm."

Dinah wiped her cheeks with her fingers. She touched her head, the hair stubbled like a beard. She said, "I will never be done. It will never be done." Her breath came short; a scream gathered down in her throat.

The gap-toothed woman shrugged. "Your hair will grow back."

Dinah ran her hand again over the burr of her skull. The scream never came up. The woman brought her some of the sour milk to drink. She sat and watched while they went back to unpacking the cart. They took everything into the round tent, boxes, bowls and pans, stacks of cloth, rugs.

Being clean was astonishing. Dinah's skin felt soft and new as a baby's. Drowsy, she was half asleep when the Mongol rider came back.

He rode in among them; he spoke to them from the saddle. She could not remember seeing him ever off his horse. He turned to her, and said, "Stand up."

She stood, moving away as she did. He nodded. "Good. You look much better." He spoke to the other women in a laughing way, and they bowed and he gave them something from his belt pouch. He turned to Dinah.

"Come with me." He kicked loose a stirrup and bent down, one arm out.

She saw he meant her to get on behind him. She slid her hands behind her. "Where?"

"To see my mother," he said. "Now, come on, nice as you look now, I don't want to muss you up getting you there."

She was afraid; she looked around as if somehow she might be able to escape. They were all watching her. She remembered them cutting her hair, the hands gripping her wrists and her head, and how she could not fight back then. And so not now. She gathered herself, went up to him, and took his arm, and tried to put her foot into the stirrup. He swung her up behind him, and before she was settled the horse galloped off.

She held onto his belt with both hands, jouncing painfully on the back of the saddle, but almost at once they were slowing down, coming up to another tent. He dropped her down on her feet, and for once dismounted from his horse.

The tent was a great circular wall made of heavy cloth, with a pointed top. It was much bigger than the one where she had bathed, and she saw it had a kind of floor under it laid down of wooden planks. People bustled around it. Some were unloading carts and carrying goods into the tent but many were just standing around. They wore coats like her new coat, but of fine shining fabric; they had fur hats on their heads. When her Mongol came after her, they burst forward toward him from all sides, everyone shouting.

"Noyon! Nikola! Noyon!"

He tramped through them, got her by the elbow, and steered her forward, through the door of the tent. Inside, he stopped a moment, still holding on to her, and said, "I am Nikola. You are—"

She swallowed. She wanted not to tell him, but she did not want to lie. She looked away. "Dinah."

He muttered at her, but she was looking around her now. She stepped into a wide round dim space. The noise from outside died away. Rugs covered the floor of the tent, like a bazaar. The space was open, with only a few thin columns for the roof. In the middle of the room in a hearth of iron were red glowing coals. Nikola nudged her onward, through people carrying in boxes and cloth to either side of the big room. A soft light filtered down through the cloth roof, mellow as honey. Nikola pushed her on across the room, across the soft cushions of the rugs, around the hearth.

In that space was a low table, with, she saw, astonished, a crucifix on it. Behind that, almost to the tent wall, stood an empty chair. Someone put a table down beside it. Two men struggled setting up a folding screen behind it.

The table, the column holding up the roof, the chair were all carved into intricate patterns. As she went by the column she saw in the carvings the glimmer of gold. One hand on her arm, Nikola forced her forward, toward the chair. The men with the screen stood up straight suddenly, and the man with the table also, and toward them all came a woman.

Dinah stopped. The woman was no taller than she was but facing her Dinah felt much smaller. Pale eyes in a dark face. Her coat was sleek as spider silk, lined with fur. On her head a fur cap. Her ears were rimmed and ringed with gold and around her neck were chains of gold. She stood with her head thrown back, as if she looked far off. Then she was turning toward Nikola, and he gave her first a sweeping bow and then embraced her, and Dinah saw this was his mother.

He said, "Girl, this is the Khatun Dokaz." He spoke to his mother in another language, but Dinah heard her name.

She bowed. The Khatun said, "My son tells me you are a Jew."

Her heart clenched. Now they would murder her. She lifted her face, eye to eye with the Mongol woman, and said, "Yes."

"The Great Shaman began as a Jew. You are a favored people. I am honored to have you among us. Come and talk to me."

Dinah went loose limbed. The Khatun waved Nikola away. She turned to the carved wooden chair and sat down. Dinah did not move. She pressed her hands together. The three-paneled screen behind the chair was painted with birds. Beside the chair was the small table, the top a shining panel of wood inlaid with loops and curls of gold. Someone brought over a gold tray with a pitcher and some cups and set it carefully on the table. There was a little chest next to the pitcher. Beside that, a tiny brazier on its own metal feet. Dinah looked back wonderingly toward the woman in the chair, who smiled at her. The chair itself was carved and figured with metal and with jewels. Set into the high back was a silver medallion—she saw at once it was a map of the world.

"Idrisi," she said. "That is Idrisi's map."

"It is." The Khatun leaned toward her. "You recognize it? Tell me your name again." She spoke slowly, carefully, as if the language were new to her.

Dinah cleared her throat. She wondered what she should say. "My name is Dinah, my lady. My father was Reb Moseh ben Maimon, of Baghdad—"

When she said that, suddenly, her heart burst, and she began to weep, not for herself, nor even her father, but for Baghdad, gone to dust. She put her hands to her face.

"Ah, well," the Khatun said. "Come sit down. Tell me why you are crying." With her hand she drew Dinah forward. Beside the big chair was a stool, and Dinah sank down on it.

"You ruined my city," Dinah said. She was gushing with tears. Everything she had suffered poured out of her. "You destroyed us."

"This happened," the Khatun said. Her hand lay on Dinah's shoulder; her fingers pressed and kneaded, as if she would push her into another shape. "And you have been hurt and you have lost all. We did this to you. You see only that we destroy. But we are bringing in a greater world. We must wipe away the old world first, to bring the new. We are gathering all the peoples of the world together again, as we were meant to be, under the most high God, as the earth lies under the sky."

Dinah lifted her head, astonished. The Khatun smiled at her. Her hand shifted to Dinah's cheek. "You are welcome here. You are my guest."

Dinah lowered her head. She could not think this into anything straight. She felt suddenly exhausted. The Khatun touched her again, soft.

"Your father was a rebbe—was he a scholar?"

"There were thousands of scholars in Baghdad."

"And he was one?"

She sighed. "Yes."

"And you are a scholar? You recognized Idrisi's map. You speak Arabic. What else?"

Dinah blinked at her. "Hebrew. Some Farsi."

"Can you read?"

"Some. Hebrew."

"Can you read Latin? Can you read this?" The Khatun reached down to the table and took something from the floor beside it, and held it out.

Dinah took this up, a scroll of reed-paper. Black ink marks crossed it, lines and circles, and she could make nothing of it for a moment, until part of a word swam up at her, and she saw the marks as letters of the Latin alphabet. "Frere," she said. "This is French."

She began to weep again, tears trickling down her cheeks. The Khatun took her by the chin and turned her face up.

"Why are you crying now?"

"You murdered him," Dinah said bitterly. "Him I knew who spoke French." She rubbed at her eyes.

The Khatun patted her cheek. "Ah, poor thing."

Dinah turned her face away. This kindness gave her nothing to defy. Across a space covered with rugs Nikola stood watching her. The Khatun took the scroll out of her lax grip.

"You have endured much, and yet you live. You interest me. You will stay here, I shall find you some duties. Now share chah with me."

With her finger she beckoned over a stout woman in a long shining gown.

This woman went to the little table. She poured water from the ewer into a cup, and set the cup on the brazier. After a moment it was bubbling, and the servant emptied it quickly into another cup, filled it again, and set that on the brazier. When this cup was boiling, she dumped out the water in the second cup, filled it again with the fresh boiled water, and opened the little chest.

A heap of dry leaves filled it. A wonderful aroma escaped it. The servant sprinkled several of the leaves on the water, and from the table took a round of wood and fit it over the top of the cup.

Dinah murmured. The Khatun said, "I learned to drink this in the east, when my lord and I were there for the kuriltai." She spoke as if she and Dinah had known each other for years. There seemed no space between them, as if they were old friends. The servant was going through the whole process with a second cup. When she was done, she took the wooden lid from the first, and kneeling down held the cup out with both hands to the Khatun.

Dokaz stood; she took the cup, held it up to the sky, then to right and left, then toward the ground, and then back and forth. She sat again, and sipped up the steaming drink. "Aaah," she said. "The eyelids of God, the Han call this."

The servant gave Dinah the second cup with far less ceremony. Dinah held it, uncertain. She thought briefly again of Persephone, but the delicious smell filled her nose and made her mouth water. She lifted the cup. It was hot, almost too hot to drink, and she sipped cautiously. The savor flowed over her tongue. She felt suddenly warm and happy. Looking to the Khatun, standing there above her, she smiled.

\* \*

The women had one side of the big tent, and the men the other. At night they slept on mats on the floor. During the day they sat and gossiped and waited to be told what to do.

They took the rugs out into the sun, shook them, beat them, and brought them in again. They kept the fire going in the iron hearth, carrying in dried dung to fuel it. They took food here and there. Dinah obeyed. They gave her a broom and she swept. They gave her a bucket and she went for water. The work was steady but easy. She felt light, hollow, an empty skin. Everything she knew was gone, the household she had managed, the father who had ordered her life, the city that had contained her. She had nothing to hold onto. She watched the other women, and did what they did, stood waiting to be fed, used a certain part of the latrine. Slept on the floor.

She learned words. The tent was a ger, the clear fermented milk was airaq. Nikola was a noyon. Thank you, please. She learned names, like Jun, the big breasted woman who gave them all orders. Tulla, slight and pretty, who could speak some Arabic.

There was a baby, which they brought to her often; he cried a lot, even with his honeytit to suck on. His mother had died.

Tulla said, "He die too, alas. So be it." She patted Dinah's shoulder and said something in Mongol.

But Dinah loved to hold him, to have something, anyway, to care for. She took him outside, to the edge of the platform, in the sun.

The camp spread out around her. On either side of this ger was another, just as big, and around them all a little open ground, like a dry moat. Beyond that the gers crowded the long slope as far as she could see. Once she thought it must have been grassland but now the ground was beaten to dust. She sat with the baby in the sun, sang to him as he cried, and lifted her head into the warmth.

He slept, after a while. Cradling him in her crossed legs, she leaned down past the edge of the board floor and smoothed the dust with her hand. With her finger she traced letters in the dust. Some other children came out of the ger, the little girl and two boys. One of the boys was the Khatun's youngest son, Nikola's brother. This gave him nothing with the other boy, who was bigger and picked on him. They both went off quickly toward the horses in the open ground. The little girl came over to Dinah and sat down.

She said something, which Dinah thought meant, What are you doing?

Dinah said, "I'm trying to write, khatun."

The little girl giggled. She probably didn't understand but she liked being called by the honored word. She leaned on Dinah and watched, and Dinah drew the letters of the Latin script in the dust with her finger.

She remembered how Dokaz had reacted when she recognized the French. If she could remember this, she could find some favor. Once, she had studied this. Her father had often needed help with his library, and she had learned to read the titles of scrolls and books in the Hebrew and the Latin scripts. She thought the Latin letters had some order but she had no idea what it was. The Hebrew script began with Aleph and so she put the Latin A first, and slowly she remembered others, and said their sounds, and drew them in the dust.

The little girl beside her moved closer. Dinah looked over; the child was drawing in the dust, looking carefully at what Dinah did, and copying it.

Dinah laughed, and hugged her. The child shrugged her off and she drew away.

She had fourteen letters in the dust when Nikola came.

He rode up on a spotted horse, without saddle or bridle, which nonetheless came straight beside his mother's ger door and then stopped. He slid off, and the horse wandered over toward the other horses, in the open ground, where the two little boys were trying to scale their legs. Nikola came over beside Dinah and sank down on his heels.

"Your hair is getting longer," he said, and reached out toward her head.

She pulled back away from him, and he lowered his hand. He looked down at the dust. "What are you doing?"

She stared down at her hands in her lap; she cradled the baby. Her heart was pounding. She did not dare look at him, or he might try to touch her again.

She said, unsteadily, "This is lettering. An alphabet. But not all yet."

He frowned at it. "You know this. That's good. But—for me—" He put his hand down in the dust and swept all her letters away. "Tell me what is west of here. You knew Idrisi's map, my mother said. Make me a map."

She stifled down a rush of anger. She reminded herself she did not own the dust. The baby was waking anyway and she found his sap and gave it to him.

She said, "I am not all so sure where we are now. Here is Baghdad." She remembered all the maps she had seen of the trade routes east and west. "Here is Damascus, and here is the edge of the sea, and here is Constantinople." She drew the straight vertical shoreline of the Middle Sea, and made dots in the dust for the cities. "Here is Cairo." The baby was howling; he had soaked himself, and needed tending. She started up. Nikola got her by the arm and pulled her down again.

She swallowed. Her arm burned where he had touched her. He said, "There is—somewhere—a golden city."

Startled, Dinah gave a shaky little laugh. "What?"

"The city of Jesus? Sah-lem."

"Jerusalem," Dinah said.

"Ah, then it is a real place."

"Not made of gold," Dinah said.

"How do you know? Have you been there?"

"No," she said, with another shaky laugh. Nothing was made of gold; Baghdad itself had been only stone.

"So." He smiled at her.

She said, "Very well." She looked down at the map. She did not want to tell him where the Holy City was. She made a random dot. "There is Jerusalem. Now. Answer me, then. What is a shaman?"

"Someone who goes between here and—" He nodded up, toward the sky. "She said that? She means Jesus. He hung himself on a sacred tree so that he could reach the overworld. That's what shamans do."

That was not how Dinah understood Jesus. She got up, holding the baby. "I have to take care of him."

She went back into the ger; Nikola followed her. As she went through the door of the ger, his hand brushed her backside. She licked her lips. If he attacked her she could not stop him. She took the baby back over to the corner where they kept his fresh clothes.

* *

Ever since they moved off onto this part of the steppe, Dokaz had been expecting some message from the Mongols in the north, and when an emissary came, she had him brought before her right away.

He was one of Berke's sons, harsh and coarse; the north wind made them so. He stood in front of her, in the middle of the ger, and said, "The Khan of the Golden Ordu has sent me to tell you to stay out of our pastures."

She sat straight in her chair. The blocks under it put her at eye level with him. She said, "This grass is not yours. We have rights here, and we are here, and you are not."

He bared his teeth at her. Put his hands on his belt. "The Great Khan, praise to his name, gave all west of the River of the Chumash to Jochi, the eldest son--"

Dokaz spat to her left. "Jochi was not his son."

Berke's son bridled up. She glared into his eyes, her jaw set, and waited for him to speak.

He said, finally, "That is not material. The Great Khan accepted the lord Jochi. And left him all this pasture which you are now treading on."

"West of the Chumash. North of the Sea of the Georgians. "

"Do not make us settle this in the old way."

She held still a moment, her mind hot. She considered coming forth with a threat of her own. Just words. She said, "The Khakhan has sent us here to do his will, the Khakhan, the Lord of the World, even of you."

The emissary pulled his lips back from his teeth again. "Do not make us settle this in the old way." He turned on his heel, with no courtesy, and walked out, his men following him.

She leaned back in the chair and put her feet on the stool. Nothing ever ended. This was an old sin that kept causing trouble. Before he became the Great Khan, Temujin was just another young man with a handful of followers. When a greater man's army attacked his camp, he fled, leaving his young wife behind. After a year he got Bortai back, but she was with child, after all that time in the ger of his enemy. Temujin owned the child as his, because what had come on his wife was through his fault. He named him Jochi, the guest. Now a generation later , a hundred days' ride away, the name still fell like a rock in to the soup.

She did not think Berke Khan would attack them here. Temujin's bequest to his eldest son had included vast territory but no Mongol army. Berke commanded a dozen tumans, good men, steppe men; with them he and his father had beaten the Rus, the people west of the Chumash, who were very many, and rich, subduing them as far as Rum itself. But they were not Mongols. In her mind she went through the meeting she had just had, so that when Hulegu came she could tell him exactly what was said. But she did not think Berke would attack them and she would say that also.

* *

Dinah fed the baby milk and honey, rocked him and sang to him, and he seemed happier. She had him now all the time. At night he slept in the hollow of her body. During the day she carried him everywhere. When the khatun's leftovers come down to the women, she mushed up bits of meat and poked them into his mouth. The other women were glad to have him off their hands and patted her and nodded.

She learned more words, help, and where, and the colors red and blue. She learned that the name they had told her for the baby was just the word for baby. She began to call him Moseh. Only in her mind at first. When the other women bounded onto horses and rode off to the lake, she climbed on a horse and jounced along with them. They swam in the lake, taking turns standing watch to keep the men away. When she took off her clothes her arms and hands were brown, but above the elbow so white the other women laughed.

Dokaz sent her with Jun to the bazaar to buy chah, and she went with the baby on her hip.

The bazaar was on the flat ground, in among the gers, a row of stalls and awnings and people selling things. Most of these people were not Mongol. Dinah drifted along past the stalls, heaps of figs and apples, nuts, jars of honey. A tinker, mending pots, selling them. Jun whispered something, and drew her toward a tray of little jewels.

"Oh, they're beautiful."

These were crosses, necklaces and earrings, mostly silver, or at least silver looking, with chips of glittering stones. Jun moved on soon but Dinah stayed, poking among them, looking for something Jewish. The merchant was watching her narrowly and she stepped back, embarrassed, and then in the stall behind him, behind a screen, someone called to him.

The merchant turned and answered, and they were speaking French.

She hovered, listening. She got some of it. She went back to the counter, and the merchant swung back to her.

She said, stumbling, "Je vuv-veux menorah? Shofar?"

He looked at her as if she were witless. She had said it wrong. "Ah," he said. "Une Menorah." Leaning on the article. He leaned toward her and rattled off some words.

She got the gist of it; he was asking if she were Jewish, and she said, "Ah, oui." And tried again. "Je suis—"Oh God, she had forgotten the word for servant—"une femme de la Khatun."

The merchant was entering into the spirit of this; he leaned on the counter, and spoke slowly and carefully, broadly smiling the while. They talked back and forth. Then another customer came to his counter and he waved his hands at Dinah, shooing her off, and went to sell something. She walked down the lane of the bazaar after Jun, who was in the little crowd listening to a man play a kind of lute, and took her along to buy the chah.

Thereafter she went by the bazaar as often and she could, and she stopped by that merchant's stall and they spoke in French.

* *

She was in the ger, laying down a rug, when there was a stir and a shout and the door thrown back, and a man came in. Everybody in the ger at once stood straight and still, and Dinah, as always, did as they did.

From the other end of the ger Dokaz strode, and as she came on she sang, in a high joyous voice. The man stopped inside the door; he was not tall, but square, solid. He flung aside his hat. His long black moustaches hung down to his chest and his eyes gleamed pale in his sun-darkened face. Other men crowded in behind him, going to one side of the ger. Dokaz came up face to face with him and bowed to him, and he bowed. She held out her arms, palms up. Their eyes locked. He stretched forth his arms over hers, and they both leaned forward and touched their noses first to one cheek and then the other. They straightened, still holding each other, and they both bowed again, several times. Then they walked together through the ger to the back, and disappeared behind the painted screen.

Beside her, Jun muttered, "Hulegu, the Il-Khan. The grandson of—" She gestured up. Dinah had seen there was someone they would not name, who was not, she thought, Jesus. But their Jesus was different from the one she had learned of, not the son of god, not god at all. Jun nudged her. Around them the other women were moving eagerly into the middle of the ger. "Come along," Jun said. "Now are the gifts."

"Gifts."

They all crowded together into the center of the ger, around the hearth, and by the altar, and suddenly all around her they were calling out.

"Welcome home, father Hulegu! Welcome home from the hunt!"

Whistles and cheers followed this. The Il-Khan came out from behind the screen again. Dinah saw again how stout he was, how he walked as if he owned the earth. He came up before the ger's welcoming people.

He bowed. They all bowed, Dinah among them.

He said, "Pleased am I to be back among my children, the people of my heart. Kitboqa!"

Two men came up, carrying a rug rolled up. They unrolled it on the ground between the servants and the Khan, and on it was a great heap of gold and silver and ribbons and tassels and little bowls and cups. The Khan bowed again, and all the people bowed. Then the Khan went back behind the screen and the officers who had brought up the rug stood beside it, and one by one each of the ger's people went up and received something.

Dinah went up last, her eyes lowered. All she saw of the tall man by the rug was his hand, holding out a silver coin.

She went back to the women's side of the ger, and Jun came up at once. "Let me see."

Dinah showed her the coin. "Why is this?"

"The Khan took this all in a raid, and he shares it with us all, least to greatest, because that is our way." Jun held up a little brass bell, which tinkled. "All I got was this. Maybe Kitboqa has his eyes on you."

Dinah held the coin out. "Do you want it?"

Jun burst into a smile, took the coin, and gave Dinah the bell. Dinah rang it softly; she thought the baby would like it: better than the coin.

* *

Hulegu, who missed nothing, said, "Who is this popeyed girl with the odd hair?"

Dokaz was helping him get out of his deel, which he had worn for days, riding, and which stank. She said, "My Jew. Nikola found her among the people brought out of Baghdad. She is a clever bit, I think she will be very useful. Where did you go?" She took the filthy stinking coat out to the opening by the screen, where someone could take it away to clean, or maybe just burn, and bring another one.

He sat down on the low bed, yawning. "I went south, to the salt, to see what was there."

"And what was there?" She came back, and he pulled her onto his lap and they wrapped their arms around each other.

"Cities, ready to surrender." He stroked her hair. "They have much, so much. In the harbor at Basra there were ships from beyond the salt, and goods piled on the shore. Mongke will be pleased."

She leaned against him. They had loved each other since they were children, long before they married, when he had come to her clan to court her older sister. Her older sister now lived somewhere else. He had other women sometimes but between them there was perfect trust. She had never needed another man. "Then we'll go down there next?"

"No. those places are already yielding, and there are bigger prizes to the west. Damascus. Cairo." He was sliding her clothes away, his hands searching, but he yawned again; tired, he would want only to sleep in her arms. He said, drowsy, "Whatever lies to the west." They lay down together.

* *

The baby Moseh fattened, and sat up. She taught him to clap hands, and they sang together, sitting in the sun. Then Jun too would sometimes sing, and Tulla, the four of them sitting out before the ger spilling out music. Jun sang in an eerie voice, high and low at once.

They were working harder. With Hulegu there the place was much busier. His officers came in and out, in and out, tracking the place full of dust. One day they all were suddenly put to packing up. Everything in the ger had to go into boxes, and the boxes outside to an unending row of carts. The men lashed rows of carts together, side by side, front to back, into a great square on wheels, and all the ger's people, and many others besides, gathered around the tent and lifted it up into the air and set it down on top of the square. Then rows of horses drew it slowly away over the treeless plain, rocking and swaying above the trampled ground like a cloud fallen to earth.

The people went along after it. Jun offered Dinah a horse but she wanted to walk; the ger was going so slowly she could easily keep up. She walked up to one side, out of the dust, Moseh on her hip.

She heard a horse coming up behind her, and turned her head. Startled, she saw one of Hulegu's chief men. He dismounted and walked along beside her, leading his horse.

He was tall, and not Mongol: a broad, high-cheekboned face, light skinned. He stared at the baby Moseh a moment.

"Who is this one's father?"

She hugged the baby closer, like armor. "I don't know. His mother died. He is an orphan."

His face slackened; he looked away a moment. She picked up her step, looking around for Jun and the others.

He said, "Your name is Dinah." He drawled the a, as the Mongols all did.

"Yes," she said.

"I am Kitboqa," he said. "I am great in the Il-Khan's favor."

"I've noticed that," she said. She saw how he puffed himself up as he spoke, throwing his chest out, making himself bigger.

He said, "I have my own ger."

She saw now where this was going. She held the baby snugly against her. "I am happy with the Khatun Dokaz."

"She has said I might have you."

"I am happy where I am," she said, again, but her throat went dry. Moseh sensed this, and gripped her sleeve with both fists. Tilting his head back, he gave Kitboqa a dark look.

He said, "You need not come with me now." Turning to his horse, he gathered up his reins. He gave her a quick look up and down. "Later," he said, and bounded into his saddle and rode off.

She watched him go, her skin creeping. The baby called out, "Ama-mama—" And pulled on her sleeve. She held him tight, and turning forward again she walked quickly, to catch up to the ger.

* *

Around midday, Hulegu galloped up to Dokaz, who was riding along out of the dust; he had been all morning going around talking to his soldiers. She sent a woman to bring airaq and figs, which she knew he lusted for. He sent his men away with a look, and she sent the women off with another look, and they rode along stirrup to stirrup, sipping from the leather flask and sharing the figs.

"Did you think about what I told you—about Berke?"

Hulegu shrugged. "He knows what I am doing here. If he thinks he can sneak up on me from behind, he will, the cur. But I don't see anything to do about it until he moves."

"He's an old man," she said. "He will do nothing. But his sons might."

"What ails this pop-eyed woman of yours? She turned down Kitboqa."

Dokaz snorted at him. "He's got no charms, Kitboqa. Not for women, anyway."

"What's wrong with him? He' s a tuman commander. His father was some kind of chieftain."

"I don't like him much either." She thought Kitboqa smiled at those above him, and snarled at those below. "You give him a lot of power."

"I'm thinking over the horizon. I won't have all these Mongol tumans here forever, Mongke will need them, or Kubilai. I want a Turk commander I can trust, because those are the men I'm going to have."

Dokaz thought this over. Hulegu was right, she knew; she admired his broad sense of this. Still, she disliked Kitboqa, if only because her sons did. And he was a rude man. She said, "I wonder why that one."

"He's clever and he's brave. We have to get the best out of every man we have," he said. "Let every man think he could be Temujin."

She nodded. He saw Kitboqa in a different way, maybe better than she did. She said, "Do you want me to talk to Dinah?"

"He's broody over her. Yes." Hulegu shrugged. "I suppose, if she doesn't want him, there's no way to force her. Unless, you know, she is really a slave."

"She is my guest," Dokaz said, sharp. She saw a use for Dinah. "I do not hold my guests as slaves."

His teeth flashed behind his moustaches. He said, "You are always the north star to me." He leaned forward and sniffed her cheek.

\* \* \* \*

They stopped before nightfall, but only to camp; they would go on in the morning. The ger's women spread out beds in the open and made a fire, but Hulegu did not come. Nor Dokaz; Dinah kept an eye out for her, as the night settled down, and the firelight made a little room in the great darkness. She lay down to sleep but she could not sleep. She kept thinking of Kitboqa, and her body felt stiff as a corpse. She imagined it all broken, down there, the channels of her body hanging loose, like the roots of an uprooted tree.

Then suddenly in the dawn light, she was jolting awake. The others stirred around her; she got up, rolled her bed and stowed it, got the baby some gruel to eat. Already the ger was starting off on its great slow passage over the earth, its peak swaying back and forth.

Then Dokaz rode in among them all, on the gaudy brown and white horse she loved.

"Soon," she cried. "Take heart, all of you, we've found a good place with a lot of water. Ha!" Abruptly she bent down and scooped Moseh out of Dinah's arms and set him on the saddlebow before her. "What a little man!"

Dinah clung, desperate, to the side of the horse. "Khatun—" Moseh was gaping around, his eyes wide and his mouth open, his fists full of the horse's mane.

"Oh, what a mother," Dokaz said. She jiggled the baby up and down. "I won't keep him. Isn't he the ugly little thing, though?" She beamed down at Dinah.

"Khatun—" Dinah gulped. Now she could speak about the other thing but she was suddenly afraid. She gave Dokaz a pleading look. "Kitboqa—"

"Ah," Dokaz said. She nudged her horse to walk along, still holding onto the baby with one hand, but the other she stretched down to Dinah. "Here, now. He has no knack for wooing, I expect."

"I want to stay with you," Dinah said.

Dokaz' fingers squeezed her shoulder. "He would make you a good husband. You would have a household, your own children. You should consider this. You won't be a girl forever."

Dinah gulped, and looked away. "I—What happened to me, I—" She brought her gaze back to Dokaz. "Maybe I can never have children."

The Khatun's face drooped, and she reached out one hand to her. "Don't say this."

"I want to stay with you."

Dokaz was still regarding her sadly, and her hand brushed Dinah's hair. She blinked a few times. She said, at last, "This is your choice. You are not a child anymore, but you make your choice." She slid the baby down into Dinah's arms. "By tonight we'll have the ger on the ground again. Things will be easier." She gathered her reins and rode off.

* *

In the afternoon they came to the edge of a shallow lake, and there they laid the ger back down on the ground, which took much digging and smoothing and rearrangement of the dirt, and then fitting the boards of the floor together. When that was done, and the ger laid on the floor, Hulegu with a crowd of his officers appeared and Dokaz went to greet them with the usual ceremony.

Dinah hung back; she saw work to do. One cart was full of rugs and beds and she got a rug she could carry by herself and took it into the huge, dim room, and while she was near the wall laying it down she heard someone come in behind her.

She glanced over her shoulder, and wheeled quickly around. It was Kitboqa. She saw purpose in his long narrow face, and she backed quickly away from him.

He said, "I will not let you say no this time." He reached for her.

She shrank back but he had her by the sleeve of her deel. She whined in her throat. He reached for her with the other hand. "Listen to me. You are like me, not them. I can—" Then behind him someone came into the ger.

It was Nikola. Seeing him, she struck away Kitboqa's reaching hand. Kitboqa let her go, and turned, putting himself between her and the Mongol prince.

He said, "Get out. I'm busy here."

Nikola looked past him to Dinah, and shortened his gaze to the big Turk. Kitboqa was much taller. Nikola stood with his head back, his chest out. "No," he said. "Leave her alone."

Kitboqa swayed; he gave off a stink of rage. While the two men glared at each other, Dinah darted past him toward the door. She heard Nikola laugh, behind her. She fled out into the sunshine and the crowd of other people.

Jun gave her a sharp look. "What's wrong? What happened in there?"

Dinah shook her head. "Nothing. Nothing." She went in among the other women, comforted by their numbers.

\* \* \* \*

One day the French merchant told her, "Bohemund is coming."

"Bohemund," she said. Vaguely she knew this was the Prince of some Crusader city, off to the west by the Middle Sea.

"There will be people here with money again," he said. He complained often of the Mongols' wanting to barter with him, offering him horses or blankets or goats, but not money.

Then back in the ger, the Khatun summoned her in behind the wall of screens  In the dim space, Dinah greeted her in Mongol, with a bow.

"Well, good for you," said the Khatun, and spoke on in her own language. "We are having some people here from the west, in a few days—"

"Bohemund," Dinah said, and put her hand over her mouth.

The Khatun's eyes widened in surprise. "How did you know that? I only heard a little while ago."

"In the bazaar, Khatun."

Dokaz laughed. Her gaze rested on Dinah as if she had grown wings. "Ah well. That's where the news is freshest, always. Anyway. When they come, will you help me? I need to find out all I can about them."

"Yes, of course." Dinah made another bow.

"Good. We shall see how this goes."

* *

In the bazaar the next morning, just as she came to the French merchant's booth, shouts sounded, and the crowd shrank quickly back, out of the lane. Dinah craned her neck to see over the shoulders in front of her. Men ran by with sticks, chasing the crowd out of the way, making room for a huge grey horse. The man upon it carried a banner with a cross. He wore armor, his helmet bright in the sun. Behind him came more Christian knights, riding in rows.

Among them came one in gilded armor, whose horse danced this way and that, half-reared, snorted, as the knight waved around him. From either side came cheers. Behind her, the French merchant called out, "Prince of Antioch! God save the Prince of Antioch!" That brought a few more whoops.

The gilded helmet jittered by her. Then, in the crowd of riders just behind him, she saw Rikart.

She gasped. He was dead. She had thought him surely dead. He wore mail, under a loose white sleeveless surcoat, but no helmet. On his head a flat-brimmed peasant's hat of straw. She shrank back, but he did not look her way. Among a dozen other Christian knights he passed her by.

He would not know her if he saw her, she thought. She was another person now.

* *

Later, the Prince and some of his men came to the ger to present themselves to Hulegu and Dokaz. Jun took the baby for her, and Dinah wrapped her head in a cloth to cover her hair, tightened her belt, hooked her coat up close to her chin. She waited by the side of the ger, watching the Franks come; relieved, she saw Rikart was not one of them.

When they went into the ger, she followed. In the men's side of the ger were the jugs and cups for the greeting ceremony. She stood there, the other people staring at her, while the Franks filed in and arranged themselves, six men in two rows. From the side of the ger Moseh called out to her but she gave him only a quick smile, her eyes always watching the Franks.

They were looking all around at the ger. Some lamps shone, here and there, and the place gave off gleams of gold. Before them was the hearth, and then the altar, but the two chairs beyond that were empty.

With the men serving, Dinah went up to give cups to the knights. To her surprise, the jugs were full of wine. She wondered where the Il-Khan had found this. Going along the row, she filled the cups.

Bohemund, in the middle, was jiggling a little in place; he looked quickly around, as if he expected a chair, and took the cup from her without even looking at her. He spoke a rapid French, sharp-edged. "What a place. Reminds me of the Venetians, a little gold here and there and a man thinks he's a king."

The others all laughed. Behind the Prince a short, square man said, "Yet they're Christians. See the cross?" He pitched his voice to reach Bohemund's ear; Dinah went to fill the next cup. "We can use them, sir. God sends us what we need to do His work." He crossed himself.

"If you ask me," another man said, "Rikart is right."

She gripped the jug tighter, her heart thumping. Calmly she went on to the next man, the next cup. From behind her someone clutched at her behind. She twitched out of the way. Looking up toward the wall, where the Mongols stood, she saw Nikola scowling, his gaze aimed past her.

In the front of the ger, by the door, was the cask, and she went there to fill the jug. Back in the center of everything Hulegu stood up in front of them all, held his cup up and down, back and forth, and said, "God above us give all peace. Greetings to the Prince of Antioch."

In the front row of the Franks, the short man piped up in Latin, "Pax nobis, O Domine! Ave, Princeps Antiochus!" He leaned toward Bohemund and said, low, in French, "Peace to everybody." Bohemund leaned closer to hear him, half-turning his head. Not a Latiner. He held up his cup.

"God grant us all the strength to do His will. I greet the Lord Hulegu, conqueror of the Caliph!"

That rattled back on through the translators, God granting all, and Hulegu conquering. Everybody drank. She went down the line to Bohemund again, to fill his cup again. As she did, she looked past him, to the man who had said Rikart's name.

Tall and lean, this one, with a red cross on the chest of his white surcoat. She knew that meant he was a Templar. She dropped her eyes quickly to the jug.

Now Bohemund was presenting gifts, each one with a chain of words in several languages, up and down. She did not see how they would get anything done this way. Hulegu also had gifts. The Franks stirred, restless. The short man beside Bohemund tilted toward the prince again and said, "Get to the Sultan Yusuf somehow. Tell him we have a common enemy."

She kept moving, her eyes lowered, cup to cup. But her ears tingled from listening. Bohemund cleared his throat, and said, "Conqueror of the Caliph, we are here to honor your great victory. But also, to tell you, we stand with you against the Sultan, we are ready to fight side by side with you against Damascus! Christians together!"

That turned into a flurry of excited Latin and then Mongol. Hulegu answered that all honor went to the Khakhan but he would convey this to his brother. As for the Sultan in Damascus, that would happen as God intended it. They drank again, with many gestures.

The man behind Bohemund said, "Ask him for a private hearing tomorrow. See if he'll come to us."

She filled up his cup. The Templar said, "Do you think he's a nitwit?" When she lifted the jug he waved her off. She drew back.

Bohemund and Hulegu nattered a while about meeting again. Hulegu was hunting in the morning; for a while it sounded as if he wanted to go off at that by himself and meet Bohemund later, but gradually they came to the notion that the Franks could try their hands at this as well. The Templar said, between his teeth, "We aren't allowed to hunt." The stubby man beside Bohemund said, "Catch him at his ease, sir. We can keep up with them."

The Templar rolled his eyes. Dinah poured them all more wine. Now they were winding this down. More speeches about peace and glory went up and down the ladder of translations. Somebody stroked her again. Then they were filing out into the blazing spring sunlight.

She went to wash up the jug and gather cups but at once Tulla came and said, "The Khatun wishes you."

Dokaz was sitting in the back, behind the painted screen, drinking chah. When Dinah came in and bowed, the Khatun said, "Sit down, please. I saw you, that was daring, I thought, and I hope useful. What did you find out?"

"Just what you heard, Khatun. The Prince wants to ally with—"he almost said "us." Instead, she said, "The Il-Khan, against the Sultan in Damascus. The man behind him was urging him on."

"That man. Did you hear his name?"

"No, Khatun."

"Find out, if you can. What about the others?"

"They're Bohemund's men. Except one, the man in the white surcoat with the red cross."

Dokaz was pouring her a cup of chah. "Who was that?"

"I think he is a Templar. He is against this, I think."

"Templar."

"They are knights. Monks. Brothers of the Order of the Templar of Jerusalem." This was coming to her in bits. How to explain. "They fight for the Cross, for Jerusalem. A little army." Very little, compared to the Mongols, she knew. "They have Acre, I think. Much of Acre. The big city on the coast."

Dokaz frowned, her fingers tapping on her cup. Dinah lifted the cup to her lips and sipped the steaming brew. The Khatun said, "Find out some names for me. That one man, I saw how he spoke to the Prince. If we can influence him, we shall have done something." She smiled. "You did well, Dinah. Thank you."

The chah warmed her; the praises warmed her more. She sipped the tea, content. Going out, with only a little listening, she found out the small man was a Genoese named Simone de Bonafaccio.

\* \* \* \*

Then in the afternoon, in the new bazaar, she came around a corner and Rikart stood there.

He stared straight at her. He paid no heed to Moseh. He said, "Why are you here? Why are you staying with them?"

"I have no choice."

"What a lie that is. You never lied before. They destroyed Baghdad. Everything beautiful and wonderful in Baghdad is gone. Your father's city. Have you forgotten that?"

She said nothing. She thought she had put that behind.

"They will do that to every place they come to. They hate cities. Listen to their prayers sometime. They want only endless grass, and horses, and the great blue sky."

"There is nothing left for me back there. My father is gone, Baghdad is gone."

"Damascus and Aleppo come next. Then Acre, Antioch. Jerusalem, what's left of it."

"They will win."

"Ah." He stands back. "That's not what matters." He stared at her. "Gilbert can always find me. If you change your mind, I will help you."

\* \* \* \*

Yvain de Foret-le-Garde, Grand Marshall of the Templars, had deliberately taken a slow horse; he watched the hunt gallop away up the long slope beyond the lake and sat back in the saddle and let his reins loose. The Mongols on their infernal ponies were racing on ahead of Bohemund but the Prince was doing his gallant utmost to keep up.

The Mongols were hunting with eagles. The Marshall fought down a pang of envy at that, he would have loved to have seen that. In the sky, out there, he thought he still made them out, those faint specks. Below, the earthbound leaders of the hunt were disappearing into the slopes and draws around the lake. Cranes, maybe. Even hares, he would have liked to see that.

But now, up along the wide undulating plain, here came another rider.

He let his horse amble. The wind swept out of the east here, smelling of the steppe, wild and bitter. The hunt had begun well north of the Mongol camp, which stretched out across the open plain under its usual yellow cloud. Jogging through the tall grass, Rikart Rannulfsson rode up to him.

"Well met," Yvain said, and they shook hands. "I thought perhaps you had gone. Where have you been?"

"I went looking around," Rikart said. "I know some people here."

Yvain had heard that Rikart had once lived with the Mongols, that he had married a Mongol woman. There were a lot of wild stories about Rikart the Ghost. Yvain looked the younger man over. Rikart had cut his beard and let his hair grow. He wore a red silk Mongol shirt over his mail. He looked half-Mongol.

"You were in Baghdad when they attacked, I heard. How did you escape?"

"I ran. I fought, but mostly, I ran."

Yvain grunted. He would have liked to know more, but the look on Rikart's face held him back. He said, only, "What have you found out?"

"This is a huge army. They're saying fifteen tumans, and it may be all of that."

"A tuman is what?"

"Ten thousand men."

Yvain swallowed. His eyes drifted off, toward the yellow cloud.

"The proof is the horses. Their horse herds are grazing the land for six days' east of here. They must have over ten hundred thousand horses."

Yvain scratched his beard. Such a number was impossible. However it did mean they had to move constantly, always seeking new grass. This, he thought, explained much.

"Worse, for our sake," Rikart said, "is these men are mostly Mongols. The Khakhan has sent the best of his home forces here, with his own brother commanding. They have a few Turks, Naimans, Kipchaks, some very high up, but this is an army of well-armed, well-trained men with very good officers. They have a big purpose here. Baghdad is just the beginning."

"This Khakhan is their Emperor? I have heard another word, a name—Tema--gan--"

"Temujin. He gathered them together, two generations ago. They were just steppe clans then. He made them into the Mongols. Turned them loose on the world. Hulegu is his grandson."

"Bohemund thinks we can make use of them."

"Bohemund is an idiot."

Yvain laughed. "I wouldn't turn my back on him. He hates you. What you said to him yesterday did you no good with him at all."

"Yes. I am leaving, I don't trust Hulegu not to move on me, either."

El Shab'h, the outsider, everybody's enemy. Yvain said, "Come to Acre. Maybe we can convince my brothers."

Rikart shrugged one shoulder. The hunt had vanished in among the rumpled land along the head of the lake. He said, "You and your brothers won't stand a day against them."

The skin of Yvain's neck roughened up. "God wills it," he said. This gave him less comfort than it once had. He laid his hands on his saddlebows. "Who else? You think you can rouse Damascus against him? You think Yusuf would listen?"

"Put it in a poem," Rikart said. "Write it on the rear end of a pretty girl."

Yvain laughed again. That left only one other, and he said, "What about Egypt?"

At that Rikart straightened, and his eyes came back to meet Yvain's. "Do you get along with Baibers?"

"Holy Blood," Yvain said. "Does anybody get along with Baibers? Not even the other Mamelukes get along with Baibers, which is why he's outcast. I was thinking about Qutuz." This was the Mameluke Sultan of Egypt.

"We make an alliance. You," Rikart said. "As many of the other Christians as we can. Qutuz and the Mamelukes of Egypt. Maybe Yusuf. That's a solid wall against them. But it must be solid. Baibers and the Bahriyya Mamelukes control the center of the wall, the Jordan Valley and south."

Yvain said, "Such a thing has never happened. At least, not for very long."

Rikart swept his arm out, toward the yellow cloud, the distant camp, the hundreds of thousands of horses. "Such a thing as this has never happened."

Yvain lifted his reins. "We shall see, then. Come to Acre. At the very least the Venetians will pay you well to talk to them." He nudged his horse, turning back toward the camp; the Il-Khan had provided them with a good larder and a fine southern wine. Turning brought the whole plain before his eyes again, the vast clutter of the Mongol camp, stretching it seemed over the edge of the world.

He blurted out, not thinking, "How can we beat them? Has anybody ever beaten them?"

"No," Rikart said. "Never." He nodded stiffly. "They say that's God's will."

He backed his horse quickly away. "Until seeing," he said, and galloped off down the slope.

# CHAPTER 3

## Caravanserai

The merchant Gilbert d'Baalbeck, with five camels and four servants and a chest full of money, left the Il-Khan's summer camp and went south and west, toward the Euphrates. The road was poor, but Gilbert saw no need to ride in company; the Mongols took their tolls but they kept the place free of bandits.

He had come into the country by another road, from the north, from Armenia, and so what he saw on the road west surprised him. The Mongol army had come that way, in the winter, to attack Baghdad, and they had left nothing behind them. It was midsummer, and the fields on either side of the road should have been sprouting green, busy with the rise and fall of the shadufs and people stooping to pick weeds, but he rode through fallow lands. Empty. The houses he saw were burned out. He met a caravan coming the other way along the road, and once an arrow messenger galloped by, but nobody lived here anymore.

For a while the road ran alongside a canal, dry as bone. The date palms that grew in clusters along the bank were already drooping, the fruits withered like the testicles of old men.

That canal bed led to another, wider and deeper, in which, also, no water ran; but looking across he saw that the land on the far side was a lake, reflecting the blue sky, a watery sheet studded with brush and low trees. His little caravan crossed the canal, and came up the western bank onto a marsh. Water covered everything, only a few inches deep.

It was still and flat, and a smell of rot rose from it. The faint buzzing of insects sounded around it. It was like a desert, only of water. The road was invisible. The cursing drovers slid down from the camels , which grunted and backed up and flattened their ears. They hated getting their feet wet. Gilbert stopped his horse. He knew what had happened, the Mongols had broken the levee to the north, and the waters of the canal had come through the breach and flooded all this land. He let the drovers argue a few moments while he peered around. Far ahead across the watery land he saw a thick dark stub poking out of the water. He called over the head drover and pointed this out to him—the next milestone on the road. The drover grunted, went back to his camel, and they all walked off sloshing through the muck. As they left the canal behind them, the water turned ever more shallow, until it was only a surface sheen, but the road was buried under silt.

Silt also covered the milestones, the stalks of the abandoned gardens. They passed through a village, where the houses were falling apart, their roofs gone, the marks of the flood knee high on their walls.

The waterland fell behind. They crossed bare thorny scrub. Now, at last, he came to the main road, running east and west. This was the Diocletianus, an old road of the Romans, and he could see another caravan almost at once, far ahead of them; the drovers saw that also and called to each other, as if just seeing someone else meant they were less alone. The road took them quickly on to Raqqa where they crossed the Euphrates.

On the north bank he paid the Mongol in charge of the ferry depot, and he paid the ferryman, and on the south bank he paid the Sultan's agent in charge there. This left his money chest considerably lighter.

Now he looked for a larger group to travel with, but saw nothing. Hurrying along the Roman road, he came at noon to the caravanserai at Resafa. He could have gone on another half day's travel but he decided to stop. He would not reach Palmyra for days, and the desert ahead was a dangerous place. If he were patient he could pick up some traveling companions here.

Resafa had been a bigger city once. Now little of it was left but the caravanserai, which had taken over an ancient building inside the walls. This was a square stone fort, with no roof. Cloth awnings and wooden stalls lined all the inside walls; there was a well in the middle. Carved along the tops of the walls were scrolls of Roman work. The kitchen, he knew from long usage, was excellent.

The master of the place took his money and gave him a good corner. Gilbert's men tethered the camels, and the master sent a boy over to haul water and hay and shovel away the dung. Gilbert walked up and down in the afternoon sun, stretching his legs. He meant to reach Acre by midsummer day, when the Venetian fleet would arrive, and unless something happened bad in the next week or so he would do that easily. He fell to thinking of the silver in the chest, the little pouches of gold coins; even when he had paid off his men he would have a weight of money in his hands.

He thought of going back to Italy. Maybe it was time to go back to Italy.

The master of the caravanserai fell in beside him as he walked. He said, "You came from east of the River?"

"Several months now I have been in the bazaars of the Il-Khan," Gilbert said, proudly. Most merchants he knew had refused to go east after the fall of Baghdad.

"Ah! And how did you find that?"

"I made a lot of money," Gilbert said.

"They didn't rob you?"

"They took their fees and taxes. They have other things to do." He talked about the caravans he had seen, bringing the wealth of Baghdad and its treasurehouses and bazaars into the camp of the Il-Khan.

"What do you think? Will they stay on that side of the river?"

Gilbert wanted to think so. He wanted to believe that in spite of everything nothing had really changed. The Mongols were only taking the place of the Caliph. Everything would be as it had always been. He thought uneasily of the ruined fields he had seen. Without the canals working, it would be hard to bring that land back alive. He said, "I don't know."

"What they did to Baghdad—" They were strolling around the courtyard, and they passed the boy hauling a load of dung out toward the gate. The master's voice fell to a murmur; with a jut of his chin he indicated the boy. "He survived it. Somebody found him on the road, half-dead."

Gilbert gave the boy a quick glance. A scrawny Arab boy, eight or ten years old, bent against the weight of the hod he was dragging along. He got to the gate and stood a moment, breathing.

"What does he say about it?"

"Nothing. He won't talk. Not a word. Whatever they did to him stopped his tongue."

Gilbert said, "I saw them. They are not so bad. If you give them what they want, they let you alone."

The boy suddenly snapped up straight, looking out, and turned toward the master. His face was bright. He shot the master a fierce look and threw out one arm, pointing.

The master said, "Someone is coming. We'll talk later." He got up and went to the gate.

\* \*

The new arrival was Bohemund, the Prince of Antioch, one of the Crusader lords. Gilbert had marked him in the ordu of the Il-Khan, but Bohemund had never summoned him and Gilbert had seen no reason to invite himself. That was different now. He watched as Bohemund's retinue, nearly forty men, horses, packs and squires, spilled into the caravanserai, taking the best places, noisy and demanding. The Arab boy ran among them, carrying water and hay. After a while Gilbert strolled up to the Prince of Antioch, who sat on a camp chair in the center of his space, with all the bustle around him. The master of the caravanserai himself was pouring the Prince a cup of wine.

Gilbert hovered, shuffling his feet, and Bohemund saw him and motioned to him. "Come up. Who are you—yes, Guillaume, is it not? You were in the bazaar at the Il-Khan's camp."

"Gilbert d'Baalbek," Gilbert said, pleased. "I am, my lord, I am most elevated that my lord remembers me."

Bohemund drank deep of the wine. "There weren't that many white faces. You're an agent of the Venetians."

Gilbert bowed. "I am a free merchant, my lord. I have a seat in the guild hall in Acre."

Bohemund said, "Which belongs to Venice." The cookservant brought in a platter of flat bread, the Arab boy on his heels carrying fruit in a wooden bowl. They set these down and rushed off again. Bohemund's knights gathered around the table and the jug passed among them. Gilbert waited patiently for Bohemund to notice him again. He saw no purpose in expounding to Bohemund about the complexities of governance in Acre. The Prince sprawled in his chair, and Gilbert saw his chance and went around the table, took the ewer from the back table and filled Bohemund's cup.

The Prince drank it down. "What is it, then? Gilbert, right?"

"Gilbert, my lord. I am traveling west, and I wondered if I could keep company with you and your men, the roads being full of bandits here."

Bohemund looked him over. The Prince was a young man, handsome in the ruddy golden way of the Franks, with bright blue eyes. His beard, redder than his hair, was a mass of oiled curls. He said, after a while, "How much can you pay me?" He lifted his cup.

Gilbert pressed his lips together; he struggled with his face. He said, "My lord, I am a subject of the Kingdom of Jerusalem. Surely—"

Bohemund flapped a hand at him. "Yes, yes. Come along. Keep up." He was drunk. "I'll take a tithe. Where are you going?"

"Acre, ultimately, my lord. I only need an escort as far as Palmyra, probably."

"Come with me, then." Bohemund swung around to talk to the other men around him. "But everybody has to pay the tolls." He laughed. "Sit," he said to Gilbert. "Eat."

Gilbert dropped onto the bench, delighted. He reached for bread, for fig jam and soft white cheese. The Arab boy was hovering nearby. Clearly the knights awed him. The master of the caravanserai went around directing his servants—only the two men servants, Gilbert saw; he kept the women hidden away inside.

They were talking about the Mongols; how small they were. How many.

"Hand to hand, we can beat them. Carve them up like pigs."

"They don't fight that way."

"Like with the sand-monkeys. Pin them where they can't run."

Bohemund overheard this, and said, "They are Christian men, like us." He lolled in his seat; the drink softened his face. "We won't have to fight them."

"Not like us," said another man, stubbornly. Clearly they had had this argument before. "They're Nestors, they're not like us. You heard Rikart."

The Arab boy jerked his head up; probably he did not speak French, but he had heard something in that. Gilbert poured himself more wine.

"They are Christian. They're friends." Bohemund leaned forward. "We have the same enemies. Once we convince them of that, everything will go well."

The other man said, "I hope you are right, my lord," in a voice that suggested he thought otherwise.

Bohemund gave him a fierce, drunken look. He lurched up onto his feet and lifted his cup. "Friends! To the Mongols! To Hulegu! May he save us from the Mamelukes and give us back Jerusalem! Hulegu!"

His men roared, drinking with him, but from their midst suddenly the Arab boy erupted toward Bohemund, shouting.

"No! No!" He rushed at the Prince, his arms milling.

The master reached him in one stride, wrapped an arm around him, and held him down. The cookservant came over and between them they wrestled the boy still. Bohemund jerked back, his head up,.

"What does this? Who is this?"

The master shouted, "My lord, pay no heed--he is silly, he is weak-minded, who knows what he meant." He slapped the boy hard on the side of the head and dragged him off.

The boy struggled in his arms. His voice croaked out. "He was cheering—them. "He lashed out with his fists and feet. "He was—cheering—" Gilbert got up and went to help. By the time he reached them the boy was sobbing, limp, and mute again. They took him into the back of the caravanserai, to the master's quarters, and locked him in a storeroom.

* *

Daud curled up in a corner of the room, on a heap of empty sacks. His insides were boiling, and he burst into tears again, burying his face in his hands. A kind of raw terror filled him. He leapt up, and went around and around the room, swinging his arms and breathing hard. He had to run but he was pent here, the walls around him like a shell.

In another corner was a sack of dates and he fell on these and ate until his stomach was full. Then he wept again. After a while, sitting with his back to the wall and licking the date sweetness from his fingers, he realized that he had to get out of here.

The memory of Bohemund oppressed him. He had thought—they were knights. He had heard Rikart's name. He had thought—

He was tired but he was afraid to sleep, because of the dreams. He found himself up on his feet again, walking around and around. He could not stay here anymore. He had been here too long. He swung his arms back and forth. He was thirsty now and he went to the door, which was locked, and tapped on it until Mina came. She opened the door and looked in, and shut the door again, but in a moment was back with some bread and water in a jug. She put her finger to her lips and closed the door again.

He drank the water. He had been here too long.

He remembered—they had said Rikart's name.

He had seen the Caliph's army drowned in the tide of the Mongols, Rikart among them, but he remembered also that people called Rikart the Ghost because he escaped from everything. Maybe he had escaped even from the Mongols. Daud decided he would go to find Rikart. Thinking that made the whole whirling mess settle down around him. He sat down, his back to the wall, and ate the bread.

* *

In the morning Bohemund's steward came to Gilbert, demanding money. Gilbert was packing his camels. The night before he had divided his money up, so that he did not have to expose it all at once, and now he made a show of unhooking his purse from his belt and counting out twenty pieces of silver to the steward.

This was a stocky, short man named Simone, a Genoese. He took the coins, but his eyes were on the pouch; Gilbert knew he was guessing at the amount left.

He said, "I don't like these. Don't you have isaacs?"

Gilbert shrugged. "I have some Egyptian dinars."

"Gold?"

"Absolutely." Some of it probably was gold. He said, "I have dirhams."

"From where?"

"Armenian."

"Let me see the dinars."

Gilbert produced the three battered coins. The steward wrinkled his nose, but he took them, and slid them along with the other money into his own belt pouch. He shrugged.

"Ride at the back, so we don't have to put up with the stink of your camels."

Gilbert bowed, very deeply, so it was more an insult than a grace. "As the Prince desires." Simone sneered at him and left.

They went off along the Diocletian road. Bohemund and his knights chattered and made their horses cavort around the road, and they kicked up more dust than the camels. By midmorning, Gilbert saw that the Arab boy from the caravanserai had come after them.

The boy stayed well behind them, perhaps thinking he was unseen, but he kept pace. Later, when Bohemund decided to stop for the night, Gilbert sent one of the drovers back to fetch the boy into their camp. There was no caravanserai here, only a spring, with some little ruined stone buildings around it. Many people had fled this part of the country, since the Mongols moved in. Nobody knew who was lord here, and the place was full of

Bedouin thieves. The boy silently went around hauling water for the camels. Gilbert saw he avoided even looking at Bohemund.

In the morning they went on again. The road was straight and true, as the Romans had always built. The first heat of the summer baked the hills around them. The road ran between two low grassy rises, and from all sides suddenly horsemen rushed in around them.

Gilbert jerked his mount to a stop. He saw at once these were not Bedouin; they rode blooded mares and he recognized their blue coats. He looked quickly around at his caravan. The drovers were bunching the camels together. The boy sat on top of one, his hands on the hump, looking startled. Gilbert heard Bohemund call out, and turned forward again.

On the road, the Prince was wheeling his horse around, face to face with a tall rider with a badge on his turban. Gilbert stiffened, his stomach tight. He glanced right and left. The Franks were outnumbered more than two to one and the Mamelukes surrounding them carried their bows ready across their saddles.

Bohemund shouted, "How dare you block my way? Do you know who I am?"

The Mameluke amir said, "You can pass, but you will pay me. As to the rest, I think you are the Prince of Antioch. For that, you will pay me double."

The Mamelukes, bunched all around, gave a low general laugh. Bohemund braced up. His men were watching him, intent. He sat silent a while, staring into the Mameluke's eyes; Gilbert grew fearful they would fight. He saw no way the Prince could win, and clearly Bohemund thought so as well, because after a moment he tipped backward slightly in his saddle, his chin up, and said, "This time, Baibers, you get your way. But my time will come."

Gilbert gave a little shake of his head. Up there, the Mameluke amir's white teeth flashed. "I look forward to that." He waved a hand. "One dinar a head. Two for you." His eyes swiveled around, toward the rest of them, counting, and he saw Gilbert. "A dinar for every kaffir."

Almost in unison, the drovers all called out the declaration of faith. Gilbert said, "The boy is sahih."

Baibers had gone back to his staring match with Bohemund, but he heard this, and he turned back toward Gilbert. He was younger than Gilbert. A train of horrible stories followed him. His face was hard as a blade. "Let him say so."

Gilbert said, "He has no speech." Except, he suddenly remembered, that outburst against Bohemund. "He was in Baghdad when the Mongols came. He survived. Whatever happened there took his voice."

Baibers nudged his big bay mare around and jogged a few steps toward them. His gaze fixed on the boy. The child stared back. Gilbert wished he had said nothing.

"I will take him, then," Baibers said. "For your passage."

Gilbert blurted out, "He is a child—"

"Or all your money."

Gilbert clamped his mouth shut. Baibers waved a hand, and a Mameluke from the swarm around them came up, reaching for the boy on the camel. The boy shrank back, casting a pleading look at Gilbert, but the Mameluke got him by the arm and swung him down. Another of the turbaned riders lifted him onto the back of the first man's horse, behind the high-cantled saddle. The boy gave Gilbert one last, frightened glance, and they all rode off.

* *

Daud gripped the cantle of the saddle with both hands, to stay on; they rode at a quick trot back through the hills. The long grass was dry and yellow on the slopes. He glanced around him at the other men, riding all around him. They were still looking back over their shoulders, but one by one they were sitting down deep in their saddles and sheathing their bows.

The beaten path they followed wound through the cleft between two hills, steep and grassy, rounded like breasts. Daud's rider was near the last of the pack, and the boy watched the side of the road. He thought he might be able to slide down off the horse and run, if he found some cover. There was no cover. He caught the eye of the nearest of the riders, staring at him. Daud turned quickly forward. His mouth was dry. He wondered what they would do to him.

Around the shoulder of his rider, through the dust of the horses, he could see a fortress on the high ground. That was where they were going. He glanced around him again; the land fell off sharply at the edge of the road, down into a ravine. He could run—The rider near him pushed his horse up alongside him and glowered at him.

Daud hunched his shoulders, facing forward again. He watched the rider from the corner of his eye. He had grey streaks in his beard. His face was sun-darkened brown but his eyes were pale. Daud's insides felt like hot iron. He kept his eyes on the rider ahead of him.

They rode up to the gate of the fortress and half the men stayed outside, but Daud's rider and the grey-bearded rider followed the rest into a court-yard. At a nudge from the grey-bearded man Daud slid down from the horse. The men pushed him ahead of them, on across the courtyard toward the stone tower, and inside.

They came into a wide, dim space. Overhead were the beams of a ceiling. Around the walls were rolls of carpet, saddles, pots. The floor grated under his feet, unswept. He had a moment to think he had kept the cara-vanserai better than this, and then one of them pushed him and yelled at him.

He jumped back, all his hair on end. They were gathering around him. He thought he saw knives in their fists. He spun around, looking for a way to run, but they were all around him. One grabbed him, and Daud kicked out, yelling.

They closed on him. He could hear them laughing. He flailed out with his arms, striking blows, and their hands were all over him. They pawed at his body, his face, his arms. He was falling. He screamed again.

"Stop!"

Abruptly, they let go of him. He lay still, panting. He was lying on the dirty floor of the tower. The men around him had backed away, were staring at him, round-eyed. He sat up. One man remained beside him, the grey-bearded man, who squatted down on his heels.

He said, in slow Arabic, "Are you mad? Are you raving?"

Daud sat there, panting; he thought of the hands gripping him, of the laughing. Maybe, he thought, maybe that didn't happen. Not that way anyway. He shut his eyes. His whole body throbbed.

"He doesn't talk," someone said, from the crowd watching him. "That's what the merchant said. Where is Baibers? This was his idea."

The bearded man put out a hand to Daud. "Here. Come. Sit and eat something."

Tamely Daud let him lead him to the wall; he sat against the wall; he felt drained empty, slack as an empty skin. He began to cry, not aloud, just tears trickling down his face. The grey-bearded man put a cup into his hands; there were bits of lemons in the water.

"Drink."

He drank. The water trickled down his throat and into his stomach and made it all alive again.

The grey-bearded man said, "Rasul." He tapped his chest. "My name."

Daud wiped his mouth. Then across the dim hall the tall man was striding toward him.

Daud stood up, dropping the cup, his back to the wall. This was the man who had taken him from Gilbert, his eyes like pale chips in his face.

Dark, weathered face. One eye had a white dot in it. His forehead was bruised. Daud's stomach churned. Now they would kill him. But he could not move; the tall man's stare pinned him like a lance against the wall.

Rasul said something in another language. The tall man grunted. He reached out and wiped a hand over Daud's cheek, wet with tears.

In harsh Arabic, he said, "You are my slave now. If any asks you, say that you belong to Baibers. Rasul is your brother. Listen to him. Obey me."

Daud could not move; he licked his lips.

"They said you were in Baghdad. Is that so?"

Daud nodded.

"Yet you lived."

Daud shut his eyes, tears leaked down his cheeks again. He gasped for breath.

A hand fell heavily on his shoulder. The tall man said, "You will tell me, someday. But now you are with us, so you will bear yourself as one of us. Remember. We follow the will of God. My will. Obey me. Come. The time for prayer is on us."

Daud shivered. Around the hall some of the other men were spreading out their carpets in rows, facing the far wall. He stood. He did not know what to do now. His mother had taught him some prayers but he had not been to madrassah, and living in the Reb's house he had seen nothing of Islam. Rasul stood beside him. Rasul led him out of the hall, back to the courtyard, to the fountain there. He washed his hands and face. He knew to do that. He thought of another mosque, somewhere else, and his mind whirled up a blur of rage and fear. He followed Rasul back into the hall. Rasul had spread a carpet down, but there was none for Daud. He stood there, trembling. Rasul took his hands and put them together, palm against palm. Rasul began the words, and Daud remembered them, the oldest words, spoken even in Eden.

"There is no God but God--"

He was still weeping, but he remembered what the tall man had said. These were magic words. If he said this and did this, they would take care of him. He was safe. For now. He was never really safe. He bowed and knelt and put his forehead to the floor, grateful. But even bent to the ground like that, he told himself, nobody owned him.

* *

They all slept on the floor of the hall; the men had blankets and carpets but Daud lay down on the stone floor. He was afraid to sleep, as always, but sleep came over him, and he saw the eyes again, floating in the dark. He sobbed, in his sleep.

Then someone touched him; he startled, but he only came partway out of the dream; he thought his mother had come to console him. She murmured to him, she wrapped him in her shawl. He fell into a deep sleep and dreamed no more.

In the morning when he woke, Rasul was beside him, and Rasul's blue coat was wrapped around him. He leapt up, and went away; he had to piss anyway.

They prayed again. Rasul brought him a handful of dates and some bread. The other men stretched and laughed; they put on the mesh shirts they wore, and over that their blue coats, lapped right to left. They spoke together in that other language. They stood close together, bumped each other, gripped each other's arms as they talked. One turned to Daud and held out a handful of dates, and when he hesitated, banged their fists together, nodding and smiling.

He ate many of the dates. He loved dates.

The other men went into the courtyard and Daud followed. They all had bows in their hands, and they lined up at one end of the courtyard, jostling each other into rows. Then by fives they stepped forward, still in a neat line, and each five lifted their bows and shot, in unison, like a dance.

At the far end of the courtyard, three sacks stuffed with straw hung from the wall. These were the targets. Swiftly, in rows of five, the men stepped forward, raised their bows in a single motion, and shot. The straw bags filled up with arrows. Daud stood there, intent, watching. He saw Rasul, among the last five, go up, lift his bow, and shoot, and Daud ran toward him, not thinking, his hands out.

The grey-bearded man laughed at him. "Yes, yes! Here. Take the bow." He held out the bow and an arrow.

Daud did not know how to do this; he gripped the middle of the bow with his right hand, and Rasul laughed again. "No. Here." The other men were watching. One called out something in that other language. Rasul stood behind Daud and put the bow properly into his hands.

"Draw with your thumb, like this." Rasul held up his right hand, the three lower fingers curled tightly to his palm, and his thumb and forefinger crooked. Standing so close he brushed against Daud's body and the boy stiffened, but the bow fascinated him. He lifted it, the arrow in the string, and tried to draw it. His arm shook with the effort but he could only move the string back an inch.

"Draw toward your mouth," Rasul said. "Not your shoulder. Elbow straight back. Hold your left arm tight as you can. Try again."

He struggled, barely moving the string. Rasul laughed again. His hand clapped roughly on Daud's back and the boy jumped and the arrow flopped off to one side.

Everybody laughed. Daud gave Rasul a hard look and went off to get the arrow. Over and over he tried to draw the bow but he could not.

Back in the hall, Rasul brought him to a chest, and opened it, and took out clothes. These smelled like dust and mold. Rasul shook out some loose leggings; when Daud put them on the bottoms puddled on the floor. Rasul rolled them up, and they tucked the waist around Daud's waist and cinched it with a sash. Next was a shirt, like the others, too big, so Rasul folded it to make it fit.

He said, "We fix." He took a leather pouch out of his coat, held it up, and with a tweak of his fingers pulled on a thread coming out of it; a needle followed after the thread. Quickly he stitched up the folded bottoms of the leggings. Daud stood, shivering, the touch abhorrent. When Rasul stopped to get more thread he ran away. He stayed far away from Rasul.

In a little while they saddled up and rode out of the fortress. They gave Daud a horse to ride, a little mare, the color of dark sandalwood. They rode fast and he had to struggle to keep up. That night, when he finally slid down from the horse, he could barely walk.

They were camped by a well, in the open, and the men sat close together around a little fire. Daud was fighting off sleep. He listened to the voices around him that he could not understand. One of the men put a coat around him. One by one, the others fell to sleep, or went off to walk guard, but Daud kept himself awake until Rasul had lain down, and he could tell the older man was asleep.

Then he went over behind Rasul, and lay down with his back to the other man's back, and curled up. And then he slept.

* *

Rasul showed him how to pick up the little mare's feet, clean her neat round hoofs , and trim off the rough edge. When he tried to do this Daud's knife slipped and he cut himself. Rasul swatted him. "Pay heed!"

Daud gave him a dark look, and Rasul hooted. "Oh, what a look, little man!" and knocked him flat. "For that, go haul water for all of us!"

Daud brought water for a dozen horses, all the while hot as a blister. His hand hurt where he had cut himself. They went to prayers; he went through the whole up and down, up and down, the bowing, but his mind boiled against Rasul.

He thought he would run away. But there was nowhere to go.

He named his horse Friend, although he never said that aloud. Rasul gave him a bow of his own, with its own case, and some arrows. He slept against Rasul's back but during the day he would not let him near him, and Rasul stopped trying. At night when the eyes came he bit his sleeve to keep from screaming.

Another man, big heavy bearded Boglu, brought him bread and honey. "Come here, I will help you sew your clothes. You look like a harem doll in that."

Daud trembled. Sitting down cross-legged beside him, Boglu smiled at him, and made a gesture.

"I am helping you. Don't be a fool."

Daud swallowed. Boglu's eyes met his, steady and mild. Daud made himself stand; Boglu had a needle, and he gathered up the waist of the leggings and made many small looping stitches. "Turn," he said, twice, and Daud turned. Now the leggings hung better, not flopping around his ankles.

His needle moving, Boglu said, "I was a boy, I was sold. Perhaps older than you. Sold as a slave. I was nothing. But then God found me and made me a Mameluke. " He gave Daud a deep look. "So, you see. You have your fortune." He paused, looking around, his brows lowering. "This is not where we belong, this scrubland. You should see Cairo. Trees everywhere, the river, the gardens. And so full of life. Bazaars. Good things to eat, and women." He turned back to the waist of Daud's leggings and made a knot. "The panther will get us back there. " He bit the thread. The panther was Baibers.

Daud pulled off the shirt, which draped him like a tent, took the needle, and fumbled with the cloth. Boglu took the side, and folded it over. "Here, see. Just run a seam along here, and we'll cut off the extra. You can make that into a belt."

Daud pushed the needle in and out of the thin, slippery fabric. Boglu said, "We can't go back to Cairo now because Qutuz hates us. Qutuz is the sultan. He wouldn't be sultan save for us, but he's forgotten that. " He sighed. "I dream about Bahri. Here, kuçuk, you have to do better than that." He took the shirt and pulled out Daud's raggedy stitching.

* *

In the morning there was the same thing, they prayed, they ate, they shot their bows. He tried to draw the bow again, and this time, he got the string to his chin. The arrow sailed off toward the target, dipped, and skidded on the ground. All the men gave up jeers and jibes, but Rasul smiled wide in his beard. "Better. You are doing better." Daud swelled, light with pleasure.

* *

Since he could not understand the Mamelukes' language, the way they acted spoke to him like talking. Their hands made their own words, asking for things, telling jokes. Stopped for midday, he watched two men bristling, standing closer together, their noses almost touching, so near when they shouted they sprayed each other.

Then suddenly they were standing back, stripping off their coats, their shirts. The others gathered up. Their voices rose. The two in the middle rushed at each other, wrapped their arms around each other, grunting and thrusting with their legs. The watching men whooped and screamed names and cheers, thumped each other on the back, clapped hands.

The smaller man sidestepped, and the bigger man crashed down hard onto the ground. The tall skinny man next to Daud turned to him, caught his arm, said in Arabic, "See how Moro is using Yaqi's own weight against him, there, see that"—and hugged him. Daud pushed him away. On the ground, the big man reached down to his belt for his knife.

"Ayyiaaah!"

Yaqi lunged to his feet, the knife in his hand, and from the crowd the bay mare burst in between them. Baibers in the saddle was roaring at them. He spun the horse, driving the two men farther apart, and bounded down to the ground. The bigger man, Yaqi, stood with his head thrown back, but the knife was in the dust at his feet. Baibers got him by the hand. He was still shouting at them both—at them all. and He leaned the other way and held out his hand, and Moro, the other man, slowly came up and took it, and Baibers dragged them together. He forced their hands together. He stopped shouting, and the crowd around fell breathlessly still.

The two men stared at each other, and then abruptly they lunged together again, but this time to embrace one another. Baibers stepped back. They stood apart, and clasped hands, and smiled, and then everybody went off to something else.

They reached a wide stone road, running east to west, and almost at once came on another caravan. Baibers went among those people and got money. He led the Mamelukes away into the west; he rode around them all, making sure they stayed close together.

Rasul, riding beside Daud, said, "Where we are going, now, The Sultan of Damascus rules. He is nothing. We have served him before and fought him before and he's always nothing. But now we have to get across the river and go to the coast, and who knows? He might make some trouble for us."

Daud thought, Another sultan. There were too many sultans.

When they stopped in the afternoon he took his bow and an arrow and went off beyond the edge of the camp and shot at bushes. The land here was flat and dry, running east toward the mountains like strips of blue cloth along the edge of the sky. He lost the arrow and stood, tired, looking east.

Back there, over the edge of the world, was Baghdad. What Baghdad had been, once. He thought there was something he should tell these men about Baghdad, but he didn't know how.

He could not remember much. He remembered people screaming. The smoke. "No, please—no—" His throat clogged and his eyes burned with tears and he stood, dumb and miserable, locked fast. That way was Baghdad. He could not think of Baghdad. He could think of nothing.

After a moment he drew in a deep breath, as if he had not breathed for hours. He thought again that he could run away, he could go back to Baghdad, somehow. There was no Baghdad. Finally he went back into the camp, where the other men were making ready for the evening prayers.

* *

They went on, more westerly now, into the sunset. Around them the hills loomed brown as lions. They came out through a gap in the hills into a flat wide valley, and after the desert this seemed beautiful as a garden, all green with fields and orchards. They passed through a village where the people cowered in their huts. Where goats grazed in the thatches.

Rasul said, "We are under the sultan's eyes now."

He spoke to Yaqi, who was riding on his far side. That man said, "No army outrides us. Nothing can catch us." He said this in Arabic, so Daud would understand.

"We're coming to the river. We'll find out."

Daud stood in his stirrups to look around. In the fields beside the road, people in white thobes, under broad brimmed straw hats, stooped among rows of low bushes. Up ahead he saw against the sky a brown ridge. Something on it strange, like a thumb sticking up; as he rode along he made this out to be a tower with a broken top.

The Mamelukes were drawing rein around him. He looked quickly over at Rasul, who was scowling ahead of them. Out there a voice called out sharply. Rasul settled back in his saddle, unhooked the waterskin on his saddle, and drank. He handed the skin to Daud.

"Somebody ahead of us." He swung toward Yaqi on his far side. "I told you so."

Daud drank the musty, lemon-flavored water and gave the skin back. His nose itched from the dust. It was almost noon when they would stop for prayer and maybe they would just start praying now. He looked around again, uneasy. Beside him Yaqi opened his bow case and drew out his bow.

Swinging toward Daud, Rasul said, "Stay close by me. Stay under my arm." He reached down to his saddlebows, and unslung the circle of his shield.

Daud gripped his reins. He wondered what was going on. The men were drawing in closer together, moving forward stirrup to stirrup. At a walk, first. Then at a jog. Then, suddenly, at a full gallop, and around him, the Mamelukes were drawing out their bows.

Somebody was shouting—a lot of shouting, and Rasul turned to him and bellowed, "Watch! Watch out!" Like a wing sweeping over him the shield swung above Daud's head. Rasul's horse jostled against Friend and the mare staggered. Daud almost went off. He sank his fingers in the mare's mane.

A rain of arrows pelted down around them, pinging off the shield. His blood leapt. A white panic flooded him and he crouched low over the mare's neck. That made it harder to stay on and he pushed himself upright again. Then the ground in front of them disappeared, the horse was skidding down an embankment, and they were splashing into the slow-moving water.

Ahead, past a dozen other riders, he saw the dark river running over rocks. Shallow there. He tried to steer the mare that way. Rasul wasn't beside him anymore. More arrows flew toward him; beside him a horse let out a shriek, staggered and fell into the water. Then the horses around him were slamming to a stop, knee deep in the river. A wail went up. Past the rocky shallows he saw, ahead of them, on the far bank, a dark swarming mass of other horsemen. Above them a long green banner floated, curling like a snake's tongue on the wind.

An arrow clipped his arm. He flinched. There was nowhere to go. He looked around for Rasul but did not see him. Around him the horses stamped and shied in the shallow water, the men turning, their eyes wild.

Then Baibers galloped up past them all, into the gap between Daud and the enemy on the far bank.

After Baibers the rearguard of the Mamelukes followed in a stream, shooting their bows as they charged. The men around Daud all roared and followed headlong. Daud wrenched the horse's head around and kicked her in the ribs. She pinned her ears back and stuck her nose out and hurtled forward, packed among the other horses. Daud's stirrup banged into the stirrup of the horse beside him. The tail of the horse in front of him lashed Friend's shoulder. One of a hundred, Daud flew across the shallow riverbed, toward the screaming dark mass on the far bank.

He had forgotten his bow. He got it off his back, while Friend plunged and galloped with the others, and tried to string it. Around him the Mamelukes were screaming the name of God. Just ahead of Daud an arrow struck a rider and threw him backward out of his saddle, and Friend jumped over the falling body and bolted on. Daud gave up with the bow and clung to his horse with both hands.

The horses before him bounded suddenly upward, and then Friend was scrambling upward, onto the far bank of the river. For an instant they all slowed, jammed together. The horse before him reared, its saddle empty. Abruptly they were charging forward again, and now, through the thin rank of riders in front of him, Daud saw men out there in front of them, turning and running away.

Then there was a howl of voices, and a horn blasted again. They were stopping. Friend slowed to a trot and then a walk and stood, among the other horses, blowing hard. Daud leaned both hands on his mare's withers. He was in the middle of the road, among a crowd of Mamelukes. Almost at Friend's feet, a body sprawled on the stone pavement, and beyond, another. All around him the men were whooping, clapping each other on the back.

He looked ahead; he could see only the dust of many people riding fast away. Above the dust was a streak of green. He realized those were the men who had attacked them. They had won a battle. Dazed, he wondered if he had done anything good. Baibers rode up before them on his bay horse.

"Praise be to God, who has given us victory!"

They all shouted. Daud opened his mouth, but nothing came out. He looked around again for Rasul. He was thirsty; he licked his lips, looking around for water.

Boglu was riding up toward him, leading another horse. At the grim look on his face, his brows down and his mouth tight, Daud stiffened all over, warned. He looked past him, to the horse Boglu was leading.

Rasul lay there, across the saddle. Rasul hung there, facedown, dead.

Daud gave a violent shudder. His throat closed. He slid down from the saddle and went to the body, and put his hands on Rasul's back. The other men gathered around him, weeping, all hugging him. He remembered the shield covering him. How Rasul had protected him, and he lowered his head and sobbed.

The horn blew again. They had to ride again. Numbly he went to Friend and mounted, and steered her back to ride beside Rasul's body. The fields where they had just fought were covered with green vines, trampled into the dust, and pieces of flowers. His eyes kept turning toward Rasul. He wanted to tell Rasul something, but it was too late. He didn't know what it was anyway. The sun was sinking. Soon it would be night.

\* \*

Just across the river, below the hill where the ruined tower stood, was a meadow, and here Baibers brought his men to camp. They were battered, many hurt, and several dead, and in the meadow they first went together and faced Mecca and prayed to God who had chosen them to bring him victory.

Boglu and some others laid Rasul down on the ground, and straightened his clothes. Daud brought water and they washed the dead man's body. Baibers came among them, looking each one in the eyes, and spoke to them all.

Baibers said, "Rasul is with God now. God has taken him. Don't grieve, but rejoice for him, that he has won paradise." His hand lay heavy as a blow on Daud's shoulder.

Daud stood among them, empty. Everything that came to him went away. They dug Rasul down into the earth, and everybody laid stones over him.

He took care of his horse, brushing her and picking up her feet and combing her mane. This soothed him. Darkness fell. When Boglu put food before him, he ate, sitting with the others, but separate. Sleep was coming. What came with sleeping frightened him. Then Boglu draped an arm around him, as Daud had often seen him do with Rasul, and held him against his side. Daud let out his breath, relieved, and shut his eyes.

\* \*

In the morning they shot their bows. When his turn came Daud drew the string back, as always the power in the bow resisting him, defying him. He saw the sack of straw down the way and he thought it could be the man who killed Rasul. He shot, and the arrow sailed wide past the sack.

He saw how it curved in the air, and when Boglu gave him another arrow he kept that curve in his mind, and drew the string back.

Then the bow came alive. It arched in his hands, part of him. He foresaw the flight of the arrow through the air, and he let go the string and the arrow pierced the sack through.

All the men around him cheered him, and they thumped his shoulders and pulled his hair. He stood, letting this happen, staring down at the arrow, and he ached that Rasul had not seen him do it.

\* \*

After midday prayers, a file of men rode up toward their camp, and above them floated the green banner.

Daud saw them, and leapt to his feet; but he could see they weren't here to fight. Baibers was going out to meet them on his bay mare, all alone. Daud frowned, struggling to make sense of this. His hand, unwilled, was on the knife in his belt.

Behind him, Boglu chuckled. He said, "I think we're changing sides again."

Daud startled all over, shocked. Boglu was sitting on the ground, eating an apple, and Daud looked around the camp and saw them all sitting, or standing idly, or talking, none of them caring at all what was happening. He swung forward again. He could see it was true, by the way Baibers held himself, the way the other men spoke to him.

They were asking something of him. And he was agreeing to it. The men who had killed Rasul.

Boglu said, "Well, it doesn't matter to me. It's all one war, anyway."

Daud sat down, to hide the shaking of his body; a black rage took him. He raked at the hard ground with his fingers, thinking of Rasul. He wondered how Baibers did not hate these men with their green banner. Why he did not strike them down.

He thought Baibers talked a lot about God. But he meant himself.

The next day they rode out across the valley, following an old road. Daud was still angry; he thought of riding up to Baibers and sticking his knife in him. On either side the fields stretched away across the plain. Here and there an orchard made a pond of shadow. They passed by a broken wall, where beggars sat and women called out. In the fields beyond people rose and dipped, picking something into baskets. Here was flat ground but to the north two low long hills rose, covered with trees.

Boglu said, "This place is full of stories. Ibrahim and Isa walked here. See that hill? That is where the Giant lived. Goliath, which the shepherd boy slew."

Daud lifted his head, the story familiar to him; he remembered the shepherd boy's name. He almost spoke, but did not.

The Bahriyya stopped at a caravanserai and drove out most of the people to make room. Daud went around drawing water for the horses, and finding good hay in the heaps of old stuff behind the building. Boglu came to him and said, "I am going to the city here, to bring out the merchants. Come with me. I would like to see you laugh again."

Daud followed after him, his whole mind dark. They followed the road a few miles and came to a town. A stone wall ringed it, and they went up to the gate.

There, by the gate, stood two men wearing white surcoats with red crosses on them.

A sharp shock passed through Daud, like a slap. The two men were watching them, and as Boglu led him into the archway of the gate, one knight held out his hand to stop them.

Boglu said, "I am Bahriyya, on business of the Sultan, let me pass."

The big knight said, "Just you and this one? Where are the rest of you?"

Boglu waved vaguely behind them. The two knights looked at each other; the one who had not spoken only shrugged. The big knight said, "How long are you staying?"

"We'll be gone by sundown. We're just going to the bazaar."

The knights exchanged another look, and the big one stepped back.

"Go on, then. Don't give me any trouble."

Daud's heart was thumping. He rode after Boglu through the gate, and the Mameluke held back so that Friend came up even with him. Boglu leaned toward him.

"Templars. They have a quarter here. Demons of the Franks. Someday we'll drive them into the sea." He grunted.

They were riding down a narrow cobbled street between high buildings but ahead beyond the roofs was an expanse of sky, over a wider space. Daud swallowed hard. They came out into a great square, all lined with stalls and awnings, crowded with people. A fountain gurgled in the middle. Daud thought Boglu surely would hear the thundering of his heart. Would see the purpose in his mind. Boglu was headed toward the far side of the bazaar. Daud looked quickly around.

In front of a stall selling bread, Boglu swung down from his saddle, looped his reins over his arm, went forward to talk to the merchant. Daud slipped down from Friend and ran.

He went through the thick of the crowd, dodging and darting among people, a woman carrying a basket on her arm, two men talking with many gestures, a boy leading a donkey. Behind him, he heard a yell.

"Kuçuk!"

He dashed around past the fountain, headed back toward the gate where they had come in. Somebody grabbed for him but he ducked. Then to one side, he saw a white surcoat with a red cross.

He swerved that way. The square ended here in a row of buildings. Where a narrow way opened between them stood two more of the red cross knights. He heard again, behind him, Boglu's shout.

The knights saw him coming. One stepped forward; Daud slowed. The knight held out one arm, but he was looking past Daud, toward the square, and suddenly he was waving Daud on.

The boy flew into the narrow way, into the dark little street. He turned into an alley, panting, and stopped there. Peering around the corner, he saw the two knights standing side by side in the opening, facing Boglu. He could not hear what they said but he knew by their looks the knights were turning Boglu off. Daud went off down the alley, all his skin humming, wondering what he should do next.

# CHAPTER 4

## ACRE

Rikart came to the land gate of Acre around dusk, just before it closed for the night. The warm sea wind was rushing out of the west, smelling of the harbor, salt and rot. The last long daylight shone on the pale walls of the city. At the gate a servant was lighting torches. The Templar guards came out to meet him, and he showed them his pass and was let in.

Vespers bells were ringing. The long street that stretched from the gate to the harbor was full of people hurrying to get home. He had been alone for a long while, riding here, and the crowd made him jittery.

The last light hung in the sky, the rooftops like a jagged black staircase against it. Up the low rise ahead of him, the old minaret was a stump. No call to prayer went out from that.

He turned off into a narrow street that ran along the foot of the land-wall, coming to the inn called Grasper. He put up his horse in the stable at the back and hid his pack and his sword under the manger. There was no one else in the barn and only two other horses; he forked them all down some hay and went out.

Going down the dark street he came to another gate, torchlit, three pikemen in striped doublets lounging around a turnstile, where another pass got him through.

This street was quiet, hard against the sea; he could hear the waves on the rocks just beyond the wall. He passed an enclosed garden, its walls dripping jasmine. He was the only person on the street now, his footsteps loud in the dark. At the corner, on the wall above his head, was a wooden balcony. A light shone inside, streaking yellow through the slats in the walls. He stood beneath, and called out, "Bella. Bella! The cat's come home."

For a moment he stood looking up, and then the slatted window opened, and a plump white arm reached out, and dropped him down a key. He walked around the corner to the alley, to the postern door, and let himself in.

* *

Isabella da Benefrio stretched her arms up, arching her back, and nestled down into her silken covers. Rikart was across the room, naked, his back to her, his arms thrust out to either side like a cross. She had seen him do this often; she knew not to speak to him while he did. She let her eyes enjoy him. He was lean and hard as a whip. The flair of his shoulders narrowed into a slim waist and the smooth arches of his backside. Down one shoulder ran a long old scar. He had recently cut his hair and his beard, maybe when he was among the Mongols. He stood utterly still in his cross for what seemed an impossibly long time, his arms steadily flung out. She thought of breakfast. He lowered his arms and turned toward her.

He smiled; he came back and threw himself on the bed. "Bella," he said. He gathered up one tress of her long fair hair and curled it around his finger. "What a Bella, Bellissima." He tugged on the tress.

She bent down and kissed him, and let him roll her into his arms. In his arms she was a girl again, heedless, lusty; she gave him back all she knew of the ways of love. For a while she forgot breakfast.

Later, sipping sweet hot apple tea, she said, "You can't be here tonight, alas." She was hoping he would rouse at this, and change her mind.

He was putting on his clothes. He said, "What you wish, Bellissima." He turned and smiled at her. "I'm just glad you let me in last night." Standing, he pulled his leggings up to his waist and tied the string. "Tell me a few things. Have the Genoese come back?"

Disappointed, she said, "No. At least, not openly. Probably they are trading through somebody else." The Genoese had been run off the year before. Still, everybody who traded in the Holy Land had to have a place in Acre.

"What about the Hospital? Didn't they just elect a new guardian?" He stamped his feet into his boots.

She lay back on her pillows; she knew this market as well as the other one. "Yes. Hugh Reinall. Do you remember him?"

"The Englishman." He pulled his shirt on and then his surcoat, stained and threadbare. She would have her seamstress make him another. "How are they and the Temple getting along?"

"Each keeps a separate quarter. The Templars watch the gates and the streets. The Hospital oversees the harbor." Which meant, she knew, as he certainly knew, that they did nothing: the Venetians controlled the harbor, as they had done since they drove out the Genoese.

"Have you heard anything more about a new Crusade?" he said.

"No, have you?"

"This and that. The Pope is a ninny. There's nobody else to do it, they're all fighting each other. Who sits on the city council?"

"The council has not met for months. There is someone I know who will want to talk to you."

"Venetian?" he said.

"Well." She did not have to answer that. He flashed another smile at her. His beard was growing back, a dark line along his jaw. She said, "I will arrange it. Where will you be?"

He stooped and kissed her again. "Here. Whenever you let me in." His mouth moved from her cheek to her lips. She put her hands on his chest. Then he was straightening, he was going, and she lowered her hands to her lap. He went out the door like the ghost they all called him. She shut her eyes. This was useless. He had no land, no money. He had no title. She sighed, and called in her maid to help her rise and dress.

* *

He went down toward the harbor, on the south side of the promontory. Below the looming yellow walls, the wharfs stretched like fingers into the shallow bay. The water was blue as lapis, except where it broke white on the rocks. Here on the south edge of the city, round-bellied cargo ships packed the water hull to hull, wooden tubs that wallowed in the chop. He walked along the quayside, threading his way through the lines of porters carrying bales and sacks and boxes up to the warehouses just inside the wall, and other lines of porters carrying bales and sacks and boxes down to the ships. A seagull screamed.

Ahead the promontory narrowed, rising into the Templars' massive tower, its forefoot in the sea. From there a point of rocks bent around in a hook to the south. Solitary in the middle of the harbor, the ruin of the Tower of Flies, where the Genoese had made their last stand, was festooned in the red and gold banners of Saint Mark.

He passed a wharf stacked up with lumber, and another sagging under bales of cloth. Beneath the reek of the shore weed, and the usual rank smells of the harbor, there ran a constant tang of pepper. He lost count of the ships in the harbor, which all looked to be Venetian.

At the far end of the harbor a stair went up the wall and he climbed it to the broad pavement at the top. From here he looked out west over the blunt end of the promontory, past the Templar tower to the blue silk of the Mediterranean, and then north over Acre, a wide clutter of roofs. He went down another set of steps into the city. He dodged back against the wall to get out of the way of a litter, borne by four men, that jogged along the roadway. Three or four other men followed, all wearing red and gold coats and carrying staves. The litter's fluttering curtains were Han silk, the fittings Egyptian ivory and gold, the wood probably from Cyprus or the Morea.

Everything came through Acre, all the riches of the world, silk and gold and furs, pepper and sugar, lumber and money. Especially money.

From a vendor cooking his wares over a brazier he got a skewer of lamb chunks dumped into the bowl of a palm frond. The vendor ladled a thin stream of yogurt over the meat. This tasted of dill. Rikart leaned up against the wall to eat it.

The crowd walked by him along the roadway, merchants with their servants, bravos in their gaudy plumed hats, workmen hauling goods and tools. He heard people speaking Italian, not the long slurred Venetian accent, something else. A procession of monks came slowly along like a great dark caterpillar. Two knights in the black surcoats of the Hospital sauntered by him and gave him a hard stare. Sea gulls spilled over the wall, also watching him, floating in the air like angels. He ate the last of the lamb and went on west along the foot of the great wall, past a row of warehouses. From the steps of a little church a whore gave him a lewd, crooning call.

He walked down a crooked lane and came on a patch of burnt out buildings. Hollow blackened holes of windows in the sooty white walls. Vines climbed up over the roofs and poppies grew out of the pavements.

He was surprised nobody had taken this over; the Genoese had been gone for months. A cat hissed at him from a doorway. He went on to the next street, and into the Greek quarter.

The street widened, suddenly full of people. Just ahead of him the great bulk of the Templars' tower blocked the high sun.

He stood there a moment. The tower cast its shadow on him. His father had been a Templar, until the Order betrayed the Emperor Frederick. Then his father had left and gone to Jerusalem as a pilgrim, married Rikart's mother. But when the Order called him, he went back.

Rikart remembered his mother sobbing. His father saying, "Go to Baghdad. Go to Reb Moseh. I'll meet you there when this is over." His hand on Rikart's shoulder, steering him out the door to the courtyard.

The servants were already packing everything onto donkeys. They had only until sunset to get out of the city. The old man, his father's squire, waited by the wall with their horses. Rikart had been ten years old then. He had known nothing. His father sank down on his heels before him, his face gaunt behind the grey sweep of his beard.

"Take care of your mother," he said. His hand on Rikart's shoulder squeezed tight. "Remember me."

"Papa," he said, and his throat closed up. His father walked to his horse and they rode away.

Months later, in Baghdad, they heard that he had died at La Forbie.

Some people thought the Order of the Temple itself had died at La Forbie.

He gathered himself. He had to try this. He took the pass from his belt pouch, and went across the street to the gate into the tower.

\* \*

"My brother Sir Yvain says you accompanied him and Prince Bohemund to the camp of the Il-Khan."

"I did," Rikart said. A servant had brought him a stool to sit on. In the depths of the stone tower the room was cool, even in the heat of the summer, and the men sitting before him were bundled in their cloaks. Braziers smoldered in a circle all around them.

The Grand Master of the Templars faced him, smiling. His plump hands, armored with rings, rested on his knees. Rikart wondered when he had last held a sword. A servant stood there with a cup and the Master took it and drank, and waved it on toward Rikart.

"What was your purpose?"

"I carried certain messages," Rikart said. He sipped from the cup and passed it to Yvain de la Foret, on the Master's right hand. Rikart did not know the other two men sitting there. "Also I wanted to see what Bohemund was doing."

"What was he doing?"

Yvain would have told him this. "He wants the Il-Khan to take Damascus for him."

"He's nothing if not ambitious. Who else was there? Any other Christians? Any Venetians?"

"Not that I saw. There were a lot of merchants."

"Bohemund is making an alliance with the Il-Khan, then."

Rikart gave a little shake of his head, and said nothing. Yvain sat back in his chair. One of the other men leaned forward, scowling in his thick black beard.

"What, then?" this man said, in a harsh voice.

"This is no alliance. Antioch is subject to them now. They will require a tribute. Eventually they'll send somebody to take over the power. Bohemund can still be Prince but he will have no power and they will take all the money."

The Master laced the fingers of his hands together and set this fist on the table in front of him. The smile had drained from his face. "You saw their army?"

"Yes." Yvain would have told him this, too.

"One hundred thousand men," said the scowling man. "This is impossible."

The Master's face suddenly flushed red above the curly yellow gloss of his beard; his eyes opened wide. "I question what we can do." Quickly he looked from one side to the other. "Perhaps Bohemund is just being prudent. We haven't been able to put an army in the field since La Forbie." He cracked his doubled fist down on the table.

One of the men on his left said, under his breath, "We could stand up for what we believe in." This was a younger man, with a wispy blonde beard. The knight beside him put a hand on his arm, holding him back.

The scowling man said, "One hundred thousand men? I don't believe you."

"More than that," Rikart said. "You can't do it alone." He glanced at the man who had just spoken. "We need an alliance."

"With whom?"

"The Greeks. The Sultan of Damascus."

The scowling man snorted. "The Greeks are busy with their own wars. Yusuf is hopeless. Saladin's heir. What a fool." The others laughed.

Rikart drew in a breath. "The Mamelukes in Egypt."

At that, they all started up, their heads rising, and a low rumble of anger stirring among them. The Master leapt up from his chair and paced away across the room, his hands behind his back. The scowling man thrust himself forward.

"The Mamelukes! Qutuz? Baibers? Are you mad? After what they did to us at Mansurah?"

Rikart kept silent.

The young fair-headed man who had just spoken said, "Will the squints march on Damascus, then? When will this happen?"

Rikart said, "They mostly fight in the winter. Right now they're up on the steppe, fattening their horses. They'll go after the Kurds and the Assassins first. When they're done with them, they'll come on us."

"Mark you, they hate whom we hate," the black-scowling man said. "There is a sign in that." He shot a harsh look at the younger man, whose companion was tugging on his arm again.

From the far side of the room, his back to them, the Master said, "The Mongols are Christians. The Pope has commanded us to greet them as brothers. And we are forbidden to have anything to do with the infidels."

The scowling man said, "We can make a deal with the Mongols. We hold Acre. That is more sway than Antioch."

"You don't hold Acre," Rikart said. "The Venetians hold Acre."

"They will follow us. Acre is the center of everything."

"Baghdad was the center of everything," Rikart said.

The Master came back, and sank into his chair. The scowling man slid back again, deferring to him. The Master said, "I heard the barbarians leveled Baghdad to the ground."

"Close enough."

The cup came around again to the Master and he drank. He daubed at his mouth with a napkin and shrugged. "A beautiful city."

"They burned the House of Wisdom. They wrapped the Caliph in a carpet and trampled him to death with their horses."

The Master shook that off. "His God abandoned him." His lips pursed. His pudgy hands stroked each other.

"What happened to Baghdad will happen to Acre eventually."

"We can find a way. If they are Christian, we have common ground in Jesus." He crossed himself. "And they need us. Acre controls the trade. They want money as much as anybody."

The scowling man said, "Perhaps we can join with them against the Mamelukes."

Rikart gave out a soft grunt. He met Yvain's eyes a moment and the Templar cocked up his eyebrows.

The Master said, "We will discuss this. Stay close by. Perhaps I will call for you again, when we have decided. I may ask you to carry a message for us back to the Mongols."

"I'm not going that way," Rikart said.

"You can make your way there."

Rikart said nothing. The Master was smiling again. He folded his jewel-encrusted hands over his belly. He said, "You will profit from it." He waved his hand. His eyes did not meet Rikart's. "You may go."

* *

Before he reached the checkpoint he knew someone was following him.

At the gate, he showed his pass; the man following him hung back there, by the corner, a small man in a short Greek coat.

Once through the gate Rikart broke into a run, turned a corner, then another, dodging down a narrow twisting lane. Heavy coils of jasmine and rose vines draped the stone walls on either side. Ahead, he knew, the lane ended flush against the city rampart.

Where a palm tree grew close to the wall he scaled the tree and swung over and lay down among the vines on top of the wall and watched the street.

Beneath him an old man ambled by with a stick and a pack. Then two boys going the other way. Rikart waited.

The man in the Greek coat appeared at the mouth of the lane, looking around. In one hand he held a short sword. Uncertainly he drifted nearer; he stopped to peer through a gate. Rikart slid his hand down to his belt, where his knife was sheathed, but did not draw it. The Greek came closer; he lifted his head and scanned the walls, and Rikart vaulted off the wall and landed on him.

The sword clanged on the street. Under Rikart's weight the wiry body writhed around on the ground, face down, and with a violent lurch flung Rikart off. Rikart rolled over and from hands and knees lunged into the other man, drove him down again under him, and got hold of the wrist with the sword. They thrashed together in the ground. The Greek swung an elbow at him. When he recoiled, the Greek twisted around and tried to butt him in the face. Rikart got his feet under him, and stood, using his grip on the man's sword arm to haul the Greek to his feet. He wrapped his free arm around the Greek's throat.

The sword clattered to the street. Rikart jerked the Greek's right arm up between his shoulder blades. The Greek's other hand gripped Rikart's arm where it crossed his throat.

"Why are you following me?"

The Greek panted. He clutched at Rikart's arm. Rikart lifted him half off his feet and swung him hard against the wall and leaned on him. Holding him tight against the wall, he let go of the Greek's wrist and drew his knife.

"Why are you following me?"

The Greek said, muffled, "I heard—I heard—" and stopped. With a groan, he worked at freeing his right arm, still pinned between his back and Rikart's chest. Rikart leaned his whole weight against him.

"Tell me and I'll let you go."

"Liar!"

"Tell me and find out."

The Greek said nothing a moment. Rikart had him wedged against the wall, snugged up by the throat, and he raised the knife in his free hand and pricked the other man's nose.

The Greek gasped out, "I heard killing you would get me a lot of money."

"From who?"

"I don't know—I just heard—"

Rikart slit the side of his nose.

"Antioch! Antioch! Oww!" The blood gushed down his face. Rikart let him go, and stepped quickly backward. The sword lay in the street and he kicked it away. The Greek wheeled toward him, his hands to his bleeding face. His eyes glittered. Rikart knew he was lying.

"Go," Rikart said. "Explain how you got that. Go, you pig." He went quickly on up the street, before the watch came on them.

* *

He went back to the inn Grasper, and sat down on a bench in the back, by the wall, where he could see the door and the rest of the room. The room was full of people drinking and playing dice. A girl went around with a jug, filling cups; she brought him a cup and he gave her a quarter dinar. He was still twitchy from the fighting and he drank the wine down and beckoned her over to fill the cup again.

The Templar Yvain came in from the street. On his heels was the blonde-bearded boy who had spoken out to the Master. Rikart slid his stool back against the wall behind him, and watched them approach through the crowd, and the eyes of the everyone in the crowd follow them.

"We could go into the back," Yvain said. There were private rooms in the back.

"Why bother?" Rikart said. "There are spies everywhere." He nodded toward a nearby bench. "Sit."

They pulled stools around on either side of him. Around the room, several men were still watching them steadily. Yvain stretched his legs out before him, crossed them comfortably at the ankles, and took a cup from the girl with the jug.

"Thank you for speaking as you did, today," Yvain said.

"I'm sorry if I disturbed you. What are you, a rich men's drinking club now?"

The boy shook his head and looked down at his hands. Yvain said, "You did more than you know."

"We will not ally with the squints," the boy said, between his teeth. "I came here to die for the cross, not for some prince."

Rikart said, "Somebody in there is doubling on you. Who was that who kept speaking around the Master?"

"Gianpaolo di Busceglia?"

"Unh," Rikart said. "Venetian?"

"I think he's Cypriot. He's new. Very well connected."

"Somebody tried to kill me, right after I talked to you."

The boy straightened; he and Yvain exchanged a look. The boy said, "They're afraid of you."

Yvain gave a half-shrug. "A lot of people hate you, Ghost. What happened?"

"Look for a man with a slit nose."

"Ah, you let him escape." Yvain smiled. "This is why we always go two by two, you see. Are you staying here?"

"Not past tonight. I'm leaving Acre in the morning. I'm not carrying a letter to the Mongols for you."

"That will not happen," the boy said.

Yvain said, "We will do what we can." He held out his hand. "Be careful. Keep me informed."

Bella de Benefrio lay back on the cushions of her chair, enjoying the gentle sway. They were moving briskly down the great street, but the four bearers were masters of this; they kept the chair upright and steady even at great pace and around corners. She pulled back the curtain and looked out. The great houses along this street all hid behind their walls; people thronged up and down. Ahead was the Templar checkpoint. She was early, the church bells not yet ringing. She liked to go into the church a little after all the rest, so that they all turned and watched her come in. The chair slowed in the crowd waiting by the checkpoint, and looking out across the street, she saw on a far corner another little crowd, and someone juggling.

She rang her bell. Leaned forward. "Mitri. Over there, see? There's a show."

The bearer on the left front shaft gave her a quick nod and called out to the others. They swung the chair around, keeping it level, and made for the far corner. Bella pulled the curtains back.

The juggler was standing on the steps before a gate of iron palings; his costume of green and yellow bright against the dark rails. Three balls whirled in the air before him. The crowd, mostly children, let out whistles and yells. Bella saw a woman, just down the way, also in green and yellow, and now this woman came up and began to toss more balls into the stream. The juggler's hands blurred. He spun five, now six balls higher and higher, and then suddenly he was throwing them one by one toward the woman, and she was catching each one, tossing it up, and passing it back in an intricate crisscross.

The crowd whooped. Bella laughed, delighted. Then, suddenly, Rikart was there, beside the chair.

"Bella," he said. "I'm glad to see you here."

"Oh," she cried, happy, and put her hand out. He took hold of it.

He said, "I'm glad for the chance to say good bye to you. I have to go."

"Do it properly. Come to my window tonight." She would get rid of Gianpaolo.

"No—somebody is trying to kill me. Something might happen to you."

"Trying to kill you." She looked all around, alarmed. "Why?"

"I tell the truth so some people want me dead."

He held her hand, but he was watching the jugglers. Abruptly she felt him stiffen. She looked where he was looking. All she saw was a scrawny Arab boy in a thobe too large for him, carrying a brass bowl through the crowd to collect money. She fished in the cushions for her purse. The boy came closer. Rikart was staring at him. She started to speak, to remark on this, and he said, "Daud? Daud!"

The boy jerked his head up. His eyes widened and his mouth opened, and he spoke, in a croak like a rusty gate. "Rikart," he said, and dropping the bowl, he rushed into the knight's arms. Bella drew her empty hand away.

\* \*

After his first croak the boy stopped talking. He kept hold of Rikart's sleeve. The jugglers wanted money to let him go, since they had been feeding him, and Rikart gave them an isaac. With another isaac he bought a little grey donkey for the boy to ride and by noon they were going out the gate of Acre.

The Templar at the gate recognized him, and drew him to one side. "My lord Marshall bade me tell you when you came this way that we fished the body of a man with a cut nose out of the harbor this morning." He handed Rikart back his pass. "Go with God, my lord."

"God help us," Rikart said, and went back to his horse.

\* \*

At a caravanserai on the coast road, as Rikart was building a fire in their brazier, the boy burst out, "I killed someone." Then he wept. He said no more. Rikart, in the habit of silence, let it be.

In the morning, when he thought he had gone off by himself to stand in his cross, he turned around and the boy was there. The boy said, "What are you doing?"

"I'm supposed to be praying, but I don't," Rikart said. "I just stand there as long as I can and wait for something to happen."

The boy smiled at him. He said nothing. They went on down the road. Rikart studied him; Daud was taller, thinner than before. Sunburnt brown. He moved with a quick, nimble purpose, like someone much older. Somehow he had learned to ride and he kept the donkey up to the big horse's pace. Rikart remembered him, back in Baghdad, and could not see that boy in this one.

The coast road thronged with camel caravans and donkeys, horsemen and many people on foot. Off on the glittering blue sea, ships rowed by, or far out there, floated under sails like clouds. The sun blazed. Rikart had one more letter to deliver, in Damascus, but he was in no hurry, and he intended to go somewhere else first.

That night they stayed in the grand caravanserai at Ramla. Not far from here a handful of Templars had set to flight Saladin's army of thousands, but now this was part of the realm of the Sultan of Damascus, and the Temple was a crew of watchmen. He still rankled over the meeting in Acre. The innkeeper came, and with many bows said a certain man would have Rikart join him for supper, and said a name Rikart knew.

Rikart hesitated; he had seen enough of Italians in Acre. But he thought he might hear some news. He followed the innkeeper across the way to a private room.

This was carpeted in many layers, and silks hung on the walls. On cushions by the low table sat a great heap of a man in a velvet cap and the loose gown of one who did not ride a horse. Rikart went over, and the man greeted him, not getting up.

"El Shab'h. We've met before, remember?" He spoke Italian, with the musical northern accent.

"In Tyre," Rikart said. He sat down on the carpets; the boy stole in close behind him. "You were looking for pepper."

The big man chuckled. "You have a good memory." His eyes flicked at Daud. "Your saddle-boy? I didn't know you went in for that kind of thing."

Rikart stared at him, blank, until the other man looked away with a shrug and said, "Well, eat something. Try the grapes, they're excellent."

Rikart fed himself. On the table was an array of dishes, cheese and fruit, olives, yogurt, pastries stuffed with fig jam, thin slices of roasted lamb. The Venetian said, "Are you come from Acre? How is the weather there?"

This was a way of saying something else. Rikart said, "Oh, it seems calm enough to me. No fighting in the streets, anyway." He slipped a bait onto the hook. "Before then, I was in the east."

The merchant's eyes widened. "Baghdad."

"There is no more Baghdad." He ate grapes. "I saw the Il-Khan."

The merchant's head bobbed. "Did you. Tell me. Will they keep open the trade routes, do you think?"

"If you pay their price," Rikart said. He gave the boy some meat and bread and a handful of olives.

"I have heard they are Christian. Prester John, wandered off into the east, returned to the family hearth. Is it true there is another swarm of these barbarians north of the Georgian Sea?"

"The great khan Temujin had four sons. Each got a part of the empire. They've been killing each other off for years, and there's only two families left, really. These coming at us are the sons of the youngest son. The ones above the Georgian Sea are the sons of the eldest."

"Are the ones in the north as many as the ones in Baghdad?"

"Yes, I think so. Probably. Most of them are likely not Mongols."

"Who then?"

"The Mamelukes' people. Kipchaks. Turks."

"Like a plague of locusts. Maybe it's God's will."

Rikart said, with some heat, "That's easy." He hadn't even gotten around yet to discussing standing up to them and the damned Venetian was already giving up. "That's a manure pile."

"What do you think?"

"I think if God wills what happened to Baghdad then damn God." He thought the hook was swallowed; he said, "What is going on in Constantinople?"

The Venetian made himself busy with some roasted meat. "While we hold Constantinople we're secure."

"Yes? Where is Michael Paleologus?"

The Venetian's face twitched. He swiped harshly at his mouth with a napkin. He looked away a moment and then turned and glared at Rikart. "The Greeks are beyond contempt. They don't know what's good for them."

"I've heard Michael has taken his army down into Epirus. Is that so?"

The merchant said nothing.

Rikart said, "I don't think you can hold Constantinople too long without Epirus."

"Our troops will defeat him there, surely. We're in a very strong position there. The Despot of Epirus, the Prince of Achaea, the King of Sicily-" he bit off his words.

"Whatever you say," Rikart said. The King of Sicily had sent an army to Epirus, then; that was interesting. There was a lot of bad blood between Venice and Sicily. "Paying him a fortune, are you?"

"Venice is the mistress of the seas and we have the greatest armies at our service." The Venetian's hand rose and fell, chopping. "This is science."

Rikart leaned forward a little. "I think if you had any real science you would have not seized Constantinople in the first place. You made nothing there better than it was before, and much of it worse."

The Venetian pressed his lips together, and his eyes glinted. "It was us or them. We're keeping the trade routes open through these perilous times. Venice is the guardian of Christendom."

"Yes, that's why you overran a Christian city."

"I'm not surprised you have so many enemies," the Venetian said, in the same gritty voice.

"Right now, we have a mutual enemy. The Mongols will come on soon enough."

"What do they want? Damascus?"

"They want Cairo," Rikart said.

"Cairo!" The Venetian grunted. "There's a reach."

"For them, not so much. They move fast. They would hold all from Cairo to the Eastern Sea. The heart of the world."

The Venetian grumbled at him. He dipped bread into the yogurt and ate it. "Many people want things. I want many things." He shifted on the cushions. "They can beat the Arabs for us. We can come out of this well."

"That's what Bohemund thinks." Rikart ate bread.

"That's his father-in-law talking. The Armenians always want to dicker with everybody. What's this I have heard about Baibers?"

Rikart shrugged. "Baibers has thrown in again with the Sultan of Damascus. At least so I heard a few days ago, it could have changed by now." At his shoulder, the boy Daud moved, and put a hand on his arm. In the welter of unfamiliar talk he must have heard something familiar.

"That is the true enemy," the Venetian said. "That damned dog of a Mameluke. All of them."

Baibers had made a life's work of beating Crusaders. Rikart said, "Baibers has a few hundred men. The Il-Khan has one hundred fifty thousand."

The Venetian shifted in his seat, looking away. "Ah, well." he gestured at the table. "Eat. We may as well keep up our strength, hah." He laughed. "We'll see what happens."

"Yes," Rikart said. "We will."

\* \*

In the morning they set off again, but soon they turned off the main road; Rikart led the way up into the hills. Daud jogged the donkey after him. He missed Friend but he had named the donkey Greyling, and he liked riding it; it was so small he could use his weight to move it around.

The country was dry, grassy, spotted with clumps of red flowers. White sheep dotted the meadows. He saw a shepherd, off across the rising slope. There were no other travelers. Grass grew on the road. They passed through an empty village, in the ruins of a much bigger place. They spent the night in the open, and Rikart sat there with him and pointed to the stars and said names.

Near sundown of the next day they came up onto a long ridge, where part of a gate stood, a tower, a wall. Beyond, the grass and the scrubby junipers were growing up over the remains of a town. Goats browsed on the broken walls. Rikart went down a narrow paved street, stopped, looked around, and turned into another way. Down toward the end of the ridge, a mosque stood, one tower, a dome cracked and fallen in. A woman in a black robe came toward them, balancing a basket on her head. Her eyes downcast, she seemed not to notice them. Rikart stopped and stood staring into an open space. Under tangles of weeds Daud could make out walls.

He said, "Rikart, what is this place?"

Rikart barked a laugh. "This is Jerusalem, little brother."

The boy's jaw fell. He gaped around him. The wind blew through the high weeds. He could hear the creak of a wagon coming up along the path. This could not be; Jerusalem was a city made all of gold, the house of God.

Rikart said, "I lived in this house." He pointed off in another direction. "Over there, Christ died for our sins." His voice shook. He stood staring around him as if he saw something else. Daud gave a shiver. He slid down from the donkey.

"Back years ago the Emperor made a treaty with the Sultan, that Christians could come into the city," Rikart said. "Frederick, the Emperor that was. When that happened my father came here. He had—he lost faith in the Templars. He gave up the cross." He lifted his arms; Daud thought it was in him to stand as he had before, like a cross, but he did not.

"Then the treaty ran out. The Sultan came to drive us out. There was a battle. My father died there. My mother took me away to Baghdad, to Reb Moseh, who sheltered us." He lifted one hand and let it fall. "After the battle the Sultan let his men destroy the city."

Daud turned back to the donkey. Some terrible dark space inside him was tightening into a knot. He wanted to get out of here but Rikart looked to be settling down for the night. The boy pressed his head against the donkey's saddle and shut his eyes, which did no good. He went off around the place, looking for wood for the fire.

\* \*

In an angle of the wall, they sat close together, and Rikart stared into the fire. He wondered why he came here; it would be that much longer to

Damascus, now. After Damascus he did not know what to do. He tossed bits of wood into the fire, brooding.

He had no way to Yusuf, and he knew he would have found no ear there, either. The Mongols probably had spies among the Sultan's court. The fire crackled; in the leaping flames he saw whole battles.

The boy said, suddenly, "In Baghdad—in Baghdad—-"

Rikart turned toward him. The boy was crying again. Bone by bone, he crawled toward Rikart, and words spilled from him like tears. "I killed them. I killed them. I made the roof fall on them." He crept into Rikart's lap like a little child. "I see their eyes. At night." In the cage of Rikart's arms he was weeping and talking as if he could not stop, giving up his memory in a spate. "I saw Reb Moseh, he was dead, and then they beat me and stole all I had. I went to the mosque. I went to the canal. Then— Then—rocks fell. I hid. There was a dead man. I hid anyway. I was hungry. The rocks fell and killed people and when I went back nothing was there. We fought them. I and a big woman. They killed her. The canal was dry. I was hungry. I was so hungry. I found a place. I killed a rat. I killed a boy. I saw—I saw—" he stopped, panting. The fire glowed on his face. His eyes stared, sunken, empty. "Everybody was dead."

Rikart closed his arms around him, and the child wept for a long while, shaking. In time Rikart let him go, and got out bread and cheese and fed it to him, with sips of water from the well. He knew nothing he could say and he thought nothing he said would make any difference anyway. Daud rubbed his face against Rikart's chest like a blind baby mouse with its mother.

"How did you get here?"

"I went on the road." His voice now flat and worn like an old shoe. "Someone found me. He took me to an inn. Someone else took me. Then the Mamelukes took me."

"Mamelukes." Rikart looked at him sharply. "Where? Which ones? The Bahriyya? Baibers' men?"

"Baibers. They were kind to me. I went with them awhile. Then I ran away. On the road I came on the jugglers and they brought me to Acre. Then I found you again."

Rikart gave him more water. "I said you were lucky. God has his hand over you."

Daud began to cry again. "I should die. I killed them. I should die."

"Not that easy," Rikart said. "Here, you've got to give me room to lie down. It's all right. Yes, it's all right. Now, sleep. It's all right."

\* \*

Daud slept, and in the darkness he saw the eyes, watching him. He made himself look at them. In the dream, he said, "I am sorry. I am sorry." He squirted tears. He saw the eyes slowly close, and then he slept again.

After that he saw the eyes again often when he slept but he was not afraid anymore, just sad.

\* \*

In the morning they went down near where the old mosque stood. Some other broken buildings stood there on a high ledge, and along the foot of the ledge were the stalls and awnings of a market. Rikart bought them meat pies. Down the way was a fountain, and they went there and drank the water. Some other people stood there, talking.

Rikart caught some of their words, and turned to listen. A tall man in a striped thobe was sitting on the wall of the fountain talking to a Jew in a skullcap.

"Well," the Jew said, "Edessa is far to the north. Practically in Armenia."

"Edessa will yield to them," the tall man said. "They were already talking about it."

Rikart said, "The Mongols are attacking Edessa."

The tall man looked over at him, frowning. "Not yet. But they're moving that way. Right now they are busy killing all the Kurds."

"The Il-Khan's whole army is marching."

"When they ride out, the earth shakes."

Rikart turned away. Daud stood watching him, the reins of his donkey in his hands. Rikart nodded to him. "The war is starting up again." He let his gaze rest on the boy, thinking this over. "You said, last night, you fell in with the Bahriyya."

Daud gave an uncertain nod.

"Baibers is crazy, and a son of a bitch. But he's a great soldier. I think we'll go find Baibers."

# CHAPTER 5

## NIKOLA'S RAID

"To al-Malik al-Nasir Yusuf, lord of some little city at the edge of the world, receive this command from the Kha-khan Mongke and the Il-Khan Hulegu. The Most High God has laid upon us the duty of bringing the whole world together, and you must now submit to us, or we shall turn you and everything you hold into dust and ash."

Hulegu let out a roar of laughter and slapped his knee. All around him the other men whooped, bellowed insults to the Sultan, boasts and praises. At the back of the ger Nikola yawned. This was like a drinking game. He was tired of all this. He was tired of standing around, but if they were still sending letters, it would go on for a while. And he hated Kitboqa.

The lanky Turk stood up there next to the Khan, his bony face shining with smiles, while the scribe read out the letter. Kitboqa had written it; Hulegu thought him eloquent. Nikola thought him a bed warmer. He had cozied and fawned his way into the Khan's favor just like a woman crowding out other wives.

The letter was good, though, very forceful. Everybody was still shouting, jumping up and down, threatening to turn the world to fire.

Nikola's older brother Yoshmut was edging through the crowd toward him. Nikola met his eyes, and without speaking they moved back by the door, where there was some open space behind the crowd. Yoshmut shifted to put his back to the council, screening them off.

"The Khan is sending me to scout ahead, across the big river here. I want you to come with me."

Nikola said, "I'm honored. When are we leaving?"

"Tomorrow. Five arban. I want to move fast. If we're ever actually going to do this we have to know what's there." Yoshmut stroked his chin. "Three horses each, supplies for two days. We'll see how it goes after that. We have to be back by the full moon."

"Joint command," Nikola said.

"Well, no." Yoshmut smiled. "I'm in command. But you're second." He slapped Nikola on the arm. "We'll have some fun. Maybe get some fancies for the khatun." Dokaz was not his mother, but everybody loved her. Nikola snorted at him, excited, and they slipped out the door of the ger and went to catch horses.

* * * *

Nikola took his arban, the nine men he had been riding with since he left Karakorum, and Yoshmut brought the nine men of his own arban, and another three arban, so fifty in all, and all from the same hundred. They left just after dawn and all morning they were riding through the ordo.

A step behind Yoshmut, Nikola trailed along his extra horses beside him on their lead ropes. They made a crowd, with all the horses, and the way between the hundreds of gers was narrow and twisting and they could not move above a walk. Then finally they came to the open, and Yoshmut led them at a steady trot off through the grassy hills, going southwest toward the big river.

\* \*

They made camp above a spring. All of them were glad to be out of the ordo and they spread themselves on the grass and drank airaq and told stories. Nikola checked over his bows and sharpened his arrows.

Old Ranga, who had served in the fireland east of here long before Hulegu came, had learned the game of chess there. He had brought a board and pieces with him, and now he set them up. Nobody else wanted to play with him, because he always won, but Nikola liked him and the game interested him.

After Ranga had beaten him very quickly in the first game, they set it up again. Somebody had shot an antelope, coming into the camp, and the smell of the roasting meat reached them. Ranga inhaled deeply and smiled.

"See? Once you get away from the ordo everything is better. Isn't this your first campaign?"

Nikola was thinking over the game they had just played, remembering what he had done that let Ranga beat him so fast. He said, "Well, three years now. I came from Karakorum with my father." He thought he had seen a lot in that time. "What's out there, do you know? What's the country like west of here?"

"Once past the big river, it's desert. Not as mountainous as up north. I was in Baiju's army when we went after the Turks up there. Those mountains are steep."

"Did you win?"

Ranga made a face at him. "Of course we won. There were a lot more of them than of us, too. Baiju said that made it all the more glorious. Which it did, of course. We suckered them into a narrow place and shot them up, like a hunting ground." His voice altered. "The sky, in that place, there was no sky. Only a little strip of blue air up above where the rock ended."

Nikola pointed to one of his game pieces. "Is this the one that goes crooked?"

"Yes."

Nikola moved the piece from square to square. Ranga leaned forward. "That's interesting." He gave Nikola a sideways look. "Did Yoshmut tell you where we're going?"

"We're supposed to find the way to some city, that's all I know."

Ranga moved another piece. Nikola thought he saw an opening, and put the crooked man up into the center of the board. A few moves later he saw Ranga had him trapped. He sat back, scowling down at the pieces, as Ranga took away Nikola's man and put his own in its place.

"See, now," Ranga said. "The game is like war. The important stuff is what you don't see coming." He smiled. "Let's eat."

* *

After a few days they were riding down through the hills onto flatter ground. The grass here was broken, ripped up to make strips of dirt for growing trees in rows. They crossed a ditch, where within the month there had been water but which was dry now.

The trees were full of fruit, but no one was there to pick them. On the ground the round globes of apples lay rotting. The grass was growing knee-high around the trunks.

They came over a little rise and saw people running away from them, far down the slope. They chased the last of these up to a walled town higher on the hillside. Yoshmut drew rein on the road; he was looking all around at the place above them. Nikola changed horses. He could smell the town from here, a dank mix of smoke and manure. He hated such places, where the walls kept out the wind and the sky and kept in the dirt.

When he mounted again, he looked up there. Along the top of the walls people were clustered thick as flies to watch them.

The gates were still open. Nikola snorted. Yoshmut said, "Look, they're trying to lure us in."

"We can feed them some arrows."

Yoshmut shrugged. "I'm not interested. They can't stop us or hurt us but they could hold us up for a while, and I want to go on."

"Your command."

"Leave it. Let's go on a little and make camp."

* *

Nikola had been riding point; he came back to the main body of the men at a gallop. It was midway through the morning. The band had stopped at a spring by the road, to water their horses. Nikola went up stirrup to stirrup with Yoshmut and said, "You have to come look at this."

Without a word his brother reined around and followed him. They loped back along the road to the little rise and over and drew rein.

"Hunh," Yoshmut said.

Along the swampy riverbank before them, the reeds and willows were winter brown. Beyond, a vast river flowed along in a broad coiling surge. Where the road came down to meet it, the water divided to either side around a flat island. The road crossed the near steam on a humped stone bridge, came down onto the island, ran along a hundred paces of flat road, and humped back up over another bridge to the far bank. On the far bank was a tower, and on the island another tower, and on this near bank, just before them, a third. Just upstream, below the dense brown willows that fringed the water's edge, a stone wharf reached out into the river. In the lee of the wharf, two or three boats lay overturned on the bank.

The towers were stone, fat and round, about thirty feet tall; the near one had a window halfway up, so maybe there was a second floor. From the top of each tower rose a little haze of smoke.

"Well," Yoshmut said. "Do you suppose they want a toll?" He stood in his stirrups, looking up the bridge. "If we get out there, with them at each end, they'll tear us up."

"We can go around," Nikola said.

"The Khan will need this bridge." Yoshmut lifted his reins. "I wonder what they have up there." He rode slowly down toward the bridge.

Nikola trailed him slightly, looking all around. On the top of the tower on the bank, he saw a sudden bustle, and behind the crenelated wall several men appeared, looking back at him, their heads and shoulders clear against the sky. One moved, pointing, and Nikola saw the stick in his hand. "Those stave bows." The long wooden bows of these people had half the range of a Mongol bow.

Yoshmut said, "They must have built the towers to cover each other, so they can reach at least far."

Nikola judged the distance between the towers to be about one hundred paces. Now he could see people moving on top of the island tower, too. The notched parapets that ringed the tops of the towers would give the defenders cover while they shot. He looked up and down the river, how the water churned and roiled through the piers of the bridge. He was not good at swimming. The way the bridge humped up meant the river probably flooded here. It was high now, flowing through the tangled willows.

Yoshmut reined in his horse, staring down at the tower. "There must be some way into that thing. They didn't fly up there." He swung back toward Nikola. "Let's see if we can force it. I don't want to lose any men, so we've got to be careful. You take everybody but my arban down here, move in as close as you can without getting shot, and make a big fuss.

Don't go onto the bridge. See if you can get them fighting." He looked up into the sky. "Give me until around noon."

"What are you going to do?" Nikola asked. He reached down for his helmet.

"Oh, I'll figure something out. Do you have any of those Han firesticks?"

"Zuchi does." Nikola put the metal cap of the helmet over his head. "He lit the fire with them last night."

"Let's go," Yoshmut said, and they rode off back toward the spring where they had left the other men.

* *

Nikola, with most of the men and all the horses, jogged on down the road toward the bridge; as soon as they came over the rise, he could see movement on top of the tower, down there by the river. He turned and nodded at Targatai, who rode up beside him. Targatai had the keenest sight of any of them.

"I'm going to get up pretty close to them. If you see any bows bend, yell."

Targatai grunted at him. With the led horses they made a big swarm, and they filled the road approaching the tower and spilled off into the brush. Nikola slowed, as they came toward the ramp up to the bridge; he waved to the men behind him to stay back.

From the top of the tower somebody called out in Arabic, "Stop right there."

Nikola let his horse carry him a little closer, just to show he didn't obey orders like that. He stood in his stirrups, looking up at the tower. "Who are you? What place is this?" He nudged the horse with his heel, turning it sideways to the tower. He jiggled the reins a little, to keep the horse on the bit.

Above him the turbaned head and shoulders leaned between two teeth of the parapet, his shape black against the sky behind him. He called out, "Never mind us, what are you doing here, squint-eye?"

Oh, ho, Nikola thought. You'll suffer for that, sand rat. He remembered the letter the Turk Kitboqa had written. He called up, "We are here to rule the world. Surrender now, or you will all die."

From the tower's top came a chorus of hoots. Other men up there he couldn't see. The turbaned head leaned down toward him, "Who tells me this? What little steppe god gave you a crown? Go on, get out of here. You won't pass here."

"Come out and make me leave, camel-knacker!"

"Go back where you came from, squint!"

"Try and—"

Suddenly the turbaned man jerked back and out of sight, and from the Mongols came a shrill "Yip yip yip—"

Nikola slammed his heels into his horse's sides and in two jumps it reached full stride. Something slapped off his helmet and the horse staggered. Nikola gathered it up on the reins as it stumbled on. The Mongols ahead of him were shooting back at the tower. In among them, he slid down from the saddle. An arrow stuck up out of the horse's rump. Targatai and Ranga were yelling orders. Mongol arrows rained down on the tower. Nothing came back; they were out of range of the Arab bows.

The arrow in the horse's rump was too deep to pull out without hurting it a lot more. He thought of killing the horse outright, but it wasn't dying. He stripped its harness off and let it go, leaving his saddle and pack on a rock above the riverbank.

He took his bowcase from his back; an Arab arrow had pierced the shell and he worried it carefully out of the leather. Taking out his bow, he flexed it once to wake it up and strung it. He rummaged around in the bowcase for his favorite thumb ring. Targatai was walking up and down behind the others, yelling at them to stop shooting, that they were wasting arrows. Still on foot, Nikola moved around toward the river, to where the road ramped up onto the bridge. He thought he was within range of the tower's bows now but either they were hunched down under cover, or they hadn't seen him yet.

He put an arrow to his bow but from here he could see nothing to shoot at. He frowned. He could not see how to move on this. The tower had good cover and a clear field around it. If the Mongols attacked across the road, the men on the tower would cut them down. Probably they had food in the towers, water too. They could wait the Mongols out. He began to look for blind spots, ways to get closer. This was new to him; he was used to running fights, ambushes, charges and feints. He had stormed the gate at Baghdad but then they had been two whole tumans, and the gate already half-destroyed, and nobody really fighting back.

He looked up at the sky; the sun was surely past noon now. He glanced around at the other Mongols, stretching in an arc along the road, and saw Targatai looking back at him. He should be giving orders. He felt stupid. He should be doing something.

Then across the bridge, out on the island in the river, a horn blew a long hollow note, and then another. He straightened up. From the stone wharf on this bank of the river, an overturned boat was running on many legs toward the tower.

From the top of the tower arrows showered down. A spray of arrows flew up from the tower on the island. Nikola waved to Targatai and shot back toward the island; the horn's long call abruptly stopped.

The running boat had reached the back of the near tower. Arrows studded its wooden hull. The boat swung up and leaned against the tower wall. Even from here Nikola heard a crash. Yoshmut had found a door. Nikola raised his bow, trying to find the right arc, and dropped an arrow onto the top of the tower.

Just above the boat, something moved between two notches of the parapet, and a head appeared, shoulders, two hands with a bucket. That was a simple shot and Nikola put an arrow through the head. The body sprawled down over the parapet and the bucket overturned in the air and showered the boat with liquid and bounced away.

Under the upturned boat Nikola could make out the men pushing through the wall into the bottom of the tower. Moments later, somebody left behind in the boat pulled it off to the side, and half a dozen horses galloped out the tower door.

Nikola paused; he was running out of arrows. He saw Yoshmut came out of the tower and dodge into the shelter of the boat. Behind him black smoke billowed out the door. A wail came up from the top of the tower. Smoke began to trickle up all around the parapet. A rope sailed uncoiling out over the edge and two men came climbing down. One screamed, in Arabic, "Mercy! Surrender--" Nikola shot that one and somebody else got the other. The Mongols flooded in around the tower, surrounding it, packing the road. Nobody up there shot back.

Nikola looked down the first span of the bridge toward the next tower, on the island. As he watched, half a dozen men on horseback raced out of it, hurrying away toward the far side of the river. That garrison was fleeing. Nikola let out a yelp of outrage. He leapt up onto the bridge; the men and horses were so jammed together on the approach that nobody could pass. He caught a stray leadrope and reeled in a horse. Swinging up onto its back, he wound and pushed his way through the clog, his last five arrows in his fist. The other Mongols were turning to chase the escaping Arabs. Already across the bridge, the Arabs were scattering in all directions. Galloping across the island, Nikola saw that the men from the third tower, on the west bank, were fleeing away too. Racing up the ramp onto the last bridge he came up on a man running on foot, a striped gown, a turban, and he shot him. Ahead was a horseman and he chased that one down also. He rode on off the bridge, but the Arabs were disappearing now into the hills.

He turned back. A body sprawled on the road. He dismounted to pull the arrows out of it.

The other Mongols were all across the bridge, spreading out along the road. Yoshmut loped up to him. His leggings and his coat were soaked to the armpits; he must have waded along the river. He smelled bad.

Nikola said, "That was good, Yoshmut. That was smart."

Yoshmut shrugged. "Forts like that make people think they're safer than they are. They threw a bucket of piss at us, did you see that?"

Nikola looked back at the river. Rolling black smoke still poured from the tower on the east bank. If they had kept horses inside the tower there would be a lot to burn. "What about these others? Should we fire them too? I have to go get my saddle."

Yoshmut nodded. "Nice job, little brother." He cuffed Nikola on the shoulder. "Let's go do that."

* *

The road wound off south. Green fields sprouted along the river, straight lines of something bushy. Ditches lined with rock led the water from the river into the fields. They passed through a deserted village, a dozen little mud cone houses on either side of the road. These people had gone somewhere nearby, Nikola thought, looking up at the hills. They would come back when they thought the Mongols were gone. The craggy hills closed in around them, and they rode over a little pass and down into the river valley again, stretching away to the west.

Beside the road was a tub carved into a rock, water bubbling in from some underground spring, and Yoshmut stopped and they watered their horses. Nikola stood looking down toward the river valley, wondering where the people were.

Yoshmut came to him. "I'm going down along this river. Take some men and go up higher and see what you can. Stay close. I'll see you in camp at sundown."

With five other men from his arban Nikola rode off through the grass-covered hills, skirting outcrops of rock. He could see this was sheep grazing land, from the way the grass was cropped, and the occasional dung. He wondered if those herdsmen were hiding and watching him. Below him the river valley wound along, green and tended. Far ahead he saw the haze in the air that meant a village. Yoshmut would come on that in the afternoon.

An old path climbed up the hill, and Nikola followed it, his men trailing behind him. The path turned steep, cut between two jutting rocks, and came out on a high plateau.

On this flat ground several old ruined buildings stood, not cones like the others but square, made of rock, long empty. Nobody had lived here for ages of ages. The place didn't smell like anything except the wild around it. The windows were worn round as snakes' holes. A tower stood on the highest ground, half caved in. On a wall among the overgrown brush he saw images.

He stopped, curious. Brambles climbed over the wall, but through them he saw markings, and he pulled away a clump of the sticker vines to see. Along the rock was a row of people, some walking, some hacking at the ground with hoes, one leading a horse. They had big sideways eyes. Beards. The outlines of this had been cut into the stone. Maybe they had been painted once. In the east he had seen pictures painted on the walls. He pulled down more of the vines, seeing what looked like writing, and more people.

He called to his men to lay up here a while and rode to the tower. The top had long since fallen in. Half the rocks were tumbled down. He left his horse at the base of it and climbed up the rocks to the uppermost course.

From here he looked over the world. He sat down cross-legged on a flat stone and searched around with his eyes. East of here, over the horizon, was his father and the army, and down below, somewhere east on the green thread of the river valley, was Yoshmut. Farther west along the green stretch, where the river bent around the toe of a hillside, was a little cluster of cone-houses. Beyond were the long shallow yellow hills. He wondered how much farther the world reached. He thought about the city below him, wondering how it had died. Far off to the south and west, the sky along the horizon looked dirty. Maybe that was another city, bigger than any of these villages.

He wondered again about the dead city below him. Those round-eyed people must have built it. The pictures made him feel as if these people were still here. Some cold thought touched him and he shrugged it off.

He thought briefly of the girl Dinah. She wouldn't let him touch her but he caught her looking at him a lot. Maybe he should marry her. He would have his own ger then. That seemed like a lot of trouble. But he liked Dinah, who was strong and clever, and he wanted to lie down with her.

Kitboqa wanted her too. It didn't bother him at all to thwart Kitboqa.

He looked up the river valley again. Where the cone-houses stood at the foot of the hillside he could see something moving. Yoshmut's band was still well down river but now, on the brown slope above the village, Nikola could just make out a dark line of many moving things. People who had heard the Mongols were coming, people running away.

He went down again to the ground, where his men were sprawled around drinking airaq and talking, and got them back on their horses and headed down toward the river valley.

When he reached the village the place was empty. In the first house he went into, the brazier at the center of the tall dim room was still full of hot coals. The floor was packed earth, covered with rugs. An overturned chest lay against the curved wall. There were no windows, only a hole at the top that let in the sunlight. He found a wheel of bread, some onions in a braid. On a shelf built into the mud wall was a jug full of something liquid; he sniffed it and his head reeled.

"Eyo."

"In here," he called, and Yoshmut came in behind him.

"Are you finding anything?"

"Not much."

Yoshmut went off around the room, opening cupboards. Nikola heard a whimper, and wheeled. He nocked an arrow. He thought the sound came from the overturned chest, and he went over and looked around it. There in the dark between the chest and the wall a little girl cowered, a baby clutched in her arms, her hand over the baby's mouth. Her enormous eyes stared at him. The people had taken away their food but left their children. Nikola imagined the arrow flying, pinning the baby to the girl, the girl to the wall. He saw no use in that. He took the arrow off nock. Yoshmut was going out the door, the jug in his hand, and Nikola followed him.

* *

They went on a little way and made camp on a bench above the river. Some of the other men had found a sheep and they cooked strips of the fat back over the fire. Yoshmut drank from the jug and soon was slumped on the ground, calling out incomprehensible things in a flat voice. The jug went around from hand to hand. When it came to Nikola he sipped at it and his head floated and his stomach heaved. He thought, this is poison.

He passed it on. It was nearly empty; soon it was all empty, and Targatai lifted it to his lips, lowered it, made a sour face.

The bad taste stung Nikola's lips. He felt once more the touch of something cold and dark. He took a horse and went out to ride around the camp. The other Mongols gathered around the fire, in the round dome of the yellow light, but beyond that the night covered everything. He let the horse pick its way along. Above, the vast sky was white with stars.

He remembered the dead city, and he wondered if those people had foreseen their end. Maybe they had thought they would go on forever. He thought, we will go on forever. He thought, maybe not.

The horse carried him step by step through the dark, the fire a soft little glow far to one side, and the infinite dark world spread around him. I don't know, he thought. I don't know anything.

All the more reason to go now as far as he could. To do as much as possible. The night sky above him blazed with the thousands of the stars. The great Khan, his Ancestor, watched him from beyond that glitter. A sudden gladness filled him. Let me be your arrow, Temujin. Let me go on forever. He lifted his face to the night.

\* \*

In the morning Yoshmut and several others were throwing up in the brush. Yoshmut looked as if he had been knocked over the head with a stick. He said nothing to anybody, only got on his horse and took his led horses on their ropes and started off down the road. With the others Nikola trailed after him. They followed the river upstream through a valley studded with fruit trees. Zuchi darted out of the pack and went off among the trees and came back with an armload of apples, red as blushing cheeks. Yoshmut was sick again as he rode. Nikola caught some of the other men rolling their eyes and thought his brother would suffer more than a bad stomach for this. They were coming to another village of the cone-shaped houses, deserted as usual, and rode into the middle of it. There were six houses on one side and three on the other, pale mud brick, with doors framed in heavy timbers. Nikola was wondering if there was anything left here to steal when suddenly the air whistled and arrows pelted down around him.

A blow on his right shoulder knocked him halfway out of his saddle. He bounded down and ran, dodging the plunging Mongol horses. Ahead the last two cones of the village stood close together, a low wall between them, and he leapt over the wall and ducked down behind it.

He reached up behind him; he could just get his fingertips on the arrow in his shoulder.

In a yellow dust cloud, the horses leapt and bucked and wheeled in the middle of the street. More arrows showered them. Quickly he saw these arrows were coming from only three of the cones, two on his right and one directly across on the left; the shooters were aiming through the doors. He had no angle here on any of them. Some of the Mongols trapped in the street were shooting back from the shelter of dead horses but most were just trying to get to cover. Zuchi raced up the street and jumped over the low wall beside him.

Nikola turned his back to him. "Help me." He shrugged his left arm out of his coat.

Zuchi said, "Hold on." Nikola felt the arrow tug, and then with a snap Zuchi broke the shaft in two. As Nikola eased out of his right sleeve he lifted the back of the coat off the stump.

"It took your shirt in with it," he said.

Nikola leaned his head against the wall. "Do it."

He felt Zuchi gather the silk shirt up around the wound and pull, and pain bolted through his shoulder. His head swam. His right arm was numb. He pulled his coat back on. Zuchi laid the arrow down on top of the wall;

fibers of silk stuck to the bloody bodkin head. Nikola took the ring from his right thumb and put it on his left, so he could draw with that hand; the ring felt funny and he chewed it a moment to soften up the leather.

Out in the street a dozen horses were running up and down, their saddles empty. Bodies dotted the street, horses and men. He could not get a good shot from here, the doorways almost edge on to him.

"Zuchi. Stay here, see what happens."

Nikola went back through the way between the houses. From the rear the cones were steep blank walls. He counted down two buildings and studied the pale mud face before him. Here and there a brick stuck out of the sheer expanse. He thrust his bow into his bow case, reached up for a jutting brick and began to climb. The wall was warm and rough. A brick crumbled under his foot and he slid down, caught himself against another outcrop and scrambled up again. The top domed over almost flat around the sun-hole, a square wide as a bow-width. He pulled his bow out of its case and strung it.

In the street below him nothing moved now. Dead horses and dead men littered it.

Through the corner of his eye he saw something moving in the doorway across the street and he jerked his gaze back to that. An arrow spun by him and he sprawled down on the lee side and inched around the dome, keeping the curving mud wall between him and the house, until he could see around to the street. Now he could see the doorway across the street without sticking his head up above the roof, and he put three arrows in through the dark opening in the middle. He was shooting wrong-handed; the thumb ring didn't fit right and even through the pad his thumb hurt where the string crossed it. Somebody else opened up on the far door too, from the alley right beneath him. Maybe Zuchi had moved. The shooting stopped.

The lane between this house and the next suddenly swarmed with Mongols. In the door across the way the tip of an arrow appeared and Nikola sailed a shot through the space just above it. The Arab arrow clattered down loose to the ground outside the window.

He heard Yoshmut shout something, down below him.

Nikola crept up the dome again, and leaned on one elbow over the hole at the top, keeping an eye on the house across the street. Through the sunhole he saw something moving in the room below him and put an arrow in that direction. The doorway across the street stayed empty. He heard the crash of the door beneath him going in, and then they were fighting and he couldn't shoot for fear of hitting one of his brothers. He got up on his knees. In the room below him somebody gave a roar of triumph. Looking down, he saw Yoshmut and the others pounding each other on the back and yelling into each other's faces.

In the house across the street, nothing moved. After a while Yoshmut came out of the house below, crossed the street, stood there a moment, and then reached in the hole in the door and opened it. He looked in and turned and waved his hands.

That left only the house next door. They had stopped shooting also. Nikola swung down to the ground. Yoshmut came back across the road. Their eyes met and Yoshmut nodded.

Nikola went around to the front of the next house. The door was framed with timbers set into the mud wall. Once the panel had been solid wood but a big piece had been recently cut out of the middle. He stood leaning against the door, his hand on it; he pushed slightly, and the door began to swing open.

As certainly as he knew his own name, he knew there were men inside with bows drawn, waiting for him to come through.

He looked around; Yoshmut had gone to the alleyway, several of his men behind him. Yoshmut bobbed his head at Nikola, and began to scale the outside of the house, as Nikola had, his feet slipping on the uneven bricks.

They would hear that inside. They would know what was happening. Nikola leaned on the door again, and it swung slowly inward.

He dropped his bow. It would be too close in there for arrows. Drawing his knife left-handed, he let the door swing almost all the way open, and rushed headfirst through it, diving toward the wall.

He landed on his bad shoulder, kept rolling. He could hear arrows hitting the mud wall and his leg hurt and he was bleeding from his chin. When he reached the wall he popped up on one knee, the knife in his hand.

They had made a fortress of the furniture on the other side of the room. He had nothing to hide behind. He ran, weaving from side to side, toward the fort, and they rose up to meet him, three men, their long bows drawn.

From the sun hole at the top of the cone an arrow took the middle of them through the chest. The others wheeled to look up. Nikola vaulted over their fortress wall. In front of him an Arab was trying to aim his arrow and Nikola knocked the bow aside and cut him open up the front.

The body buckled to the floor. Nikola slumped down on his heels, panting. He hurt all over. His right arm was numb to the fingertips. Yoshmut came in beside him.

"Are you all right?"

"Ah, well." Nikola got up. He felt sick to his stomach. The three Arabs lay crumpled in their little fort of tables and chests, two with Yoshmut's arrows in them, one with his guts spilling out. Around them were their bows, arrows, a basket of bread, water jugs. They had been ready to hold out here, to die fighting. After Yoshmut drew his arrows, Nikola pulled the bodies straight, on their backs, and crossed their arms over their chests. He thought their people were somewhere nearby and would come for them, but they had been brave and he wanted to honor them. He covered their faces with their headcloths. His shoulder throbbed and burned.

\* \*

Five of Yoshmut's band had died; every arban had lost somebody. They slung the bodies up on the backs of the dead men's horses and led them up and away from the village. There was no grassland so they went into the desert. They turned the led horses loose there and chased them around until they threw the corpses, and then killed each horse beside its rider, so that his spirit would enter into heaven as a man, on horseback. In the sky, the first curving flight of the vultures appeared.

\* \*

They made camp upstream from the village, caught some stray goats, and spitted them. Nobody talked. Nearly all of them were wounded, and they had lost a lot of horses. Old Ranga had taken three arrows through the chest. He leaned against his saddle with his eyes shut and did not stir much, even to eat. Zuchi had learned some woundcraft from a witch in the fireland east of the rivers. He went from one of them to the next and washed and poked and sniffed. He cleaned up Nikola's shoulder and daubed it with something that stank. Nikola's shirt was stiff with blood, and he peeled it off and put on another from his pack.

Yoshmut came into the firelight. He still looked sick, his eyes red, and his face green. He walked stiffly. He said, "We need to have sentries out all night."

Targatai lunged up to his feet. "Who are you to give us orders? You got us into this. You cost us our brothers. You let that stuff you drank steal your brain. I say, stand aside. Let somebody else lead us. Let Nikola lead us, he is of the golden ones."

Around the fire the other men looked at each other. Yoshmut wheeled, his eyes glinting, but he said nothing. Nikola stood up. "I remember that night, Targatai, and who drank, and you would have drunk as much as Yoshmut if there had been any left."

The other men laughed. Targatai glowered at him, and started to talk, and then Zuchi on the far side of the fire said, "Besides, I'm not all that sure Yoshmut is to blame for this. We all slacked off. We were bad soldiers."

Without opening his eyes old Ranga spoke, his voice harsh with pain. "You followed him today in the street. So follow him now."

Targatai said nothing. He gave a quick glance around, maybe to see who supported him, and the other men looked him off. Nikola sank down on his heels again. Yoshmut said, in a harsh voice, "As I said, we need sentries out all night." He said some names. Men rose and went away and other men came in by the fire. Yoshmut went over to old Ranga and squatted down to talk to him. Nikola was tired; his spirit sank. He lay down to sleep before he had to go ride sentry.

During the night Ranga died. They cast his body out with the others, killed his horse, and rode on to the west.

* *

They sorted the horses they had left so that everybody got two, with four extra, and counted out the arrows of the dead men. The hills gave way to a wide plain. Far off in the west there were purple smudges of hills. On this flat land there was even less grass, only strips of fields, newly harvested. These people harvested the river also, threading it in and out of the country in ditches. On the bushy plants some pods of beans still hung, cracked open and blown empty. The horses ate the bean plants and also the stalks of the grain left behind in the fields. Mice scurried through the overworked fields. Snakes and hares. It rained one night and in the morning water lay in sheets along the lowlands, reflecting the sky, and the little ditches streamed a foamy brown.

They passed by great pillars made of fluted stone, terraces of stone worn soft with age. They rode through empty villages, where the houses were much bigger than in the east, with square walls and roofs and balconies. Poking around in a big house, Nikola found a necklace with green jewels set in silver, a cup figured with strange designs, a gold ring.

His shoulder felt bad the first day but every day after it seemed better. Zuchi put more salve on it. Nikola kept it moving so it wouldn't stiffen. He thought Zuchi had a healer's touch. Zuchi had taken old Ranga's chess set, and when they camped Nikola played with him, and like Ranga Zuchi beat him every time. He could see afterward what he had done wrong, but not before.

South and west of here the sky was fuzzy with smoke, the haze growing higher and thicker as they rode toward it. They left the river and rode overland. Came to a waterhole, in among tall thin trees like giant feathers, where camel Arabs backed hastily out of their way. While the horses drank, Yoshmut went over toward the Arabs, on foot, taking Nikola with him, since Nikola spoke the language.

The Arabs were clustered shyly in a stand of the tall spiny trees. As always they had hidden their women. When the Mongols came closer one called out, "Stand, in God's name! Stand! What do you want?"

The two Mongols stood. Nikola said, "What is the name of this place?"

The Arab said something Nikola could not hear as words. He glanced at Yoshmut. "What should I ask him?"

"Find out where there is a city called—" Yoshmut fumbled a moment. "Alap. Alpa. Something like that?"

"Halap," the Arab said. He waved his arm, on toward the smoky sky. "Halap."

"That's where Hulegu wanted us to go," Yoshmut said, as the two went back to the band. "We're close."

* *

The next day as they rode west, a collection of roofs and walls appeared on the horizon, under the lid of its smoky dusty sky. The Mongols rode steadily toward it. Nobody challenged them. They saw some people fleeing in the distance. The fields gave way to houses, at first scattered far apart, then more and more, like a pond getting deeper. Many of the houses they passed stood inside their own walls, as if they were palaces. A stray chicken ran across their path. A flock of pigeons took off from a rooftop. Nikola could smell that these places had been lived in only a few days before, in the smoke, in the latrines. He thought there were people here still, hiding.

The road widened. After a while they could see a wall ahead, as high as Baghdad's wall, studded with towers.

They came to a cross-road, and Yoshmut held one hand up and everybody slowed down. Behind the walls, Nikola could see towers, scattered around the city, tall and thin like needles. He saw domed roofs, like the ones in Baghdad, although none of these were made of gold. The city was huge, as big as Baghdad, as big as a Han city. Near the center a high ground swelled up above the rooftops, ringed with towers and battlements: a citadel.

In the distance, a horn blew.

"What's that?" Yoshmut said.

Nikola reined over beside him. Ahead of them, a gate pierced the wall, and the two sides of it were swinging open.

Out came a column of horsemen. Their horses were much bigger than the Mongol horses, with longer legs, and the riders looked massive. As they came out the gate they picked up a trot, and the sun flashed on them, and they clanged. They wore armor. That was why they looked so big, why they glittered. The column seemed endless; there were hundreds of them, horses and riders all cased in metal, bright in the sun, and after a long while, it seemed, they were still coming out the gate.

Nikola shaded his eyes. The armor seemed made of loose pieces of metal, so the whole suit shimmered. The men carried lances, now upright. Even the horses' heads wore armor, their bodies shrouded in metal skirts. He could hear the heavy tramp of their march from here, as if they made a drum of the road.

Yoshmut gave a shake of his head. "Pretty amazing. See the archers on the walls?"

The walls and the towers of the city were black with people watching. Nikola turned his gaze back to the armored riders.

"There are a lot of them." They moved like rolling boulders, slow and heavy. Their lances poked up like rows of needles. Nikola's horse suddenly lifted its head and neighed, and all around the Mongol horses neighed.

Yoshmut said, "They look pretty solid. I want to pull them back farther from the walls. You flank out. Get well out past their line if you can."

"I don't have any heavy arrows."

"Get close. Bone tips will pierce armor if you get close enough. All they have are those lances, and maybe swords. They won't throw them, they have to come within reach of you, and our reach is a lot longer. Stay behind them so they can't charge you." He looked around. "Let's try to get them in the middle of those houses."

Nikola dismounted and changed horses. Behind them, the wide road led back westward through two rows of houses, past orchards and gardens. Just ahead of them, another road crossed it. Yoshmut called for Targatai and Zuchi, and they talked. Nikola let his old horse go, and on the fresh one jogged back to his arban.

The oncoming lancers packed the road to the gate, their lances jigging up and down as they trotted along. Nikola led his men off along the crossroad; that surface was rock hard, and he moved off to the side, into an orchard, where the footing was better. Nutshells littered the ground. He followed a footpath through the trees. He heard somebody yipping behind him, and swung around to see, through the little nut trees, the armored men suddenly swing their lances down and charge along the main road toward Yoshmut and his four arban.

A stream of arrows went up from the Mongols. The arrows glanced off the armored horses, the armored men, who barreled through them as if they were drops of rain. Nikola saw none go down. Yoshmut and his band wheeled and rushed off away down the main road, but the armored men slowed, pulled together again, making a tight rank that filled the broad space where the two roads crossed.

Probably they couldn't go very fast for very long, carrying all that weight. Make them run, then.

Nikola kicked his horse on, his men trailing after him, trying to get to the edge of the other army, but the Arabs were spreading out along the side road, keeping up with him. Ahead a walled house loomed up, and he swung around to skirt it, which put it between him and the armored line.

When he came down into the next lane, he was abruptly face to face with a dozen lancers, only forty feet away.

They charged. He wheeled, twisting to shoot back over his horse's rump, and fired an arrow into the mass of moving armor. Nobody fell. Then he was galloping into an open road, his arban hurtling on ahead of him. The enormous armored horsemen pounded on his heels. They dashed across another side road, and just ahead of Nikola, Sakim's horse stumbled .

Sakim flew off. Nikola sat back, slamming his horse back on its hocks, skidding to a stop between the fallen man and the oncoming lancers. He twisted in his saddle, arrows in his fist, his stomach clenched. The armored wall loomed over him like a great wave. His horse leapt and bounded, trying to run; he held it fast with his legs and his weight and the reins. Twenty feet in front of him he could see a face inside the helmet, the lance coming for his eyes, and he dropped his reins, yelled and shot.

Inside the helmet the face exploded in a burst of blood. The body reeled in the saddle. The tip of the lance hit the ground and shattered. Suddenly riderless, the horse galloped straight at him and Nikola's horse sprang sideways to let it go by. On the ground beside him, Sakim was drawing his bow. From the whole arban, arrows flew straight across the shrinking gap. The great line wavered. In the armored line another man fell, and then another.

From a distance of a few bow-lengths, Nikola fired three arrows into them. The road emptied. Now he could see down the street to the crossroads, jammed with more of the armored horsemen. He galloped toward them, and the nearest of those men saw him, lowered their lances and charged.

He knew now how close he had to be to force an arrow through their armor and he raced toward that point. The houses on either side shoveled the lancers into a tight pack, the horses clanging together. The lances wavered in the air. Five long strides from them, all his arban around him, Nikola spun his horse and shooting backward loosed five arrows into the enemy swarm..

His horse weaved and bounded around the bodies lying on the road. The gap between Nikola and the lancers widened abruptly and the front rank of the armored charge plowed down headfirst into the ground. As he raced back along the road, Sakim ran out to meet him, shouting. Nikola slowed to a trot, reached down an arm, and boosted him up behind him on the saddle. He wheeled the horse around again.

Armored bodies strewed the road. Beyond, in the space where the roads crossed, the rest of the lancers milled around. Yoshmut had them surrounded. Mongols filled the lanes between the houses and leaned down from the roofs to shoot at them. Arrows poured into the crowded street. Nikola pulled more arrows from his case. Sakim abruptly leapt down from behind the saddle; he had seen a loose horse.

Lighter, Nikola reined around. A few of the armored men were fighting their way out of the trap, running down the main road back to the city. The Mongols chased at their heels all the way to the gates, shooting, until the last of them got within range of the Arab archers and the Mongols all turned back. The gates clanged shut. On the walls, the people screamed and fired waves of useless arrows.

* *

The Mongols rounded up the loose horses and picked up as many arrows as they could. A lot of them had splintered. Nikola knelt by a body in the road and looked over the armor; it was made of a hundred thin leaves of metal, sewn onto a leather backing; the leaves overlapped, so the armor was flexible and still tight. He remembered how the lancers had ridden right through the first barrage. He thought, We should use something like this. He had seen Han fighters wearing armor like this, but made of boiled leather, not of metal.

They camped in the courtyard of a sprawling house, where there was a fountain, and scoured that house and the others around for food. They dragged out rugs to sleep on. Three chickens cackling in the back of the kitchen quickly wound up on spits over the fire and somebody found a goat. Yoshmut led in one of the Syrian horses, stripped of its armor and harness, and they all gathered around it.

"What a beauty," Targatai said. He leaned down and passed his hand along one of the slender forelegs. The horse sidestepped, nervous. It was taller than any of the Mongol horses, longer and leaner in the body, its hide sleek as a silk shirt, its tail highset, its neck arched. Its long head flared from a slender muzzle to wide-set eyes. Its nostrils widened, sniffing them. Nikola held his hand out and the horse slowly extended its head toward it. Its ears switched forward; its great dark eyes studied him. He thought, I want a horse like this.

In the house, nosing around, he found rolls of paper, written on, and clothes. The walls were tiled in blue and green. On a shelf were Han dishes. On the beds, fine white covers. Under one bed he discovered a sack full of money, silver rounds with faces on them. He remembered the dead city, in the hills, and the dark, cold feeling swept over him again. The people here had been rich. Now they were gone. They might come back, once he and Yoshmut left, but the Mongols would rule here and this would never be theirs again.

He went back out to the courtyard, where the others were gathered around in the growing darkness, eating and laughing. The glow of the fire was comforting. He sat down beside his brother and reached for the last of the chicken.

* * * *

Nikola said, "There's good water the whole way. There isn't a lot of grass. They grow apples. Something else, beans, nuts, something the horses ate. Little villages. They ran as soon as they knew we were coming."

"Except once," Yoshmut said, in a hard voice. "They ambushed us."

"Aha," Hulegu said. "How did you let that happen?"

"I got drunk," Yoshmut said. "I let things get out of hand."

Hulegu looked at Nikola, who shrugged. "Yoshmut led the counterattack. We took those people out, all of them. When we came to the city—"

"What city?"

Nikola made a face, trying to get the strange name out. "Lalpa. Hallapa." He glanced at Yoshmut.

"Something like that," Yoshmut said.

Hulegu smiled. "A big city. How long did it take you to get there?"

Yoshmut said, "Seven days."

"Tell me about the city."

"It's on a flat plain. High walls. It looks old. This whole place looks really old. Big solid wall with towers every hundred feet or so. I would have gone in but they sent out an army to drive us off."

Nikola said, "We need better arrows. We had only hunting arrows and they sent out men in armor."

Hulegu said, smoothly, "So you ran?"

"Well," Yoshmut said, "first we took care of their army."

"Yoshmut set a trap for them," Nikola said. "They were five or six to each of us and we crushed them. It was Yoshmut's idea and he did it well."

"But then they locked the gates," Yoshmut said. "And it was getting on to the full moon, anyway, when you said you wanted us back."

Hulegu grunted a laugh. "I think you went where I told you to go. This is excellent. You will have to draw me a map. But the mistake, I don't like that. You lost men I cannot replace. And you didn't make sure your men were prepared. There are arrow makers all through the ordo. We have plenty of heavy arrows."

Yoshmut blurted out, "I didn't expect——" His face altered. "Yes, Khan."

"I've got a task for you, which you won't like." His gaze rested on Nikola. "You will come with me."

"Where?"

"To Halap."

* *

When he went into the ger he shared with his arban and Yoshmut's, his brother was sprawled out on cushions, drinking. He gave Nikola a sour look.

"I'll defend myself, thank you."

Nikola shrugged. "I thought you did a good job."

"Yes, well. They have you in their eye now. Watch out." He lifted the cup in his hand. "You may end up a khan, who knows?"

"What did he order you to do?"

"He's sending me to take a fortress, somewhere in the north. Dirty, slow, boring." Yoshmut wiped his mouth. His breath smelled sweet.

"What is that?" Nikola asked.

"Some stuff the Franks make. I never know as much when I'm sober as I do when I'm drunk."

* * * *

He went to his mother's ger, and gave Dokaz the necklace and the cup, but he gave the ring to Dinah.

Her mouth fell open. She looked from him to the ring on his out-stretched palm and back again. Her fingers closed around the ring, and she tried it on each finger until it fit.

He stood there, smiling, and abruptly she leaned forward and put her lips against his mouth. This startled him so much he did nothing. She turned, then, picked up the baby she called Moseh, and went away, still running from him. He touched his mouth, wondering what that meant.

*  *

It didn't mean anything, she thought. But she loved the ring, with its entwining threads of gold.

# CHAPTER 6

## DAMASCUS

When Baibers was born, his mother told him, the midwife saw the white dot in his eye and tried to strangle him with the birthcord. But his mother saved him.

"I knew you were marked," she said. "Either for great evil or for great good. One or the other. You will never fall into the middle."

When he was taken captive and sold, that seemed evil. But that made him a Mameluke, a greatness hidden in the evil. That had taught him much.

Now he led the Bahriyya along the old Roman road toward Damascus. The city was a crust of walls and roofs on the edge of the plain, and long before they reached it, they came to the edge of the Sultan's army, camped there on the outskirts. A horn sounded at their approach and Baibers stopped, and sentries rode up to him.

He was looking beyond them, even as he answered their demands. The army stretched away almost to the far edge of the plain, below the great mountain there, a spread of fires and tethered horses and tents and pavilions, thousands of men. Bedouin with their black tents. Kurds and Turkmen, Armenians. His heart gladdened. The whole of Islam had heard of the advancing threat and was rising to defend the world. This was a power, now, that he could use.

If he could convince Yusuf to give him command. But he saw no other choice, the Sultan had no other choice. He turned to Boglu.

"Go find us a place to camp. Make sure there's water. I'll be back by nightfall."

Boglu saluted him. The sentries were watching him, frowning; he guessed he had missed something they said, something unimportant. He nodded to them.

"Take me to the Sultan." He would present himself at once to Yusuf, and take command of this.

* *

Trees were astonishing, thought the Sultan Yusuf; they grew up so massively from nothing, they shaped their own space and as well the space around them, they did not move and yet they dominated the world.

A line of poetry came into his mind: remember being green.

The cedar at the foot of his garden filled his eyes, its graceful float of leaves, its elegantly twisted stem. He had built the garden here, when he first took command of Damascus, because this tree was here. Someone had told him his great-grandfather had ordered it planted, on this open slope just below the city parapet. So the Sultan Yusuf himself had enclosed the tree, caused broad straight walkways to divide the space around it, ringed the whole with a wall, set a pavilion where the walkways crossed. Where he now sat, looking down past the beds of yellow and red roses upon the elegance of the cedar. Even so late in the season, with a tinge of ice in the breeze, this place was as pleasant as Eden.

*We have forgotten what we were, except in spring, when we remember...*

That poet too had fled the Mongols.

Damascus weighed on him, old as the rocks, and clogged with memory. If he lifted his eyes he would see out beyond the garden wall to the great mountain where Cain had killed Abel. Ibrahim had drunk from the fountains here. Iskander had ridden through this place on his great black horse. The gates and causeways of the Romans were all through the city, like the leavings of giants, and Roman faces still looked out from medallions on the walls. Just a little way away was the Yarmuk River, where in the time of the Rightly Guided, Khalid ibn al-Walid had defeated the Emperor and delivered al-Shams to Islam. From Damascus, Yusuf's great-grandfather had ridden out to take back Jerusalem from the Franks.

He did not care to lift his eyes. He was here, in his garden at the heart of the world, and he should have some peace.

He had done enough. He had submitted to them. Long ago he had gone there, years ago, hauled himself off along the old road to their city of horse-hair domes, given the khan his homage and several bribes. He had been surprised to find them not entirely the fur-bearing brutes he had expected, but they were, still, an unpretty lot.

Since then he had sent them more gifts. One of his sons as a hostage. Surely that was enough.

Through the corner of his eye he noted that Abdulhassan bin Al-Bakr had come out to the edge of the pavilion, and stood there, waiting to be noticed. Yusuf let him wait. This would be about the council the next day, and he had no will to think about that. He had read the letter privately already. His heart still quaked with it. He felt this all slipping out of his hands, the outrageous letter, the armies gathering steadily on the plain outside the wall, the pressure to act.

He studied the tree, its pleasing asymmetry that was also somehow balance, freedom in order, motion in stillness.

He said, "Yes, come up before me."

Abdulhassan walked around before him, bowing, his hands pressed together. "The Amir Baibers has arrived."

Yusuf stiffened. But he had known this would come. Every other important power in his realm was gathering here, Baibers surely would not pass this up. "How many men does he have with him?"

"One hundred and twenty. They are camped on the plain with the others. He wants to meet with you. Shall I send him to you?"

"No." Baibers' hands dripped blood. Killer of Sultans.

"My sovereign, perhaps it's better to see him first, before the council. Gauge his temper."

The Sultan mulled this over. He saw Abdulhassan intended him to see Baibers, and would likely keep on this way until he agreed. And perhaps the vizier was right. Yusuf saw several sides to this. But not here.

"Not here," he said, aloud. "And I will not be alone with him."

"Who else?" the servant asked.

"You. That Kurd, Al-Farasi. Sheikh Umar. Some guards."

Abdulhassan  bowed again; Yusuf had said the right thing. "As you wish, commander."

* *

Baibers could not be still; he paced across the little room to the far wall and turned and paced back again.

This was less an audience than some kind of trial. Three Kurds in their puffy trousers and sashes stood against the wall. Among several other men, a Bedou chieftain watched  from the shadows behind the Sultan. Sitting on a raised platform Yusuf looked down on him like a judge. Baibers went up before him.

"You have heard that the Mongols are moving toward Aleppo. At least let me take my army and go find out what's going on."

Yusuf was sitting slumped on the cushions, soft as bread dough, his hands limp. He frowned. He said, "Well, maybe..."

Abdulhassan, always in his shadow, called out, "Do nothing to provoke them. We will work this out. They want money--"

Baibers burst out, "They want everything! You're giving it to them piecemeal!" He gave a quick look toward the men in the shadows, to see if any of them agreed. The Kurd al-Farasi did not move. Sheikh Umar who was governor of Kerak laid his hands on the pommel of his sword.

Yusuf's face twisted as at some sour taste. "Everybody must remain calm. We must understand what—"

Baibers leapt toward him. "You must know then where they are and what they are doing! Let me go--"

Abdulhassan called, "Stand back! Guards!'

Yusuf jerked his head up. "How dare you defy me? My great-grandfather defeated the iron men at Hattin and won back Jerusalem. My family has ruled here for generations while yours—if you even had such a thing as a family, you cur, you thing off the streets."

Baibers clenched his fists. The urge to spring on the Sultan almost overpowered him and he was shaking. On two sides now the Kurdish guardsmen were moving cautiously forward. They had not drawn their swords. But their eyes were on him. His red rage ebbed a little. He turned on his heel and walked out of the room.

\* \* \* \*

Damascus was not as nice as Baghdad, Daud thought. Not even as nice as Acre, where everybody seemed to be rich. He followed Rikart through the crowded street, his little donkey traveling in the wake Rikart's big horse left through the crowd. Everybody was hurrying. A vendor called out, another, another. Meat pies. Apricot juice. Several boys ran by, chasing someone. He passed a string of camels. Out in the middle of this swarm, two people argued nose to nose over a wrecked cart. He smelled lamb, and falafel.

Rikart came to a gate in a wall, and knocked on it. Daud slid down from the donkey; he was looking all around, sniffing the air. Rikart turned toward him.

"Remember where this is, we will be here tonight. But go on, go out and around, if you want. Be careful. Get back here by sundown." He nipped something out of his purse and tossed it to the boy.

Daud caught the coin and dashed off, on foot. He looked around as he went, noticing the buildings, the trees, to make sure he could find his way back.

They had crossed a great street, coming in, and he went back that way and turned into it, a broad roofed-over stretch of pavement that went off as far as he could see, jammed with people.

Now he was Daud the Free Ranger, as he had been before. The coin Rikart had given him was a wedge of silver, a quartering of an isaac. He had seen the knight traded only in Greek money and only in certain emperors. Daud did not intend to spend this and he tucked it into his belt. When the time came he would be Daud the Quick-fingered, and pick up whatever he wanted for free.

He wandered down along the street, watching the people. Watching for Mamelukes. He saw several men in baggy leggings, red turbans, wearing jackets trimmed with metal, who had swords in their sashes and were probably soldiers but not Mamelukes. He loitered by a carpet seller's stall, watching the merchant spread out his goods. On the sweep of wool and silk he saw mazes of leaves and vines, orderly, symmetrical, red and blue. The merchant shook out a small rug that was golden when he unrolled it, and red when he laid it down.

At a bookseller's he stood on a carpet, soft under his bare feet, looking up at rows of scrolls and papers. The smell reminded him of Baghdad. He thought he would learn to read someday. In the back of the shop a man sat bent over a desk, writing with a reed pen.

In a stall under an old archway, a dark-skinned man kept a grotesque, hairy little beast, with arms and legs and a furry face. A crowd of children stood around it and the dark-skinned man made the awful creature dance.

Hungry, Daud looked longingly at a heap of pomegranates on a crate, and without thinking much he snatched one.

As his hand closed on the pomegranate someone grabbed him from behind, a fist in his hair, and a knife swung around in front of his face. He gulped. Looking up, he met the eyes of a bearded merchant. He opened his fingers and let go of the pomegranate. Now he had to be Careful Daud, who knew how to get out of trouble. With his free hand he thumbed the quarter isaac out of his belt and held it out.

The merchant's eyebrows rose and fell. He let go of Daud's hair and nodded at him. "Take it." He turned the quartered coin in his hand, and put it into his sleeve and took out several coppers, which he gave to Daud with a flourish.

Daud sat in a corner to eat the pomegranate. His heart was still pounding; he thought, Stupid Daud, who doesn't pay attention.

He went through the camel fair, the sheep fair. He watched a potter slap a great wet lump of clay down on his wheel, cup his hands around it, pump the wheel with his foot, and draw the slick grey mass slowly into a globe. This fascinated him. Mud into beauty. Like seeing the world being made. There were shelves on the wall behind him, with bits of painted pots. A memory rose; a shudder passed through him and for a moment he was sick to his stomach. Suddenly he wanted to go back to Rikart. He started off, found a way out of the bazaar, and went away through the streets of Damascus.

Almost to the place where he had left Rikart, he saw a tall man in a red cloak whom he knew.

He shrank back into an alleyway. Surely that was Boglu, Baibers' man, who had befriended him.

That meant the Bahriyya were here. He tried to see what Boglu was doing but Daud was too far away to hear anything; the Mameluke just seemed to be waiting, among several other men, at a doorway, chattering to one another. Then the door popped open, and they all went in.

He went on down the street, came to the wall where he had left Rikart, and passed through a stable gate. He found his donkey at once and wrapped his arms around its neck. The donkey snuffled at him. It had no water and he brought it water and hugged it again, and went back through the stable, looking for Rikart.

The Frank was sitting in the shade of a tree in the courtyard, talking to somebody. To his surprise Daud knew this man, Gilbert, the merchant of Acre. He sat down on the edge of the carpet, out of the way.

Gilbert said, "There are a lot of Bedouin. And some Kurds are here. Those the Mongols ran out of the Shahrazur. Their amir is al-Farasi Mohammed, do you know him?"

"Tughrul's son."

"Yes. A very wily man. He is close under Yusuf's armpit right now."

"Where else have you been?"

"Down to Egypt. Ah! This you will want to know. Qutuz has put aside the boy Sultan, he will rule alone from now on. He says this is no time for children to have power."

"At least he knows something is happening."

Daud said, "Bahriyya is here."

The Frank flashed him a smile. "You've been keeping your eyes open."

Gilbert said, "I'm glad to see you, child. I have thought of you often."

Daud shrugged one shoulder, dropping his gaze, shy. He remembered that Gilbert had given him up to the Mamelukes. From somewhere nearby, suddenly, the call to prayer began. He brought his knees up to his chest and wrapped his arms around them, listening to Rikart and the merchant share news.

With a piercing sadness he remembered how Rasul the Mameluke had taught him to pray. He lowered his head. He could not do that anymore. The entire matter of prayer confused him. He saw no purpose in it and yet they all did it, one way or another, even Rikart. But now from the house a servant was bringing a jug, and bread. Daud shook off his darkness, leaned forward, hungry again.

* * *

The tube was made of iron, as long as a man's arm; it sat on a tripod of metal sticks. The opening in the front was wide as a hand but the tube fattened going backward to twice that size. The back end was plugged. In the top was a hole.

One of the Kurds was pouring something from a leather sack into this hole. Baibers cleared his throat. He could smell a bitter tang of sulfur. He glanced quickly around; they had come out beyond the edge of the camp to witness this, to a flat barren patch of land, facing away toward the mountains. Around him the other men were silent, frowning, the Governor of Kerak with two of his sons, and the Kurdish amir, al-Farasi.

Al-Farasi was tall even for a Kurd, with a long face; Baibers thought of him as the Crocodile. Baibers turned his eyes back to the long cylinder on its tripod.

Al-Farasi nodded. The man beside the tripod stooped, took a reed from a pile on the ground, and stuck it into a brazier. The reed flamed. The man cupped it with his hand and lifted it to the iron tube, and with a twist of his wrist put the fire into the hole.

There was a hiss, sparks, and then a bang that startled Baibers almost off his feet. The whole tube lurched backward. The tripod rocked from side to side. The front of the tube vomited a spray of smoke and little bits of stuff. More smoke plumed from the hole where the fire had gone in. The roaring sound rolled away across the plain. Baibers looked quickly behind him and saw the whole camp seething, all the horses leaping and men scrambling. The man beside the tube had dropped the reed; he steadied the tripod, and began swabbing out the tube with a mop.

The sheikh from Kerak said, "Dirty kind of work."

Al-Farasi said, "I don't see much use in it, anyway, other than to scare horses." Most of the junk from the tube lay spread in a wide swath on the ground only a few feet away.

"The Han use them to knock down walls," said the man mopping out the tube. "This one must be broken, it didn't work very well. Usually it will throw much farther."

Al-Farasi lifted one hand, dismissive. He turned to Baibers, his crocodile face somber. "The Sultan, may God protect him, has put off the council. Again."

"So I heard," Baibers said. "Somehow this all has taken him by surprise." Al-Farasi had been there the day before, when Baibers met Yusuf; he had some place with the Sultan.

The sheikh from Kerak had been there as well. Some of the Bedouin out on the plain would be his tribesmen. He said, "I've heard the squints are marching west again."

"It's almost the end of the year, this is when they like to fight."

"Have they crossed the Euphrates? Does anybody know?"

"I heard something about a raiding party."

Al-Farasi groaned. One of Kerak's sons said, "There have been several. Nobody even tries to stop them anymore."

Al-Farasi said, "They tried at Aleppo."

Baibers had picked up a rumor about this; he gave the Kurd a sharp look. "What happened?"

"The squints went riding right up to the gate, merry as crickets, as if they'd just come right in. The city commander sent out the cataphracts. Two hundred and fifty cataphracts." He stopped, his lips pressed together, his eyes blank.

"Were you there?" Baibers asked.

"I heard from one who was. The squints trapped them on the road and slaughtered them. Four came back alive. Two of them had arrows in their backs."

Baibers realized his fist was clenched. The cataphracts were lancers and swordsmen. It struck him as folly to send them against archers, even a small number of archers. He had fought cataphracts and they were slow and clumsy. But the armor should have helped. He said, "Their bows are better than ours."

The shorter Arab said, "I've heard they can hit a target at half a league."

Baibers and al-Farasi, together, snorted with laughter. Baibers said, "You couldn't even see a target so far away." A ripple of doubt passed through him. He looked over and saw the Kurdish amir looking back at him.

"You know what they did to Baghdad."

Nobody said anything. Baibers slapped the iron tube in front of him with his palm and turned away. He scanned the camp before him, all these men, all these horses and swords; his hands itched to take control of them.

He started off toward the camp. The sun was just past its height, and the time for prayer was upon him. He needed to ease his mind. The Kurd fell in beside him.

"What do you think the Sultan will do?"

"The Sultan is useless," Baibers said.

The Kurd grunted, and he nodded. "Well. Then we shall see."

"If enough of us stand up to him, perhaps we can force him to do something but I've worked with Yusuf before and he cannot be held to anything very long."

The Kurd was fixing him with a steady look. "We shall see. I can count on you, I know that. I heard—at Aleppo, what the squints did, pretending to retreat, and trapping the cataphracts—that was what you did to the Templars at Al-Mansurah."

Baibers was surprised that the Kurd knew this. He remembered Al-Mansurah. The Crusader King of France had brought an army into Egypt, and the Mamelukes had stopped them at the city on the Nile. Baibers had been al-Salih's Mameluke then; he still loved al-Salih above all, who had freed him. At al-Mansurah he had seen how the Frankish knights would chase after anything that fled, and when they attacked his position Baibers ran away before them, led them into the city and slammed the gates on their heels. He had put archers on the roofs. It was a bloody day.

He said, "If we had a fit leader, we could stand against them. God would stand with us."

"We will see," the Kurd said. He laid a hand on Baibers' arm. "God willing, we have a leader now." He looked deep into Baibers' eyes. "We must force Yusuf into council. Tomorrow. Certainly."

"God willing," Baibers said, excited.


Rikart went to the Paradise Gate, which opened on the great plain where the army was gathering; he sat in the shade of the wall where he could see the army camp and also watch the people going in and out the gate. This was getting to be a large army, every day more men coming in, their tents and fires spread out across the plain as as far as the distant canal.

Keeping an army like this in any one place for very long led to serious problems. Yusuf would have to do something, soon.

He leaned against the wall, warm from the sun. The Romans had built this gate and it was a tall, heavy arch with massive flanking walls, with emblems and carvings in the bricks. Rikart sat to one side of the road. Nearby were two people playing chess, and beyond them a vendor was setting up a brazier to cook meat, a line of men already forming before him. The winter was coming on and in the shade the air bit. Two women came up from the little suk just down the wall, pinching their headcloths together under their noses. A servant with a sword followed them, carrying their baskets.

The Sultan had summoned his council and Rikart was looking to see who moved in and out of the camp. One of the guards yelled, suddenly, and strode out of the archway of the gate, waving his arms at Daud, who was trying to climb the wall. The boy backed hastily down to the ground. Rikart looked around, and caught the guard's eye, and the guard harrumphed at him and went back to the gate.

In the steady trickle of people moving in through the arch, a dusty man on a little horse saw Rikart and veered toward him.

"Al Shab'h," he said. He slid down from his saddle. "I'm glad to see you. I need money, and I have what you trade in."

Rikart recognized a Turkmen from Manjib, who worked for the Templars and the Venetians. He said, "What are you doing down here?"

The Turkmen squatted before him, wiped a hand over his face, and said, "Staying alive. Manjib is gone. The squints blew through it like a poison wind."

Rikart paid him several coins. This was valuable. "You saw this with your own eyes."

"No. Happily I was out of the city. I saw the smoke and I ran."

Which made it less valuable. But Rikart was glad to know this.

"Where are you going from here?"

"Acre." The Turkmen glanced around. "I hate this place. I hate Arabs. But I need to rest up. Get another horse."

"Go to the Hamidya suk. Look for a Jew selling gem stones, an old man named ben Job, and tell him I said he should help you."

The Turkman gripped Rikart's hand, and went back to his horse. Rikart glanced over his shoulder for Daud, and saw the boy walking along the top of the wall, his arms out for balance. The guard ignored him. Rikart turned back to the road.

A troop of men was riding up from the camp, a banner going on before: the Kurdish Amir al-Farasi. So the council was beginning. He leaned back, his eyes half-closed, plotting how to find out what happened there.

* *

A scribe read  the letter, which began without any salutation at all.

"Let Yusuf Al-Malik An-Nasir know, that we sat down before Baghdad and took it by the sword of the most high God--"

Up there on his cushioned throne the Sultan sat rigidly upright. Baibers wondered if he had a stake thrust down his spine. Baibers could not stop walking, the words of the letter streaming by him as he paced around the room. Along the walls, on the suffahs, sat a dozen other men, who said nothing and did nothing. Baibers strode from side to side, his blood on fire.

"God is against you, you wicked wretches," the scribe droned; he was a learned black man from Timbuktu and his trembling hands and low voice showed he clearly understood what speaking these words might mean, and yet he had to speak them.

"He who decides all things hath given us dominion over you. We govern the world from east to west. Nothing happens without our command.

Now we demand you submit. Return to us a speedy answer before your faithlessness shall have kindled a fire that will destroy you utterly."

In the silence, the scribe backed swiftly away, leaving the scroll behind on the table. All around the council of the Amirs, the men stirred, looked from side to side, and began to murmur to each other.

Baibers stood, his head back. "Are we men? Are we not God's warriors? If we run they will surely destroy us. God will abandon us. And rightly so."

As he said this a thrill of zealous ecstasy passed through him. He felt God's hands on him. The whole room swam with a brilliant light.

Then the other voices rose, louder, beating on him like waves. They were shouting him down. He called out, but the general roar of their voices drowned his words. Somebody threw a shoe at him. He gripped his sword, but he saw the trap before him. Here he had no chance. He shrank back to the suffah behind him, where the others made him a wide, empty space, and sat.

Now they talked about surrendering to avoid a massacre. They talked about what had happened to Baghdad. Abdulhassan was suggesting they write to Aleppo, and bid the commander there to surrender. Baibers sat with his hands in his lap, drained empty. They were going to yield without any fight at all. He lifted his gaze toward the Sultan at the far end of the room. A bolt of pure hatred left him, a flaming arrow he could see boiling through the air toward Yusuf. He clenched his teeth. This was Yusuf's fault. Yusuf was the coward here. Yusuf was the evil. He shut his eyes, gathering himself. The time to act was now.

\* \*

A blue twilight lay over the garden. The cedar tree was a shadow at the far end. Inside the pavilion, with its open sides, its fluttering white curtains, the lamps made a puddle of warmth and light. The Sultan Yusuf settled himself on the cushions; he was worn to the bone, more by the constant uproar around him than by any exertion; the men around him all seemed to be saying one thing and meaning another.

Abdulhassan was still there, still pushing him to write the letter to Aleppo. He could not do that. The commander at Aleppo was his uncle Turanshah, who would return a blast of rage and shame, call him unfit to wear the turban of the Sultan, and not surrender anyway.

Baibers, at least, said what he meant. Yusuf shut his eyes, remembering the Mameluke's blazing face. Perhaps he should heed Baibers more. He waved Abdulhassan off.

"Do not trouble me any longer with this. I want you to leave me alone."

"My sovereign wishes." The vizier bowed himself away.

Yusuf sighed, and shut his eyes a moment. He would send for the Armenian girl, who had gifted hands. Even more than lying with her he loved how she stroked and rubbed his body. He beckoned to the servant to come and help him out of his turban and his coat.

"Watch! Watch out!"

He jerked around. Four men were rushing toward him through a side arch of the pavilion. One was Baibers and he carried a naked sword.

The servant flung himself forward, his arms out, holding the charge back, and without waiting to see how that worked Yusuf dashed in the other direction. He jumped the low rail in the opposite side arch and plowed through the rose garden. Behind him the servant's voice rose. "Help! Help—" He tripped and fell, sprang up again. Raced across the grass toward the city wall. As he did, men swarmed down from the wall , going the way he had come.

He slowed, his heart galloping on. Turning, he looked back at the pavilion, where furious shadows fluttered through the soft glow of the lamps, and screams and shouts rose again. His body-servant had come up beside him, a cloak in his arms.

"Master. My lord. Please. It's cold." The man held out the heavy cloak. Yusuf let himself be gathered in.

* *

Baibers could hear people rushing up behind him. He struck down the Kurd who stood in his way and ran back through the rows of thorny bushes toward the gate. Glancing around, he saw Boglu and Moammur running with him, but Shazur was gone. He had not expected so much resistance from Yusuf's people. He had sent to al-Farasi, he had thought the Kurds would be there to help him but they weren't. And somehow the Sultan had vanished anyway.

At the gate he stopped, out of breath, and the other two men staggered up beside him. The garden was filling up with soldiers. A torch burst into flame, another.

"Moammur," Baibers said. "Get back to camp and tell them to run." He let the older man out through the gate and stood in it, his sword in his hand, and Boglu beside him.

Out there on the lawn, the Sultan's men had seen them and slowed down. They edged forward, wary, getting in each other's way. These were the Kurds, he saw. The Crocodile had betrayed him.

He realized in a flash that this had all been a trap, a Kurdish plot. From the beginning al-Farasi had intended this. Now the first men were reaching him, and they came at him from both sides. The stone pillars of the gate protected him and he hacked two of them down. Boglu dealt blows and the Sultan's men flinched back. Baibers tapped Boglu on the shoulder, and the other man slid past him through the gate.

"Remember this," Baibers shouted at the Kurds. "Remember this when the squints come for you!" He lunged at them, across the bodies of their dead, and they drew back even farther. He whirled and fled out the gate.

Boglu waited there with their horses, and Baibers bounded into the saddle. Here where the slope of the mountain came down close to the city wall, a dry wadi ran along through the gap, and he sent his horse at a flat gallop toward that opening. They had to reach the camp on the plain outside the Paradise Gate before the garrison there got word to stop them.

But then ahead of them riders appeared, coming down off the hillside, and also down from the city wall, filling the wadi, blocking their way.

He reined his horse in, and looked over at Boglu. The other man met his eyes and even in the dark Baibers understood him. He drew his sword out, and turned forward, toward the dozen horsemen waiting for him. He hoped Moammur had gotten through to his men. He raised his sword over his head.

"God is great!"

He hurtled toward them; he would kill a few, to escort him into paradise. Then from their midst a shout went up.

"Take him alive!"

Panic flooded him; better he died. He swung at the bodies surging toward him. He heard Boglu scream. Baibers' sword bit, scraped on bone, tore free, and he swung it again, but they were inside his reach now, and they had him.

* *

Rikart bowed his head a little. "Lord. Thank you for receiving me so late."

The Kurdish amir did not rise from his cushioned seat at the middle of the tent. He spoke Arabic. "Yes. I had intended to seek you out, so this was fortuitous. I have heard much of you, from people I respect. Please. Sit." He gestured toward the cushions opposite him.

It was almost midnight, but Rikart had seen al-Farasi kept Roman hours. He settled himself down on the carpet, a low table between him and the tall Kurd. A servant brought a ewer, and the sheikh waved a hand and the servant filled two cups with red wine.

Rikart said nothing, but took the near cup, and drank. Al-Farasi turned his long narrow face toward him, smiling. "The prophet would forgive me if he tasted this."

"Morean," Rikart said. "They understand the grape there."

"Indeed."

Another servant brought in a tray, and laid out small plates of stuffed figs, nuts, cheese. Rikart set the cup down, still half-full. "If you wish, Amir, we can speak Kurdish."

"Well." Al-Farasi stared at him, sharp. "Then we shall. I have heard that, you speak every language." He put his cup on the table and the servant with the ewer came forward. "Also that you know all that matters, from the Tigris to the sea."

Rikart said, "That's not true." He was having some trouble with Al-Farasi's accent.

"I understand that you have recently been in Acre."

"I have."

"Tell me, then. Bohemund supports the Mongols; will the Templars?"

Rikart gave a short laugh. "Lord, nobody in Acre is interested in anything but money."

"Are they even in the Mongols' path yet? Where do you think they will strike next?"

"Aleppo, likely. They took Manjib by storm a few days ago."

The Kurd's mouth dropped open. He had not heard that. Rikart thought, now you owe me something.

He said, "In the end, what they want is Cairo."

"Cairo!"

"Did Yusuf say anything about Qutuz? You've heard the boy Sultan is deposed, and Qutuz reigns alone?"

Al-Farasi blinked. "Not surprising, is it? Qutuz is power mad. He always has been. The Mamelukes are murderers to a man. Utterly untrustworthy."

"They're better than Yusuf."

Al-Farasi blinked again. "I think I'd almost rather the Mongols."

"That's the problem, all around," Rikart said. "Did Yusuf read the letter?"

The tall Kurd grunted. "The letter. God witness this, they are foul. God strike them down for their blasphemies!"

Rikart drew one knee up, his arm over the top. "Yet God does not strike them down."

"We have sinned," Al-Farasi said, morosely. "God's will be done."

"That's what they say."

"What do they know of God?"

Rikart made a gesture with the hand on his knee. "What does anybody know of God? Adonai, El, Ahura, Christ, Allah, who cares anymore? None of that means anything. Maybe we should let the Mongols rule us all. Maybe it is God's will. But this place is mine, and he shall not have it. That's what matters to me."

Al-Farasi's teeth showed. "It is not yours, Frank."

"I was born here, Kurd."

Their eyes met. The Kurd had something of the reptile in him, in his flat pale eyes, his long jaw. Rikart reached for his wine cup again, and then he heard the tent flap open behind him.

He turned; Daud had come in, the boy as always barefoot and draped in a dirty old thobe too big for him. He said nothing, but gave Rikart a look.

Rikart turned back to al-Farasi. "You'll pardon me, lord."

"What is this?"

Rikart went out of the tent. The Kurds had taken up the southern flank of the plain outside the Paradise Gate. From here he looked out over a field of banked campfires, peaked tents and tethered horses, quiet in the deep of the night. Daud pointed.

"I see."

Through the sleeping camp, out there, dark shapes were moving. He realized these were riders picking their way through the campfires, heading south. Steadily more of them followed, scores of men, all moving at once, in the same direction. He could not make out who they were but he saw they were coming from the camp of the Bahriyya. He saw, behind them, their campfires, still red. Their tents still up.

The tent flap behind him swished. Al-Farasi came up beside him, smiling. "Is something happening that surprises even you?"

From the direction of the city a runner panted up to them. Al-Farasi lifted his hand, but the messenger burst out, "Baibers! They've got—" Al-Farasi slashed his hand down, and the man fell still. Rikart turned and gave the Kurd a hard look.

In Arabic, he said, "Thank you for your hospitality, lord. I'll leave you to your celebrations." He glanced around for Daud, and headed toward their horses.

* *

From what the messenger had said, Rikart thought they had taken Baibers alive, and he knew where Yusuf would keep him. He led Daud around through the Paradise Gate and off to the citadel on its mound at the north end of the city. The streets around it were busy even this late and the mass of stone towers and walls was spangled with torches. Around the entry a hundred soldiers waited, holding lances. Rikart skulked along the twenty-foot wall, looking up at the towers.

All but one were dark, but in the northwestern corner tower a light shone in the top chamber. Rikart said, "That one. We need a rope." The light went out.

* *

They had bound Baibers' arms behind him with his own silk belt. Thrust him into a tiny room at the top of a tower. He prowled around the room in the dark. The window was a deep narrow slot through the raw stone, and turning his back to it, he got the cloth between his wrists against the edge and sawed back and forth.

His flesh rasped on the stone. The pain calmed him down. The blood made the silk slippery and he wormed his hands around and the frayed cloth tore and he was free.

In the dark, in the little cell at the top of the tower, he knelt and put his head to the floor, but he did not pray. He let himself hate al-Farasi. He promised himself and God that he would have his revenge.

He saw his life stretched out behind him, lit as if by lightning flashes: evil and good.

He had won great victories. But now, sunk low again. Maybe, this time, he would not rise. Maybe it was over.

They would cut his head off and put it on a pike. He would rot away. What the ravens did not eat.

He groaned. God, he thought, God help me. Or at least let me die in your service. Like a knife in the chest he felt this.

He banged his forehead on the floor. Yusuf would kill him slowly.

He could not pray. God had gone off somewhere else. Getting up, he prowled around the little room again. He stood a moment at the door listening. Surely someone stood outside. He pushed the door, which was solid in its frame, and took hold of the latch and rattled it. Nothing happened. But surely they would have a guard outside, maybe several.

He went to the window, leaning across the deep sill toward the open air. The window narrowed from the inside to the outside and he had to squeeze his shoulders together to fit deeper into the space. The tower was at the highest point of the city, and Damascus spread out before him, its indistinct jumble of roofs, the trees like dark plumes. Only, here and there, the glow of a torch or a lamp in the blue of the night. The wind touched his face. Leaning across the window's deep sill, he saw down the far side, forty feet or more to the talus at the foot of the wall.

He could fling himself out. The window was narrow but he could wedge himself through. Fly like an angel. Meet his fate. Let the wind save him or let him go. He realized he had already put his hands on the sill to boost his body up, to dive out headfirst.

No glory in that, either. He lowered his head. Every soul shall taste of death. All this world is vanity, no more.

He was trembling. He had to act, soon, or the demon in him would win out, he would dash his head on these stones and die.

The light of the moon touched the window's edge. The night was halfway gone. Above him on the tower he heard a fluttering of wings and a bird's hoarse cry. Maybe a raven. Maybe a message. He remembered how the ravens had fed Ilyas. A bird swooped away through the moonlight. They were not night birds; something had roused it. Now he heard a soft scraping above him, on the wall of the tower, and then, to his astonishment, a bare foot appeared at the top of the window.

He backed up, his breath stuck in his throat. The foot groped along the window's edge. Another dirty bony foot appeared beside it, feeling for the sill. With both feet on the sill, a dark shape stooped down into the window space, blocking the moonlight.

Only a boy. A loop of rope was wrapped around him. In the window, he lifted his head up, to wave his hand to someone above him, and when he did so the moonlight shone on his face, and Baibers gave a low gasp. It was the boy he had found near the Euphrates, the boy from Baghdad. Perched there, hanging on the rope, his feet on the window, the boy beckoned, and Baibers went out through the window.

*  *

"Put this on."

His rescuer was tall, thin, wearing a poor man's shabby white thobe. Like some Bedou he had wrapped his headcloth around the lower part of his face, so that only his eyes showed, but he was not Bedou. His Arabic had an odd accent. He was holding out a heap of cloth, and Baibers took it and shook it open.

It was a woman's gown. His gorge rose, but he saw the reason. A moment later, bundled in the burka, he was perched on a donkey, trotting along a street.

The boy ran beside him. Baibers glanced constantly at the boy. He thought, God has sent him to me again, and a thrill went through him. Another lightning flash. He was not lost.

The tall man was leading the donkey along down the straight street. It was now well past midnight, but the street was full of people, many in a hurry. The burka confined him. He could see very little, only what was directly in front of him, and that small and blurry through the mesh of the veil. He hunched down, and kept his feet up under the hem. He looked for the Bahriyya in the street, but saw none. God willing they had all fled. He remembered Boglu and his teeth gritted together. He would avenge Boglu. In the crowds he saw a lot of Bedouin. Yusuf's Mamelukes in their green jackets. Kurdish headcloths. He was tired to the bone and the steady sway of the donkey's walk lulled him to a doze.

When they reached the gate the sun was rising. Part of a little crowd of people going out of the city, they waited in line for the gate to open. Slowly the line crept forward. The gatekeepers were checking them through, looking at faces. The boy drifted off, looking around, and went up to the man leading the donkey and tugged on his sleeve.

The tall man turned his head. A horseman was coming rapidly down the street, forcing a way through the waiting crowd. His voice rang out.

"The Panther has escaped!"

From the crowd a startled wail arose. The boy came close by the donkey, glanced up at Baibers crouching on its back. At the gate, two guards appeared, carrying swords. Kurds. Baibers bit his teeth together. The Kurds were letting people go by them one at a time, peering very closely at their faces. The tall man led the donkey on, two steps and pause. Two steps and pause. Baibers' breath came short. He felt the space inside the burka close around him like a shroud. If they caught him this way they wouldn't even have to kill him. They would take him prisoner again. Parade him in this woman's dress through the streets. His donkey reached the gate, and the tall man held out his hand toward the gatekeeper, showing him something, some kind of pass.

The gatekeeper leaned in, peering into the tall man's eyes. Looking for a dot.

Baibers shut his own eyes. Under him the donkey stepped forward again; he swayed. The cold shadow of the gate fell on them. One of the swarm, they left Damascus.

* *

Hours later, in the midday, they trudged up to a spring, where several tents were pitched. The boy took the donkey away and the tall man led Baibers into one of the tents.

This was a space no bigger than the cell he had escaped from, empty except for a pack on the floor and a waterskin hanging from the center pole. Baibers lifted the burka up over his head and dropped it, taking a deep breath. Praise be to God who did not make me a woman. Going to the center pole he took down the waterskin and drank.

Lowering the skin, he faced the tall man, who was unwinding his head-cloth, and for the first time Baibers saw his face.

"El Shab'h," he said. "Well-named, you are. You walk through walls."

The Frank reached out for the skin. "The last time we met you said you would kill me." He drank. "Want to try now?"

"You have served God," Baibers said. "We are even. Why did you do this?"

The boy came in, thin as a string. He said, in a voice barely above a whisper, "Gilbert is bringing the horses."

The Frank Rikart was stripping off his thobe. Under it he wore a mail shirt. He said, "You should wait until dark, amir. They'll be watching every road."

Baibers said, "Why did you do this?"

"You know where to find your men. Go to Egypt. Make it up with Qutuz. If Yusuf got a letter, Qutuz got a letter. Make him see he has to fight." Bending to the pack , he pulled out a ragged white surcoat with a red cross on the breast.

Baibers said, "Give me the boy."

Rikart pulled on the surcoat. With a glance at the boy he said, "Do you want to go with him?"

The boy gave a little shake of his head. Rikart sneered at Baibers. He took a sheathed sword from the pack and slung the belt around his waist.

"I have no weapon," Baibers said.

"Ride fast."

Rikart went to the tent flap and out, the boy on his heels.

Baibers stood where he was. This was a sign. This was how the world was. Bad became good. Small became great. Weak became strong. Defeat became victory. He had known when he first saw him that the boy was God's messenger. Now again God had shown him the truth.

No matter how low and poor his lot seemed now, God led him by the hand, and if he came on, the world would turn for him.

He went to the tent flap and looked out; a black horse stood there, hipshot, in the sun.

He did not go at once. He had to find his men and get to the task at hand, but there was another, pressing matter to deal with. And before anything else he had to thank God. He poured water from the skin onto his hands. He was not in a clean place and he had no kilim but he was glad of heart. He felt God's hands around him. God's voice in his ears. He faced south, and lowering his arms to his sides, he bent his head, and with a fiery mind began the declaration of faith.

* *

Daud was exhausted. Rikart took him up in front of him on his saddle and the boy fell asleep at once in the cradle of his arm, a sprawl of arms and legs, gawky and light as a crane. Leading the donkey and the spare horse Rikart followed the great highway toward the coast.

People thronged along it, merchants with their trains of donkeys and camels, and many travelers on foot, women leading their children along, men carrying bundles and pulling carts, boys herding goats, baskets of chickens on their backs. They were all going south. Rikart could almost feel the rumble of the vast army sweeping down on them, although it was still hundreds of miles away.

A hundred miles was nothing to the Mongols. They could cross that in a few days. He thought of going to Acre but that was still too near. Yusuf was not ready for them; he had just lost his best fighters and the others would not follow him. Damascus would fall at a breath. He shifted the child in his arms. This road led south and west, to the Via Maris, the Roman road along the coast. He would go to Gaza, where he could keep watch on the Mongols and Egypt both.

* *

The Kurdish Emir Al-Farasi heard in the afternoon that Baibers had escaped, which annoyed him. He had planned it all so well. Baibers had played into his hands so excellently. But he was pleased, anyway: the attack had left Yusuf totally unnerved, and now with only a little suggestion he was preparing to flee, abandon Damascus to the Mongols without a fight.

Al-Farasi decided he would go to Hulegu himself with this news, which would surely inspire the Il-Khan's considerable generosity. Hulegu had to realize al-Farasi had been central to this success.

The day was still and hot; he had the tent flaps open, to let in the air. His servants had brought ice, kept frozen somewhere in a deep well even in this heat, and he had another jar of the wine left. He thought of sending for a girl, but it was still too hot. He contemplated what he would ask Hulegu for, a city somewhere, perhaps Homs. Perhaps, even, Aleppo, when it fell. The chilled wine made him buoyant. He saw himself about to be a mighty man. He wished he could have handed Baibers over to the Mongols as well.

He remembered he had been talking to the renegade Templar al-Shab'h when the news came that Baibers was taken; he thought he had silenced the messenger before he blurted anything out, but the Frank had given him a sharp look. The Frank had done something.

The wine was also swelling his bladder, and he rose, and went out to the back of the tent to urinate.

He stopped in the shade of the tent wall, but not too close, not wanting to spread the odor, and he was drawing aside his robe when he heard something behind him.

He gasped. A rope whipped around his neck and tightened and cut off his breath, and he clutched at the noose, gagging, trying to scream, flailing out with his legs, his arms. His bladder spilled, and he went black.

Cecelia Holland

# CHAPTER 7

## ALEPPO FALLS

**N**ikola climbed up the rope ladder. The bottom of the tower, high as a man's head, was made of chunks of stone, torn out of the many buildings outside the walls. Above that, the frame of massive wooden beams rose up another five such heights.

He came up onto a platform as big as a ger. The mangonel stood at the exact center of this. The long arm was at rest now. The sling lay empty on the platform deck. One of the two men who crewed the mangonel was working on the bindings and ropes, and the other was bent over the brazier, his cheeks puffed, waking up the embers.

From here Nikola looked out straight across to the tower at the corner of the wall. Beyond, the rooftops of Aleppo shone in the sun. The wall thronged with archers, who shot at anything that moved. They huddled behind the notches in the parapet; Mongol snipers kept them pinned down, but the stretch of land between the tower and the wall was empty as a desert.

The army stretched out on either side along the wall, always with that gap between the Mongols and the city. A hundred feet down from this tower, another was rising, the base already set in place, and piles of wood standing around it.

Hulegu said, "We have to do this quickly. There isn't enough grass out here to keep the horses. You see that tower on the corner of the wall. I want to sweep it clear, so our men can get under it and sap it down."

Nikola thought this was obvious. He held his tongue. He knew his father liked showing off the way he planned things. The creak of wood behind him turned his head. A single mast of wood almost twice as high as the platform stood at one corner, lashed to the structure. A long arm crossed it, strung with ropes; on this they brought up the stones.

How this worked interested him; the mangonel, he had seen, operated the same way. He swung his own arms back and forth, appreciating how similar it was. Now the crane creaked and moved; he could see the ropes moving, somebody below hauling down one end of the crosspiece. The other end rose, lifting its basket into sight, full of rocks. The men by the mangonel went over to bring it in.

They loaded the sling, attached the counterweight to the mangonel, and dropped it. With a squeal of wood the machine's long arm hurtled up, and the sling whirled around and at its full length released the rocks in a shower. The arm hit the crossbar with a thud. The rocks flew in a high arc up over the empty land and rained down on the wall.

"All right," Hulegu said. "We have the distance." He waved one hand.

Nikola looked around. The crane was groaning again. This time when the basket came above the edge of the platform, there were no rocks, only a hide sack. Hulegu stood impassively as the crew of the mangonel lifted this carefully up and laid it in the sling, handling it as reverently as an offering.

The two men cranked the counterweight back up to its high point, and while one held a twig into the brazier, the other pinched and straightened a thread that stuck out of the top of the sack. They lit this thread with the burning twig. Quickly, then, they flipped the lever on the counterweight and it plunged.

The arm flew upward. The leather sack sailed away out of the sling, and as it flew, it began to burn. The dark lump flashed, and sparkled, and suddenly it was boiling with flames, and the flames spread into a shower of fire that pelted the wall.

Even from that distance Nikola could hear the screaming. Hulegu grunted in his throat.

"A few more like that."

Nikola looked down into the empty land again, down below the tower. He could see part of the army moving up, men gathering just past arrow range, ready to move in when the wall was clear. The crane jerked alive again, the arm rising, the basket carrying another leather sack.

The crewmen bent to lift it, and the sack slipped in their hands. It rolled onto the deck, and the top split open. A thick shining water flowed from it. The crewmen reared back. Hulegu shouted, "Get it out! Hurry!"

The stuff spread over the boards. The liquid top shimmered with beautiful colors. Nikola's hair lifted; he could see something dancing in the air over the puddle, barely visible, spirits, or demons.

One crewman had run for a bucket of sand; the other just dashed to the side of the tower and scrambled over. Then, at the edge of the shining puddle, flames appeared.

Hulegu leapt toward the ladder to the ground. With a whoosh, the flames roared up over the whole spill. The wash of heat crinkled Nikola's hair and his face burned. Through a veil of fire he saw Hulegu stop, on the ladder, and reach out his arm to him. Flames leapt between them. Nikola spun around. Behind him he saw the crane with its dangling rope, and he leapt out into the air.

He caught the rope tight in both arms. The leap carried him far off the platform, and his weight bore him down faster than he expected. He hit the ground with a jolt that went all the way up to the base of his skull. He looked back to see the whole tower wrapped in flame.

A crowd was gathering to watch this, leaving a good distance around the blazing tower. Nikola ran around it, and collided with his father, coming the other way. Hulegu flung his arms around him.

"Ah, boy. Ah, my boy."

Nikola stood back, breathing hard. His face hurt. The tower was an enormous torch, a single flame, red and yellow, swirling in the wind. On the wall of the city, the people were cheering.

Hulegu said, "This stuff comes from the firelands. They call it the doomsday weapon, because it will consume the world." The cheering was loud on the wall of Aleppo. He flung up his fist toward the city, one finger in the air. "Get Kitboqa over here. We need to talk." He stamped away, his head down.

* *

Kitboqa said, "In your service, lord, I told you that stuff is too dangerous to use." The lanky Turk was taller than either of them. He had been supervising the digging of a ditch toward the wall, Hulegu's fall back tactic. His coat was powdered with pale dust. He looked almost pleased the tower had burned.

Hulegu grunted at him. "We need to hasten this up."

"Give me more men to dig, then," Kitboqa said. "We can start another trench."

Hulegu turned to Nikola. "You saw what happened. I'm putting you in charge of this. Build another tower. Figure out how to make this work." He gave the Turk a hard look. Nikola drew a deep breath, his body tingling; he remembered the flames shooting up. He did not know how to build anything. His face hurt.

\* \*

The Khatun Dokaz had taken over a compound outside the city wall, well behind the army line, two big buildings and a kitchen around a courtyard, and a garden and an orchard besides. Dinah sat in the doorway of the main house, picking through a basket of dried beans. Moseh was playing at the far end of the courtyard, and she kept watch to see he didn't sneak away into the orchard. She looked up and saw Nikola ride in.

She stood up, startled at the look of him. His face was splotched with shiny red, and the ends of his little droopy moustaches were crisp. He came up before her, and she said, "What happened to you?"

He shrugged. "Something blew up."

She said, "Oh, God have mercy. Well. Wait a moment." She put down the basket and went off through the yard, past Moseh, to the garden. She had seen aloes growing here, by the wall, and she broke off one of the fleshy green leaves. Moseh had followed her; she picked him up and carried him back to the courtyard.

"Ama!" He twisted in her arms. "Down!"

"No. Stay here." He was always trying to escape. She set him down and went back to Nikola, standing there with his burned face, hands on his hips.

"Here," she said. "Sit down." He did, and she broke open the aloe leaf, so that it oozed its thick clear juice, and dipping in her forefinger she painted his hurts.

She saw at once that it eased the pain. He sat patiently waiting while she daubed his face.

When she was done he said, "Here," and held out his hands. The palms were raw, the grey calluses along the beds of his fingers pale against the burned red skin. She squeezed more aloe juice onto them and rubbed it gently over the red spots. He leaned toward her and put his arms around her and pulled her against him.

She stiffened. He laid his cheek against her hair and they sat like that a while. She ached to run but his arm around her held her there. She could not soften herself; she sat there like a stone.

He held her tight. His lips against her ear. "Come into the orchard tonight."

She swallowed. She looked over at Moseh, who had gone cautiously to stare up at Nikola's horse.

"You have Moseh," Nikola said. "You can have me also. Jun will watch him. Come to the orchard."

She faced him. Her mouth was dry. She wiped the aloe off her fingers with the tail of her deel. She said, low, "No. You know what happened to...what happened to me. I can't." She turned her head to look him in the eyes. "Let me go."

For a moment he was still, and then he sat back, and lowered his hands. She saw a surge of temper in his eyes.

She took the ring from her finger, and held it out to him. "Do you want this back?"

He smiled at her. He took the ring, and holding her hand he slid it back onto her finger.

"Now," he said, "do what you did the other time."

She held still, alarmed. His eyes danced with a merry glint. He said, "You did it the last time."

She leaned forward and put her mouth against his, as she had when he first gave her the ring. His mouth was soft under hers, eager, a caress. Her lips parted. She realized she had put her hand on his shoulder.

She pulled back again, her hands in her lap. He laughed at her. But he only got to his feet and went to his horse.

Moseh was there, staring up at the horse. Nikola scooped up the little boy and put him on the saddle. Moseh screeched. He clung to the saddle with both hands, his face shining. Nikola sprang up behind him, and rode around the courtyard with him, and then came back to her and lowered the child down to the ground. He smiled at her. Wheeling the horse, he trotted away. She took Moseh into her arms, her insides roiling.

* * * *

Nikola found the men who had built the last tower and put them to work. The stone footing was still sound but all the wood was burnt up, and wood was hard to find here. He went around the deserted houses, looking for floors and doors and beams, and finally on a canal came on a watermill that was made of heavy balks of timber.

While the tower was going up he went looking for the man who had crewed the mangonel when it burned. There had been two of them, but one had died in the fire. The other one was squatting on the step of a house behind the army line, drinking. As soon as he saw Nikola he began to shake his head and waved his hands. "No, no, I won't do that work again, not for the Khakhan himself."

Nikola sank down on his heels before him. "Have you ever seen that happen before? Why did you drop it?"

"I didn't mean to! It was slippery. It must have been leaking already." The man, a Turk, gave a wild shrug. "Like the demon in the jug. Once it gets out, it's all over. The only other time, I was on the ground, though."

"Why did it burn?"

"The sun. When the sun shines on that stuff, it burns."

Nikola remembered the sprites he had seen dancing on the spill, phantom flames. The Turk was right about the demons. But they had to set fire to the bomb. It needed more than just the sun.

189

"What can you use to put it out?"

"Sand. Not water. It burns in water. I've heard you can piss on it."

He went to see how the charges are made. This involved mixing two liquids together just before filling the sacks. The seams of the sacks were sealed with wax, so they would melt as the sack heated up.

He said, "Make nets out of cord. Carry the sacks in the nets."

"Yes, Noyon."

He was beginning to like giving orders. He thought about the sprites again, and how the fire had started only at one edge. There had been fire on the deck already, in the brazier, which he thought had been at that edge. He went off to the weapons ger, to find some Han firesticks to use instead of braziers.

* * *

Moseh now would not rest if he saw a horse, but wanted to ride it. Several horses had gotten into the orchard to eat the fallen apples and he was constantly sneaking in there. Dinah caught him for the third time and brought him back, sobbing and flailing at her with his fists. Jun came out to take him out of her arms, and gave him a shake.

"Don't hit your Ama! What a bad boy!"

Dinah wiped her hair back off her forehead. "Thank you. Can you watch him a while? I have work to do." Dokaz was insisting she cook their meals. Dinah had never cooked very much before but she understood the kitchen here.

"I'm going to the suk," Jun said. "I'll take him with me." She shook Moseh again. "If he minds!" He gave her a stony look.

"Find me some onions," Dinah said. She leaned down and kissed Moseh's sweaty salty forehead. "Go with Jun, and be a good boy."

\* \*

"The Franks are coming," Dokaz said. Her face was bright with intent. "The Il-Khan wants me to meet them, and they will be here before the sun goes down, so we have to hurry. Make me a throne room."

With Jun and Tulla, Dinah rolled up carpets from the other rooms. Dokaz brought in some of the men to help. They spread all the carpets they could find on the floor, a thick softness under the feet, and put a suffah in the middle. Dokaz stood there, her hands on her hips, looking around.

Dinah said, "Khatun, which Franks?"

"The same ones as before. The Prince of somewhere." Dokaz wheeled. "You will listen again. Like the last time."

"Of course, Khatun."

Dokaz was already talking to Jun. "Find a house nearby, one with some furnishings still. The Franks can stay there. Somewhere I can keep an eye on them."

Dinah gathered up cushions, went to the other houses in the compound, found shawls and tall fancy urns. She and Jun piled the suffah up with cushions and draped the shawls over it. Dokaz stood frowning at it.

"I want a back to this. And make it higher off the ground."

They rummaged through the house, finding nothing, and then crossed the yard to the kitchen and brought back the tables. Jun had one of the men cut the legs off the longer table and they slid it under the suffah, and they laid the other table on its side behind it all, to make the back. Dinah put an urn on either side. She thought she should put something in them, feathers or leaves, but nothing presented itself.

"Better," Dokaz said, when they had the carpets and the cushions and the shawls artfully arranged again. She turned to Dinah. "Wine. Cups."

"Yes, Khatun." She went back to the kitchen. On the way, seeing the palm trees by the wall, she decided to put big fronds into the urns.

* *

Dokaz had sent over a couple of slaves to help her in the kitchen, a Turkish woman and a Persian man. She put them to sweeping and cleaning; the kitchen had been empty for a while and there were mice in the cupboards. They kept their heads down and they did not meet her eyes. They spoke to her only when she spoke to them, although she saw them talking together when they were not working.

She thought, What is the difference between me and them? Moseh. The Khatun's favor.

She was as polite to the slaves as she ever was to the Khan. She never gave them orders, only asked for help. Which made no difference, really, but it made her feel better.

* *

She was dumping out dishwater when the gate opened, and a parade of men on big horses rode in, one carrying a banner quartered red and blue. She straightened. Kitboqa led the way, but the men behind him were Frankish knights. Among them one, clearly the leader, big and fair-haired, calling out orders, gesturing, who she remembered.

Bohemund, she thought, excited. The Prince of Antioch is come.

Kitboqa had seen her; he cast her a single furious glance. She stood in the doorway of the kitchen watching the horsemen dismount and go into the hall. She wiped her hands and went across the yard to the hall door.

Kitboqa stood in the middle of the room, talking in a loud, false voice. Behind him the Christian knights stood in a rank.

"My lord the Prince of Antioch, Count of Tripoli, Lord of Lattakieh, Lord of Darkush—"

Up on the new throne, Dokaz sat bolt upright, but as the Turk spoke these titles a smile passed over her face. When Kitboqa was done, she leaned forward a little, smiling, and said, "I give you greeting, Prince, in the name of the Khakhan, the Lord of the World."

The knights stirred, their feet shifting. Dinah put a hand over her mouth to hold back a laugh. Dokaz knew this. Now Bohemund was waving up some men with presents. Dinah went back to the kitchen, to fetch the wine.

* *

When Gilbert d'Baalbeck presented himself to Bohemund, he saw at once the Prince did not remember him. He backed away with a bow. He wasn't here to deal with Bohemund, anyway; his task was to talk Hulegu into an agreement to let the Genoese into Aleppo ahead of the Venetians. He moved off along the edge of the hall, crowded with Crusaders, all on a roar. Near the low end of the table he found a seat on a bench and sat. His two guards stood behind him; this was still a war, after all.

At the long U shape of tables the other men drank and shouted to one another. A little way up the room from Gilbert a big German was bellowing, "Glory to God!" in a voice fuzzy with drink. A row of Franks across the way had locked their arms together and were singing.

The man on his left turned. "Been here long?" He spoke French, but with an odd accent, a young man, fresh-cheeked.

"I just arrived," Gilbert said. They exchanged names and shook hands. The other man was English. They talked a few moments about the feckless foolish English King, and then the Englishman said, "Besides, the real work is here, isn't it?" He nodded toward Bohemund. "With the Mongol army at his command, we'll take Jerusalem in a month."

Startled, Gilbert sipped at his wine. His gaze strayed around the room. He wondered how long this English greenling had been in the Holy Land. His eyes sharpened: he thought he knew the woman pouring Bohemund's wine.

He said, "Bohemund is indeed high in the councils of the Il-Khan."

"A bunch of ignorant barbarians," the Englishman said. "No match for a subtle man like the Prince. He'll have them eating birdseed from his palm. And we'll have Jerusalem again."

Gilbert said nothing. He was watching the woman with the jug. It was Dinah, he was sure of it. He remembered that she was close with the Khatun Dokaz, and now he realized how useful she could be. He wondered if Bohemund understood he was hedged around with spies. The young Englishman surged to his feet, his cup lifted high, and shouted, "Glory! Glory to the Prince of Antioch!"

A howl went up all around the room; men shot to their feet. Bohemund beamed from his high seat, and drank. A thundering cheer of his name beat upon the rafters.

The man to Gilbert's right did not rise, or drink. He said, "I'll feel better about this if we actually get a face to face meeting with the Il-Khan."

Around the great room, the crowd was settling back into place. The Englishman wiped his mouth. "When will that happen?"

"Sometime soon, I hope. He's down in the fighting somewhere."

"There are so many of them. They've got enormous towers."

"Hugh-gul will send for us." That was how they said the Il-Khan's name.

Gilbert gave a little shake of his head. Dinah was moving along the table with her jug, filling cups. He thought the Franks should keep quiet more. She came by him, her gaze downcast, and poured wine into his cup. Briefly he met her eyes, and she smiled at him. When she went beyond him to pour the last of the jug into the Englishman's cup, the young man grabbed for her, and she slid away like an eel from his hands.

The man on Gilbert's right said, "Turn them loose on the Mamelukes. I'd like to see those bastards nailed."

"Mamelukes," the Englishman said blankly. "Aren't they in Egypt?" The other man laughed.

* * * *

Nikola had run out of firebombs. He stood at the foot of his mangonel tower, looking toward the burning wall. He saw no defenders; everything that could burn was likely ash by now. The flames were dying down and Kitboqa's crews were rushing from their half-finished trenches toward the foot of the wall.

His mangonel gave its grunt and shriek again, and rocks clattered down on a part of the wall beyond what had burned. He saw nobody there either. The defenders had shrunk back beyond his reach. From far up the city parapet, a bowman leaned out to shoot down toward Kitboqa's men, released a single arrow, and dodged back under cover again before the Mongol archers loosed their storm on him. Nikola saw no sign the arrow hit anything. Under the burnt out tower, the sappers were attacking the stony ground with picks and hammers.

Hulegu rode up beside him. "Well done," he said. "You work fast."

Nikola said nothing, pleased. He looked around for his horse. Hulegu rode down toward the wall, summoned Kitboqa, and they talked. Nikola mounted his horse. Around him more men were riding up, their eyes fixed on the wall a bowshot away. Kitboqa galloped up past them, headed for the far end of the line, and Hulegu trotted up toward Nikola.

Along the foot of the tower the sappers were digging and throwing dirt, and now abruptly they all rushed back, away from the wall, up into the camp. Silence fell. Nikola caught himself holding his breath.

A rumble built into a sudden roar; the bottom of the tower blew out in a spray of earth and rock. Nikola's horse reared straight up and he brought it down to all fours and laid a hand on its neck. The wall sagged, not just the tower but on either side, and then it all collapsed in a billow of dust.

The whole army roared. Nikola's hair stood on end. He gave a quick glance at Hulegu, who held out one hand, holding him back. The wall was still tumbling down, scattering loose stones. Far away, in the city, people were screaming.

Hulegu lifted his hand. All along the Mongol line the horns blew, the men howled, and they flung themselves on Aleppo.

* * * *

Dokaz said, "I hate this house. It smells bad." She waved her hand in front of her face.

Dinah said, "I can bring in some incense." She was pouring water into the cups for chai. The Khatun was in a foul mood. Now she waved her hand again, angry.

"Ah, you don't understand." She got up and walked around the room. Dinah put the lid on top of the first cup, to let it steep, and turned to the second.

Jun burst in the door, her face flaming with excitement. "They're taking the city! Quick!"

Dokaz gave a roar. She and Jun rushed out the door; Dinah followed; Jun was supposed to be watching Moseh. The other women were hurrying around the corner of the house, where a stair went up the wall. Already, out there, she saw the smoke billowing into the sky.

Her steps slowed. She climbed the stone steps to the flat roof, where the whole household was gathered, all looking toward the city. Even her slaves from the kitchen were there. Moseh sat on the shoulders of the Persian man. She looked out, over the roofs and low walls of the buildings, toward the smoke.

Out there something heavy crashed. She could faintly hear screaming. Abruptly a wave of nausea rose into her throat. She wheeled and staggered blindly back down the stair and into the house.

Inside the door she crumpled to the ground. Her breath came short. Run away. She had to run. She could not rise, she was trembling all over.

"Ama." Moseh came in behind her. He crawled into her lap, leaning his head on her, and put his hand on her face. "Ama cry?"

She closed her arms around him, this Mongol child. Her child. Murderer's child. She found herself twisting the ring on her finger. He was in there killing people.

Moseh said, "Ama?" and put his hand on her face. "Cry?"

Then Jun was there, sitting down next to her on the ground. "What's wrong?" She put her arm around them both.

Dinah shook her head. Jun touched her face. "Don't be sad. These are not your people. We are your people now."

"I have no people."

Jun gave a laugh in her throat. "Yes, see how alone you are." She looked around. "I think the chah is ruined." She went over to the table by the Khatun's throne, where the little brazier and the cups stood.

Dinah closed her eyes. Moseh was pulling on her, his fists clutching her deel. "Ama." She pulled him against her and kissed him. All she had. Everything else was gone.

She remembered the women of Baghdad, spitting on her because she was a Jew. Was she even a Jew anymore more? She felt herself dissolving into smoke.

Jun squatted before her with a cup. "Here."

"I'm sorry," she said. "I just can't bear it." She took the cup and inhaled the mysterious aroma.

Jun smiled at her. "We are your people now." She went back to the table for the second cup. Dinah sipped at the chah, too hot to drink. Moseh slid off her lap and went off to climb on the throne. The terror slipped away, like a shadow passing. She breathed in, as if she had not breathed for hours. Jun came back and they sat side by side with their cups, not speaking. From outside there came another tremendous shout of many voices. Moseh had straddled the back of the throne and was bouncing up and down. Dinah sipped the chah, her heart pounding.

\* \* \* \*

The air stank of smoke. In the distance something boomed. Hulegu rode along the street, looking up at the citadel on its height above him. After him came Nikola, Kitboqa and some of the Crusader lords. This street had been cleared, the bodies taken away, although patches of dried blood still showed here and there on the cobblestones. The people remaining, not many, had been rounded up and headed off to the slave markets.

The whole city now had fallen into his hands save this one fortress. He saw no way to storm it; the sheer slope rose twenty bow-lengths before the walls even began, so he could not bring up siege engines, and from the walls the raghead archers could cover all the approaches without exposing themselves.

"This place is formidable," he said. "They knew their work, whoever built this."

"The Romans, my lord," Prince Bohemund said, rushing in as he always did to explain what Hulegu already knew. "Roman work is very well made." He had bright blonde hair, which he kept in a sleek pouf. He rode a big, heavy muscled stallion and he kept it tight-wound, its neck bowed to the bit, its ears back.

Ahead, the street went under a roof, the dark narrow space beneath full of Mongols. Hulegu reined his horse around into a side lane. He looked up at the citadel again, wondering how many men were forted up in there. He might have to starve them out. "Is there a well inside?"

"I believe there is, my lord," Bohemund said. Which meant nothing, Bohemund always having to have an answer.

A shout lifted his head: Kitboqa was riding toward him, with some other men. The Turk gave him a salute, reined in, and said, "There is a messenger from Damascus, my Khan."

Hulegu grunted. He looked among the other men, and one came forward, bowing, holding out a rolled paper, battered at the edges. Hulegu took it, saying, "Who sent this?" All around him the others crowded in close to him.

"A council in Damascus, my Khan." The messenger spoke Arabic. The message would be in Arabic.

"Tell me what it says."

The messenger hesitated a moment, red-faced, and Hulegu said, "Now."

"It says they will give up the city to you," the messenger said. "The Sultan has fled."

A low cheer went up from the people around him. Bohemund, on Hulegu's left, gave a grunt, his face breaking into a broad smile. "Yusuf is a coward."

Hulegu said, "We have friends there. They probably helped him on his way." He thrust the roll of paper into his sleeve. This changed his plans, somewhat, and he looked around him, judging his tools. He nodded to Bohemund, "You should go to take command of Damascus. And you." He switched his gaze to Kitboqa. "Keep the peace, since they have surrendered. Find the Sultan and bring him to me. Get down there quickly before they change their minds." He looked past them, to Nikola. "Stay a moment. I have a task for you as well."

＊　＊　＊　＊

Yusuf, Sultan of Aleppo, Sultan of Damascus, missed his garden; he missed his dinner; he missed his own bed. Yet he knew he could not stop moving. He had run away from Damascus, hurrying south along the old road that followed the western foot of the Gulan. The road streamed with people, everybody moving south.

At dusk when the call to prayer was going out from all the minarets he reached the old town of al-Shanamayn. The caravanserais and inns overflowed with people. At the serai at the southern edge of the town he made the master drive out a pack of goat herders to clear a space for him.

Abdulhassan came in, smiling. "My sovereign, I think we have escaped them."

Yusuf said nothing. He had been thinking, while he rode, and he had come to an understanding, first the suspicion and now the certainty, that Abdulhassan worked for the Mongols, that he had been working for the Mongols all along.

If Abdulhassan said he was safe, he was in grave danger.

He said, "We have to keep going."

"My lord, you should rest. This has all been so hard on you."

He could not look at the vizier. He glanced around at the three guards who had come with him, walking in from taking care of their horses, and his body servant. When the servant came to help him change his clothing, Yusuf bent toward him and murmured, "Go bid Ahmed to find us fresh horses. Do not let Abdulhassan know." This would not be hard, as the vizier had assumed a whole separate room to himself. "We have to get out of here," he said.

The servant gave him a wide-eyed look and hurried off. Yusuf paced around the room, wondering where he could go. Not to Qutuz, in Egypt. Kerak? Kerak was in bed with the Mongols. Nablus. Gaza.

He put his hands to his face. He was Sultan of Damascus and yet he had nowhere in the world to go.

\* \* \* \*

Nikola said, "My father has ordered me to go south. I'll bring you back something. Will you miss me?"

"I will," she said. "Be careful." Her eyes searched his face; he saw something new in her look. She leaned toward him and put her mouth against his, and he drew her into his arms.

"When are you leaving?" she said. Her hands rested on his chest. She shivered a moment in his arms, as she had the other time, but then she gentled. He felt himself on the verge of a great victory.

"Tomorrow," he said.

She lifted her face to him again and he touched his cheek to hers and then to the other, and brought their mouths together. She said, "Come into the orchard, then. Tonight."

---

*He said, "Tell me what you want me to do. Show me."*
*He said, "We should be married, in case we have babies."*

---

Hulegu gave Nikola command over a zuun, a hundred men, the largest force he had ever led. They traveled south from Aleppo on an old road, straight as a bowstring, with milestones and berms, through pasture and newly harvested fields. He was glad to be riding again. Prince Bohemund and Kitboqa were traveling south to Damascus and at first Nikola trailed along with them, but the Franks were moving too slowly and by the third sundown Nikola's zuun was half a day ahead of them. Along the road Nikola saw the tracks and leavings of a great crowd that had passed this way recently, but now here was no traffic at all.

They spent the night in a deserted caravanserai. Zuchi had old Ranga's chess set, and he and Nikola played. Zuchi had grown up in the firelands, where chess was a street game, and he beat him, as Ranga had always beat him.

"That bug-eyed girl," Zuchi said. Dinah had come to see them leave the ordu. "Isn't she your mother's slave?"

Nikola studied the board, his hands under his chin. "She is my mother's guest."

"But she's something else with you."

"I want to marry her," Nikola said, looking up. He caught an edge in Zuchi's voice. The other man smiled at him. "What is it?" Nikola said.

"You know Kitboqa has his eye on her."

Nikola grunted. "She told him no. She told me yes." He fixed Zuchi with a look. "She has no family. My mother has the hand over her and my mother has said she can do what she chooses."

Zuchi shrugged. "He doesn't like you. I'm just letting you know. I'm no friend of any Turk's." He nodded at the board. "Play again?"

\* \* \* \*

The wide valley was a pattern of fields, lanes of grapevines, stubbles of grain. They passed well wide of a vast walled city of domes and spires, which Nikola thought was Damascus. The flat land around was plowed and tilled and measured out with rows of stones. He disliked being steered around by all this rockwork and he rode in the fields whenever he could. With winter coming on the harvest had been taken in and the fields were bare dirt and weeds. Going on south they rode up through some hills. On the right hand the ground rose into a dry, treeless highland.

But now on the road ahead, a few dark figures appeared, running away. Nikola picked up the pace; beyond the scatter of people on foot he saw a mass of moving beasts. A caravan. Sakim rode beside him, with a horn, and Nikola signaled to him, and he blasted a long note on the horn and the zuun charged.

From the swarm ahead of them, people burst out in all directions, running. A yell went up from the Mongols, and the line spread out to chase them down. An arrow stitched across the sky, and then a swarm of arrows. Nikola galloped in among the snorting, shuffling camels. His arban came with him; they encircled the caravan, trapping the camels, taller than the Mongol horses by half with their mountainous packs. Nikola rode up to the nearest camel, which grunted and backed away, but he got hold of the lashings on the pack and pulled it open.

A great slithering mass of carpet fell out. He backed his horse away. Turning to his men, he pointed to the other camels, and they spread out to loot them.

The rest of the zuun came back. Nikola found a jug of airaq and drank, watching the men swarm over the camels. They were dumping goods on the road, mostly cloth and rugs, but from the cries and yelps of the men he guessed they were finding better things as well. Sakim rode up to him.

"This was in a pouch on a very fancy saddle." He held out a leather sack, which jingled. Nikola opened it and took out a handful of money, some of it gold.

"Unh. Well done."

Sakim shrugged. "It's way too much for one man."

Nikola dumped the money back into its pouch and shoved it into the front of his deel. "Yes, you did the right thing, it should go to my father." He had no idea what to do about the rugs. "Let the camels loose."

They left the rugs in a heap on the ground. They rode on, across flat fields again, and came to a canal. The bridge was narrow and several of the Mongols tried to jump their horses across. Two horses broke their legs and Nikola put a stop to that. They pushed their way across the bridge; with all the horses they had, this took them a good while. He began thinking of other ways to manage this: building wider bridges, filling in the canal?

Beyond a fringe of trees, a town came in sight, inside a wall. Nikola spread his men out to either side as they approached it, to encircle it. The road went straight to an arched gate, which was closed, but now he saw a little knot of people on the road, waiting for them.

He reined in, his hand up to stop the others. He was trailing several horses with him and he let the lead ropes fall so he could move fast. Down there on the road, the little crowd, maybe ten people, walked slowly toward him, waving branches over their heads.

Nikola grunted, puzzled. Zuchi came up beside him. "What's going on?"

The people with the branches lowered themselves to their knees on the road.

"They're surrendering," Nikola said.

He jogged up to the townsmen, Zuchi and Sakim on his heels. The first of the townsmen, an elder in a turban, bent down and put his face to the ground.

Zuchi said, "It's a trap."

"Maybe." Nikola lifted his voice, pulling up his Arabic. "Who are you, and what is this place?"

The elder straightened to his knees, his hands at his sides, his branch drooping. Dust covered his clothes, his beard. On the road behind him the rest of the townsmen were facedown on the ground. The old man said a jumble of sounds Nikola could not separate into words, probably names, and then, "We submit to you. We are your slaves. We ask for mercy."

Nikola shot Zuchi a quick look, and saw that he understood this. Nikola turned his shoulder to the elder. To the other two Mongols, he said, "I want to go in and see this place. Sakim, gather the rest of my arban. Zuchi, you take command while I'm in there. Hold them out here, watch, make sure nothing happens."

Sakim says, "You're going in there with only nine men?"

"Watch me." He turned back to the elder, and made his voice loud.

"I accept your town in the name of the Khakhan Mongke. Open the gate for me." He rode forward.

The elder leapt up, and the little crowd behind him leapt up; they hurried off ahead of Nikola down the road, calling out. Ahead of them, one side of the gate swung slowly open. Nikola glanced around behind him and saw his arban coming after, close packed.

They rode through the gate into a crooked little street. Nikola looked all around, seeing the narrow streets, the low walls. He saw no horses and none of these people had any weapons. The townsmen walked ahead of them, calling out, "Peace, peace," and waving their branches. On either side of the road stood rows of other men, and as the Mongols rode by they knelt down.

A surge of excitement filled him. He felt enormous, a giant over these people.

Zuchi said, "Where are the women?"

"Hiding," Nikola said. "They keep them inside." The street widened into a patch of dirt with a stone water trough in the middle. The elder turned toward Nikola, and made to go down on his knees again, but Nikola waved him impatiently back on to his feet.

"Those fields. Those are your fields."

"Yes, master."

"Did you get in your crops this last year?"

"Yes, master."

"Send half of what you took back to my father the Il-Khan." He thought maybe that was too much. He thought, When we rule here we'll turn all this land back into pasture again anyway. "If you don't send it we'll come and take it." He opened the arrow case on his saddle and took out one of his blue-banded arrows. "Show this to anybody who questions you. This means you've submitted."

The elder took the arrow, and to Nikola's amazement, he kissed it. He bowed. All around them, the other townsmen bowed and murmured, something about Allah, something about the Khakhan. Nikola let his horse drink at the fountain, pleased.

* *

They camped that night in some fields, by a canal for the water, and Nikola played chess with Zuchi. He lost the first game, as he always did, but when they started the next, he looked at the board, and suddenly saw it whole, not only as it was now, but as it could be several moves on.

He won that game. Knocking his shah over, Zuchi growled at him, and took much more time and care with the next, and Zuchi won that one.

* *

They crossed through brushy hills, through the ruins of old city. On the far side the land sloped down into a river valley, crowded with fields, olive groves. Towns, and ahead of them on the road, was another caravan.

Nikola was thinking he had dealt with this wrong, the last time, and he called up the commanders of the other arban. "I want to capture this bunch. We go down and circle them. No killing. Just don't let them escape."

The caravan was already trying to flee. In their awkward lope, the camels straggled off along the road, their drovers lashing them on. The Mongols swept down around them on both sides and forced them to bunch together, like herding sheep, and Nikola rode up between his men and the caravan and called, "Who's in command here?"

For a moment none of the camel-knackers said anything, but looked at each other, and then a man on foot came out a little way from the clump.

Nikola rode up to him. "Where are you going?"

"Sire—lord—majesty—" The Arab bobbed up and down. "We go to Balqa! Balqa!"

"Will you sell your goods there?"

"God willing, sire." Still bobbing.

"Send half of what you get to the Il-Khan. If you don't we'll come get it."

"Yes, master. Yes, my lord."

Nikola gave him an arrow. "If anybody gives you trouble, show them this."

The drover took the arrow; he glanced over his shoulder at the others, and bobbed and sputtered more words, and Nikola with a sweep of his arm led his men on.

Sakim rode up beside him, his brows lowering. "Why do you think he'll do what you say? Why not just steal what he has now?"

"He'll have more when he sells it," Nikola said. "We can't carry it all anyway."

"But will he send it to the Il-Khan?" Some of the other men were riding in closer to listen to this and he realized he had cheated them of the fun of looting. He nodded at Sakim.

"We'll come on him eventually again. He'll pay up, sooner or later."

Behind Sakim, Targatai called out, "Or he'll just run away."

Nikola said, "Run where?"

They all frowned at him. He waved his hand. "Let's go. There will be plenty to steal later on."

Sakim shrugged. Nikola wheeled his horse and led them off at a good pace.

Later when they were camped for the night when he went to set out sentries, Targatai started in on him again. "This is twice now you've let people surrender and get away."

Nikola dumped his saddle on the ground. They were in the middle of an old field and the horses were grazing in the stubble. He said, "They surrendered without a fight. You can't attack people on their knees." Several other men had turned to watch this; they were passing a skin of airaq around.

Targatai glowered at him. Nikola remembered him challenging Yoshmut, on that earlier raid, and remembered nobody else had backed him then, either. Targatai said, "Just because you're one of the golden ones—"

Nikola got the skin of airaq from Sakim and drank. "Hey, how do you know you aren't? Maybe the old khan made room for your mother. He did every other woman between here and the Han Sea." He held out the half-empty skin. "Be easy, cousin." Somebody behind them laughed.

Targatai took the skin, but he was still frowning, not sure if that isn't an insult; Nikola hung an arm around his neck. "Cheer up, cousin. We're all golden to the camel knackers."

Targatai shrugged him away. But he drank deep, and he made no more trouble.

* *

They rode through a stand of old trees, enormous grey trunks gnarled and twisted, a sparse cover of thin leaves shaped like blades. The ground was littered with fallen fruit. Sakim picked a fruit from a tree and bit into it, and his face twisted so that Nikola laughed.

"Pagh!" Sakim spat out the bite.

A scout came jogging back. "There's another town ahead."

They went on, past a row of old white columns along the road, over the flat valley floor. In the distance low hills made a blue wall along the foot of the sky. The town was a little white clump of walls and roofs. As the Mongols rode up, the gates were opening. Nikola stopped his horse. The people were coming out, waving branches over their heads.

* * * *

In Gaza Daud and Rikart stayed with a friend of Rikart's in a house close by the water. The sea drew Daud like a song. The people here had built a line of rocks out from the beach, making a protected space for boats. On the south side the waves came in on a long stretch of soft white sand, where he loved running in and out of the low surf.

The ancient road ran along the high edge of this beach. On the dunes just inland were houses and markets, where he quickly learned were divided strictly into separate quarters, as Acre had been, Greek and Muslim and Latin.

People fished off the rocky seawall . The harbor was busy with boats, brightly painted, carrying goods in and out. Not like Acre, he saw at once. These were small boats, and little markets. He plunged deep into the soft blue water, the salt in his mouth, and struggled to swim.

Other boys ran along the beach, yelling at him and throwing stones. He charged up out of the surf at them and they dodged away. With the foam coiling around his ankles he flung insults at them.

"Cross-kisser!" a lanky black-haired boy his own age yelled back. "Son of a whore!" and he realized they thought he was Christian.

He lifted his hands up, palms toward them. "Allah Akbar!" He would not be a Christian, even for a good fight.

The lanky boy came a step toward him. "You're living in a Christian house. Demetrios' house."

Daud said, "I travel with al Shab'h. I go where he takes me."

He saw that name strike them; the lanky boy glanced back at his friends. They all came up closer, their hands at their sides.

"The renegade Templar?" the lanky boy said. "Where have you gone with him? What have you seen?" He put out his hand. "I am Ahmed."

Then, on the sea wall, somebody shouted an alarm.

* *

Demetrios kept a big Greek kitchen, with several serving women; Rikart leaned on the side of the door to watch them. The one he wanted was standing at the table chopping onions. She kept her gaze away from him, but she was smiling. The cook called out, and the girl chopping onions turned her knife sideways and scooped up the onions on the blade and took them to the fire, where she dumped them into a pot. She daubed briefly at her eyes. Behind her hand, she cast a quick glance at Rikart. She had big black eyes, one reason he liked her.

Another girl said, meanly, "Mena! Watch where you're going, you might fall," and all the women laughed. Rikart shifted his body against the door frame. The women bustled around the kitchen, swishing their hips at him. He could not keep from smiling, but he made no move.

Daud burst up beside him, red-faced, panting for breath. "They're coming. They're here!"

Rikart straightened, startled. "Where?"

Daud raced off again, leading the way back out to the street, and down the hill to the big street. Rikart followed him. On the big street, a crowd was rushing toward the northern gate, where already a throng of people were gathered. As Daud led him up among them, a general wail rose.

Daud slowed, and Rikart brushed by him, going to the gate. It was closed and barred, and Rikart elbowed and squeezed his way up the stair to the top of the wall. Daud followed on his heels. On top of the wall people stood shoulder to shoulder along the wall, and Rikart forced his way in among them.

He reached back and got the boy by the arm and pulled him up in front of him, in the shelter of his body, hard against the rampart. He felt Daud suck in his breath. Out there just north of the city, from the sea to first rise of the inland hills, a wide rank of horsemen stretched across the plain.

The crowd on the wall moaned and cried out. The gate was opening. Four men on foot went slowly out; they were carrying branches from the nearby orange trees.

Somebody behind him said, "They're going to surrender."

"Thank God," another man muttered.

"They're Christians, like us." A low ripple of talk rose. "God have mercy on us."

Rikart was counting with his eyes. He said, "This is not the main army. It's a zuun, a hundred, no more than that. A scouting party. A raid." He hoped.

His back tingled. He was running out of time. He was certainly running out of room.

The crowd pushed toward the rampart, many voices calling out; he stood solid, protecting Daud. "Peace," the crowd was crying. "Peace." The little delegation walked a few steps away from the gate, waving their branches. From the mass of the horsemen a few riders jogged forward.

"Christians, like us," said the man behind him. His voice rose, edged, aimed back into the city. "Watch out, you dirty ragheads. We've got help now!"

\* \*

Smoke billowed up from the roof of the building, and then the flames broke through, coppery in the sun. In the street the mob howled.

A man in a turban rushed up to Nikola. "You have to stop this! Stop this! This is the oldest mosque in Gaza!" His own people came quickly up around him and bundled him off.

Nikola shifted in his saddle. He saw no reason to keep them from killing each other. He hated Gaza, small and poor. And falling apart. Why they even cared any more eluded him. There was nothing here. He was having to move his horses every day to new pasture and riding south he had found only desert. Even along the seacoast where the old road led, there was no grass that horses would eat. He had sent Sakim back to Hulegu for more orders. Now this.

The mob was fighting. Some other mob had come to defend the mosque, now that it was almost gone. He could not tell the difference between the Christians and the Moslems; they were all pop-eyes and cloth-heads. He wanted to get out of here. The air stank here, especially now with the smoke, and it was occurring to him more and more that if these mobs decided the Mongols were the enemy then they would be hard to deal with.

"All right," he said. "Let's go. Don't kill anybody."

He tightened his legs around his horse and it picked up a trot. The other men fanned out on either side of him, filling the narrow street. They broke into a canter. Ahead of them, the mob was shying back from the blaze, and at the sight of the oncoming Mongols a wail went up. For a moment the crowd clogged the street, shoving and pushing each other, and then they were running away. Nikola resisted the urge to ride a few of them down.

In the wash of heat from the fire he slowed his horse. Someone rushed out of a house across the way, running toward the burning building, a bucket in each hand. Close by the mosque the long fronds of a feathery tree began to burn. The man with the buckets stopped and hurled water at the flaming building, and stood back. His shoulders slumped.

"Let it go," Nikola said. There was no stopping it anyway. He led his men on down the street, making a circle of the town, as he did every morning.

Gaza sat on a little rise just behind the old road, which ran along the edge of the sea. This had been a much larger city once, but now half the buildings were empty, roofless, filled with sand. The tall palm trees dropped their leaves like dried up claws all over the streets. There were no people in the street ahead of him but in a wooden latticework balcony that overhung the street he saw something moving. Behind a wall a head ducked down out of sight. They were all in there, watching him, which made his skin itch. He rode through an old gate where only one column still stood, and turned inland, past a line of stone blocks that marked what was left of the wall. Off a hundred bow-lengths across the dry flat land, a little desert deer ran a few feet, stopped and looked back at him.

Where the old road came into the city, at the northern edge, the old wall still stood, with towers by the gate. He had moved into one of these towers. The stone walls kept it cooler than the outside, now that the summer heat was on them. From the height he could see across the city all the way south to the desert. Now the black smoke was drifting away. The fire had burned out. In a building nearby somebody called in a quavering voice. A cloud of white birds rose squabbling off a roof.

He played chess with Zuchi.

"Have you found the market?"

"Yes, it's down on the beach. People bring in fish from the sea, and there are a few stalls, local cloth, fruit, tinkers, nothing much."

"Did you talk to them? Who wrecked this place?"

Zuchi shrugged. "They're always fighting here."

"Yes, I saw that. Who was the khan here, before we came?"

"You asked me that before. I can't tell. Maybe the Greeks. There's something funny going on with the Greeks."

"Those are the people up in the north. They're not our problem yet. What about the crossers?"

"There's plenty of churches."

"No knights."

"No no. They came and left, a while ago. Mamelukes, maybe."

"Mamelukes." That word was Arabic, meaning something that belonged to somebody else. "Who are they?"

"Fighters. Little armies of clothheads. These people are pretty afraid of them."

Nikola moved his horse. "Sword-fighters?" The crosser knights used swords and lances.

"No, they're bowmen, like us. They're not even actually cloth-heads, they're steppe people, they're slaves, they were bought on the markets up north and brought here and turned into soldiers, and then they took the place over."

Nikola grunted. "That follows." He put his fists on his knees. He wondered how this place had gotten so bad. They should turn it all back into grass and start over. Somebody to fight would make this much better. "How big is their army? Where are they?"

"I don't know. There are all different armies. Everything from zuun to tumen. They hold Egypt but there are Mamelukes up here, too, except maybe they're at war with Egypt. It's really a mess here, there's, you know, all these Christian places, too, and they all hate each other."

Nikola made a map in his head. The Christians held several good forts in the desert, strong positions in important places. It only took a few arban to defend a fort. He had heard that the citadel in Aleppo was still holding out.

He needed an enemy. He hoped his father would send him orders. He stared morosely at the board, where Zuchi once again had boxed him in. He had no good moves, and he picked up his shah and laid it on its side.

\* \* \* \*

Daud threw another rock; he dodged back toward the lane between houses, screaming insults. The four Christian boys chased him along the street, waving their sticks. He pulled up in the narrow mouth of the lane; he still had several rocks in the crook of his arm and he hurled one into the nearest face. The boys flinched back.

"Watch out! Watch out!"

Daud crowed. Then somebody grabbed him from behind by the neck of his thobe.

He screeched, wheeling, and Rikart shook him like a rat. "What are you doing? You want trouble, boy, I'll give you some!"

Daud let himself be dragged back up the hill. "They started it." The Christian boys had disappeared. He lost his footing on the uneven sandy stones and scrambled to get upright again.

"Yes, you stay out of it. I'm telling you==" Then somebody was rushing at them from behind a broken wall.

Rikart dropped him on his backside. The four boys charged, the boy in front swinging his long stick.

Rikart got between him and Daud on the ground, and when the first boy jammed to a stop and his stick sliced through the air, Rikart ducked under the wild blow, caught the boy by the arm, and flung him off. Somehow he had also gotten hold of the stick. The three boys just behind saw this, and two pulled up; but Rikart was already striding into their midst, laying around him with the stick, long slashing strokes. One boy crumpled, his head bloody, and two ran limping away down the lane. The boy who had brought the stick picked himself off the ground and ran off after them.

Rikart got Daud by the arm and levered him up onto his feet. "You stay out of this. This is not going to go anywhere good. And I'm trying not to let them find out I'm here."

Daud said nothing. He knew who Rikart meant. The grip on his arm eased and he walked on his own up the hill. They reached the back door into the compound and Rikart opened it.

Daud said, "Will you show me how to fight?"

Rikart grunted a laugh. "I thought you already knew everything there is to know about everything." His hand fell on Daud's shoulder again, stroked up over his hair. "Yes. In the afternoon, when everybody else is laying up."

\* \*

Later, in the courtyard, Rikart handed him a stick, long as Daud himself. "Hit me."

Daud took the stick; he looked over at Rikart, standing there, smiling, bare-handed.

"Hit me."

He swung the stick two-handed back over his shoulder, and Rikart reached forward under his cocked arms and poked him in the chest. He fell.

"See?" Rikart said. "Keep your feet under your hips, your hips under your shoulders. Stay bent. Keep everything in front of you."

Daud balanced himself. Behind him on the far side of the yard someone had come out of the kitchen to watch. He lunged at Rikart, jabbing the stick at him, and Rikart swatted the blows away, shifting sideways, backing up, never quite there, the blows never landing. Daud changed his grip on the stick, and immediately Rikart stood up straight, his hands dropping.

"No. Hold it with both hands the same way. Knuckles up. Otherwise—"

He took the stick, and held it straight up and down, with his hands crosswise. "Hit it."

Daud lashed out, a roundhouse swing; the butt of his fist struck the stick hard, just above Rikart's hands, and it spun out of the knight's grip. Daud's fist hurt.

"See?"

Daud made a sound in his throat. He cast a quick look toward the house; several people stood on the steps watching. Rikart grasped the stick in both hands, knuckles up, and jabbed with one end, then the other, tipped it up and down, in and out. He held the stick out to Daud.

"Try."

Daud took the stick, and did what he had seen Rikart just do. At first it felt odd. Rikart dodged him easily. But holding the stick this way let him use both ends, and jabbing back and forth he managed at last to clip Rikart's elbow.

"Good." Rikart held his hands up. "Play with it. We'll do some more tomorrow." He reached out and clapped Daud on the shoulder, rubbed his elbow with the other hand, and went off across the courtyard, toward the woman who stood in the doorway of the kitchen.

\* \* \* \*

There had been a covered suk once in Gaza but the roof had fallen in. Instead, the city's merchants set up their stalls on the beach, under a line of palm trees, south of where the fishing boats moored. Rikart went down there in the early morning, before the crowds came, to meet Gilbert, the merchant of Acre.

The Genoese was sitting on a suffah under an awning behind a wine merchant's stall, knees widespread, a cup in one hand. Seeing Rikart he beamed. "Well, well. You're here. I was wondering where you had gotten to. They are very annoyed with you, up north, Bohemund has offered money for you. They think you had something to do with Baibers escaping from Damascus."

Rikart snorted. He sat on his heels in the shade. "What is going on in Acre?"

"I haven't been to Acre, I just came from Aleppo."

"Ah? From the Il-Khan's ordu?"

"Indeed. I made a lot of profit there, they are rich. Homs has surrendered. The citadel of Aleppo finally fell, and the Il-Khan, to his glory, let the survivors go free, in honor of their valor."

Rikart said, "Where is the Il-Khan now?" He was noticing how smoothly Gilbert spoke of the Mongol general.

"He has gone back up onto the steppe, to spend the summer there. He has little more to do, now that the Sultan Yusuf has been captured."

"He couldn't even figure out how to escape."

"His own people handed him over. His staff was all spies."

"Where are you going now?"

"Egypt. I carry a message from Hulegu to Qutuz."

Rikart sat up straighter. "Don't do that. Send somebody else. Somebody you hate."

Gilbert's eyes widened. "They have given me a handsome purse. He said Qutuz would reward me as well."

Rikart shook his head. "I'm warning you. Don't do that. Did you see Dinah?"

"She came to me often to practice her French. She is high in the favor of the Khatun. Some say she is married to the Khatun's son."

"Ah." Rikart lowered his eyes. He thought of her in a Mongol's arms. He said, "I was married to a Mongol woman."

Gilbert said, "I have heard this."

"You know I was born in Jerusalem. My father died at La Forbie when I was a boy. My mother took me to Baghdad. I grew up there. I knew, always—Reb Moseh was kind, it wasn't that. I didn't belong. I had no place. Left over from someplace that didn't exist anymore. I went on east, I fell in with a family on the steppe. This was ten, twelve years ago, I was just a boy still. I came to love the—the youngest girl. Her parents didn't like that, I had no ger, I had no family. So we went off together by ourselves. When our, our baby was born, she died. The baby died. And I came back here."

"Is that why you hate them?"

"I don't hate them. I liked a lot of them. But they are wanton. They destroy more than they make. We can't let them come here."

"They are here."

Rikart shrugged. "Yes. Yes, they are."

* * *

Before noon, he went back up to the house on the hill where he was staying, not to the house itself but to the orange grove behind it. In among the squat, gnarled trees he stood, facing toward Jerusalem, and stretched his arms out into a cross. But he did not pray, or try to pray. He thought about Jarga.

She was always there in a part of his mind but talking about her had brought her back in full. She had been even younger than he was, barely 15. Wild, and merry, a laughing girl who could outride all her brothers, shoot a bow with the strongest of them. She had flung herself into his arms. "Show me how to do that." He kissed her. She had smelled like the steppe after a rainstorm. Her hair a thick mass against his face. His, his alone. Alone, he stood, his arms aching, his mind aching. Her brothers had not liked that they were together, and he and Jarga went away. Leagues from her family, he had made them a little ger, just big enough to lie down in. they hunted, herded some horses. They told each other stories. He tried to play the lute. They could escape, he had thought. Be only themselves, each other, out of the world. Fool, fool. The world had swallowed him up and spat out a husk of him. A ghost. He was weeping, tears dripping along his beard.

He felt around him some confinement, a membrane of time; if he could break through, he could go back there, be that boy again, who loved Jarga with all his heart.

He could not hold out his arms anymore. He had failed again to find a way to pray. He went lead-footed back toward the house.

\* \* \*

The Khatun Dokaz went out onto the porch of her ger. They had come back up onto the steppe, not far from the salt lake, had pitched her ger on a rolling slope facing east. The rest of the ordu was scattered off over the lower ground to the south and west, so she was out of the smoke and the bustle. From her porch she looked out over the endless grass, stirring silver in the wind. Horses grazed across it. The wind rose into her face, sweet and wild with the scent of wormwood.

She had brought back musicians she had found in Aleppo, and some new furnishings, and she was thinking how to place these in the ger. Far down the plain something was moving toward her. She was still pondering the arrangement of tables when she saw this was a horseman, struggling along up the slope.

His horse staggered as it galloped, exhausted. A messenger. She felt a tingle of foreboding.

Then what happened that often happened: in the space of a breath, the whole world changed.

\* \* \* \*

"He died of some kind of flux," the messenger said. He was trembling with weariness; his face was crusted with dirt. "Many of the army have it. They're laying siege to a Han fort on a mountaintop and the wells are poisoned."

Hulegu reached out and gripped Dokaz' hand, but his gaze never wavered from the messenger's face. "How does my brother Kubulai?"

"God willing Kubulai Noyon is well enough."

"Who have you told of this?"

"No one, Khan."

"See that continues," Hulegu said. It would be impossible to keep such a secret very long, the death of the Khakhan.

He made a sign to one of the guards behind the messenger, who came forward. "Care for this man, who has ridden hard in our service. Now all of you, go."

They emptied the ger. At a look from Dokaz even the women went out. Hulegu sat slumped in his chair, his gaze on the floor, remembering his brother, trying somehow to keep hold of him, who was now gone forever.

His wife's hand gripped his. After a while, he turned to her and said, "We plan and plan, and our plans all come apart like thistledown."

She said, "All praise to Mongke Khakhan. May the Great Khan himself welcome him into the overworld." A tear ran down her cheek.

"I have to go back," Hulegu said. "All this—will have to wait."

"Will it be as bad as the last time?"

"I'm sure it will be," Hulegu said. When Quyuk died, who had been the Khakhan before Mongke, it had taken years to elect another, and some deaths in the family. "Everybody will have something in it." He looked deeply into her face. "Will you come with me?"

Her eyes widened. "Of course. Where you go I go." She raised his hand in hers and laid it against her cheek.

"Good." He had known she would say this. She understood the court much better than he did; she handled people better. He shut his eyes. "Ah. My brother." Mongke had always led them, kept the three brothers together, while the rest of the family told dark spells at midnight and stabbed each other in the back.

"You want Kubulai to be Khakhan," his wife said.

"We agreed on this long ago. Yes."

"Will we take the whole army back with us?"

"Most of it." He faced her. "You see the problem here. I can leave a tumen, to hold our position here. But there's Berke."

Jochi's last son. Jochi the Guest. The boy Temujin's beloved wife Bortai brought home with her from her captivity. Temujin had let her be taken, and he accepted Jochi as his son, his eldest. But everybody knew. And now Jochi's son Berke held the north and west part of the world, just beyond the Turkish mountains, with a dozen tumen.

She said, "You think if we leave he will move in and take over what we've built here."

Hulegu thumped his fist on the arm of the chair. "We are failing the Great Khan. Temujin left us the world, to bring it all together into one. The task not even done yet, and we're letting it fall apart again." But his eyes brimmed. "Ah, Mongke," he said. His brother's face rose in his memory. He remembered the night they had talked it all out and decided to propose him for Khakhan. How calmly Mongke had taken that up. In front of them all he had grown suddenly bigger.

Dokaz was right, he had been a great Khakhan; he had built the framework of the empire. But now. Now, once again, the world trembled on the edge.

Berke would feel none of this. The shadow on his father's birth had shunted that family out of the elections. Berke would see only a chance to advance himself, get back at the people he thought had disinherited him. And there were other factions, other princes, the younger sons of Hulegu's father, his uncles and their sons, each one with some small mixture of Temujin's fire in him. This was not going to be easy. He folded his hands together in front of him, thinking about his army, and the forces against him, and how best to balance it all; he thought over the men he commanded, and how to use them.

He turned to Dokaz. "I could use Nikola in Karakorum. He's smart. He learns fast. I'd like Kubulai to get to know him."

She met his eyes steadily. Without even speaking he saw she resisted this. But she put his hand to her cheek again. "We must make a sacrifice in Mongke's name. Let me light the fires."

* * * *

The Khatun Dokaz called up Jun and Dinah and the other women. "I am to leave at once. You must make me ready for that—you know what I will need. And you must pack up the rest of the ger, and take it down and load it into the wagons, and bring it after me." She nodded at the women. "Listen to Jun, who knows best. And to Dinah."

When she said this, Dinah straightened, her mouth soft. She had been gloomy since Nikola left. The Khatun was glad to see her more happy. She went into the back of the ger, and settled herself, and made a prayer.

She knew what would be going on in Karakorum. No enemy like your brother when you both wanted power. At the last kuriltai, after Mongke's election, the sons of the previous Khakhan had revolted and tried to overthrow him. Their mother had stirred them to it, the witch Oghul Ghaimish, and when the rising was put down, the council ordered her wrapped in felt and thrown into the river. Dokaz still remembered the old woman's screams, not of fear but rage. She who had sat beside the man who ruled the world. Who, some said, had ruled that man. Dokaz remembered the days and nights of wild disorder in the ordu, the throngs of people, the shouts and whispers.

If the witch had won, likely Dokaz in the river. Her sons trampled to death or put to the sword.

She knew Hulegu would yield to her on this: that Nikola should stay here, in this out of the way corner, while the great killing ground of the kuriltai went on. She would take Dinah, and the grandchild in her belly, who would be in little danger. But she would leave her son behind.

She knew Hulegu would have to protect their hold here from Berke, probably two tumen, which he would leave on the grassy upland west of the salt lake. To keep the Arabs under control another tumen, likely somewhere near Damascus. He could call on also the Franks who had submitted, Bohemund chief of them, and now she saw more the real value of Hulegu's policy there. She would try to get him to leave Nikola in command of that tumen.

This was a reach. Her son was still so young. And there was Kitboqa. Already she foresaw that Hulegu would expect the glum Turk to take command here. That meant even more that they needed someone in that army who could keep watch. She had no faith in Kitboqa. She would talk this over with Hulegu; she knew how to win him.

\* \*

Rikart peeled the rind off an orange, all the while staying back in the shadow of the stall; he had seen the Mongols rode often through the suk. The summer heat baked down and the breeze off the sea felt good on his back. He put a piece of the orange into his mouth. The juice spurted sweet across his tongue. The fruit merchant came up beside him.

"Al Shab'h. Seeking interesting news?"

Rikart had already given him half an isaac for the three oranges. He said, "What do you know?"

"The Greek has failed. He attacked Constantinople, and the Venetians held him off."

Rikart grunted. The fighting in the old empire did not interest him. He thought Michael Paleologos would win in the end but until he did the Greek empire would be no use to anybody. He said, "Who is the Mongol commander here? Do you know his name?"

The shopkeeper shrugged, his face sagging. "Who can talk to them?"

"Try. A lot of them speak Arabic." Even now one of the Mongols was riding by along the old road, his short-legged shaggy little horse at a soft trot, and the man as if he grew there on its back. It irked Rikart that they often rode alone through the city, as if no one could harm them. The Mongol reined off suddenly toward a stall down the way. "Like that one."

The shopkeeper made a face. "Let Zayed soil his hands." He made washing motions with his fingers; his mouth pursed in his beard, as if he wanted to spit.

Rikart held up a silver coin. Money made everything clean. The shopkeeper sighed, and plucked the piece away. "I will find out."

"Also how many there are. If they're planning to stay long in Gaza. Where they're going next. Where the rest of them are. Who does Zayed talk to?"

"Everybody."

"Acre, the Templars, Qutuz?"

"Anybody."

"Baibers?"

The shopkeeper licked his lips, his shining eyes directed elsewhere.

"Where is Baibers now?"

No answer. Rikart fingered up another coin. The shopkeeper eyed it, his lips curled. Rikart said, "Shall I ask Zayed?"

The shopkeeper snatched the coin away. "In Al-Arish."

Rikart said, "Hunh."

"So I have heard. Who knows?"

If Baibers were on his way to Egypt, Al-Arish, on the coast halfway to the Delta, was as good a place as any to stop, and the Mamelukes had a fortress there. Rikart ate the rest of the orange and put the other two in his sleeve. One for Daud, one for Mena. The sun was high. The heat shimmered off the road, off the flat roofs of the houses across the way. Soon everybody would go inside. He moved off around behind the stalls and walked away down the beach.

* * * *

The kitchen was dark and smelled of fish. Daud half-carried, halfdragged the sling in the door and across the room, and dumping it by the oven began to stack the wood against the back wall. The three women who did all the cooking here were sitting in the shade outside the doorway, one mending clothes, and one holding a baby; they watched him keenly, as if he might set the place on fire.

"When you're done with that," the tall one said, "clean the ashes out and take them to the garden and spread them around. And then sweep the courtyard."

Daud said nothing. He knew Rikart was behind this, keeping him busy so he would not go out into the streets. He had been all morning gathering wood in the orange grove. He found a scoop and a bucket and knelt in front of the oven door to ladle out the ashes. The women went back to talking.

"You know he won't marry you," one said to another. "Why bother?"

The one sewing gave a low chuckle. Her name was Mena. Daud lifted the bucket of ashes and lugged it away to the garden.

When he came back they were inside, chopping vegetables and patting out flat loaves of bread. The baby was asleep in a basket in the corner. They had lit the oven and the kitchen was much hotter. Half the wood was already gone. He put the bucket away and went for the broom.

The tall woman gave him bread with cheese and a pat on the cheek. "You're a good boy," she said.

He ate; he swept, starting at the kitchen door, and working his way across the courtyard. When he came on a heap of horse dung he went for a shovel and took that off to the garden, too. All the while he watched the sun roll across the sky. It was already after noon. Soon everybody would go into the house for the afternoon quiet time. His muscles burned, but more, his heart burned to be free. He swept and swept, until as if by accident he had done everything except the gateway itself, and this he swept very quickly, threw the broom into the corner, and ran.

No one called him back. He raced away down the street into the city, watching for his enemies.

The stillness of afternoon had settled over Gaza. The street was empty. Even the beggars who usually sat by the wall were gone inside. He stopped near the top of the hill, and looked down toward the sea where it lapped blue against the beach, thinking of cooling himself in the surf. But instead he ran off down the other slope, toward the gate.

The city wall was all broken down, and anybody could get in almost anywhere, but the gate was still important enough that the Mongols kept a watch on it. Daud had been studying them for a while, thinking how he might pull the gate down on them.

The Mongol by the gate lounged against the wall, not knowing how in Daud's thoughts he was about to be crushed under a fall of rock. He wore a gaudy red shirt with sewing on it. Daud squatted in the shade across the way, pretending to sleep. Another Mongol came up, carrying a leather flask of something, and the two men drank and talked. An old man riding a donkey ambled up the road, and coming to the gate, showed them a piece of leather with a mark on it, and they waved him on through. Daud dozed off. For a moment he dreamt of Baghdad, as it had been, alive and full of people.

The clatter of hoofs woke him. He lifted his head from his arms. A horse was galloping down the road, its coat black with sweat. Reaching the gate, the rider called out sharply and flung himself down from his horse.

The gatekeeper said something, and the horseman answered with a gesture and ran to the nearby tower, where the Mongols were always going in and out.

Daud got up, staying back by the wall. Somebody came up to lead off the messenger's horse, and the gatekeeper asked him a question and the other man shrugged.

Then the door to the tower burst open, and several Mongols rushed out, all yelling at once. Daud could make out nothing in the jumble of voices, except for a name he had heard once, repeated over and over. A crowd of other men gathered and somebody stood in the tower door and called out and talked a moment, in a rushed, high-pitched voice, saying that name again, and the crowd let out a single moan. Daud turned and dashed away.

He ran off up the hill, toward the Greek quarter. Here the people were just coming out from the quiet time, opening their gates, and the street sellers coming out. Two boys he knew were walking along the street, carrying fishing nets, going down to the beach. He would have gone with them, usually, but now he ran on. At Demetrios' house, he pushed the gate open and ran across the courtyard. Someone called his name. Racing around the corner of the big building toward the back door, he collided with two people standing in the shade, locked in an embrace.

He backed up. Rikart and Mena sprang apart, the woman hastily pulling her dress together, Rikart's hands sliding out of her clothes.

Daud stammered, his eyes down, backing away, his face heating up. Then he remembered. He blurted out, "Something has happened."' He lifted his eyes to Rikart. "Something bad. A Mongol brought some news, and they are all sad. They kept talking about Mongke."

Rikart's eyes widened. "Where did you hear this?"

"At the gate. The messenger came in from the north."

Rikart grunted at him. He turned to Mena, and spoke to her in that other language. She put one hand on his chest. She lowered her gaze, and spoke in a dry, resigned voice. Rikart kissed her forehead and went off. As he left, he laid his hand quickly on Daud's shoulder.

The woman turned to Daud, her eyes frowning. "Well," she said, and reached out to him. "Come inside, naughty little boy. You must be hungry, after your adventures."

\* \* \* \*

The women kept him there the rest of the day in the kitchen. He helped Mena fold house linens and put them away. She didn't talk much but her wide dark eyes went constantly to the doorway. The other women were carrying trays of food away to the big house. Mena sighed, wiped her forehead on her wrist, and turned toward the board, where they made bread, and with her back to him Daud inched his way to the door.

"Stay where you are," she said, without even looking around. "Don't you dare sneak away again."

"I have to make water," he said.

"Use the pot in the corner."

He did not have to piss, but he went to the corner anyway, where a curtain hung over a narrow closet. They hung herbs on the wall but the place still stank. When he went back out, Rikart was there.

Daud went up to him, glad, and the Frank turned to him and said, "I am going. You stay here." To Mena, he said, "Take care of him."

Daud said, "I'm coming with you."

Rikart put a hand on his shoulder, as if he would pin him to the ground. "No, not this time." He looked toward Mena. "Keep him here." He lowered his eyes back to Daud; his mouth kinked. "If I don't come back in a few days, stay lucky, little brother." He turned and went out the door.

Daud stood where he was. He felt as if he were on fire. He had been right, something important had happened. Mena was staring at him; he knew better than to try to go after Rikart. She said, "Here. Take this around to the big house. Come right back." She gave him a jug. He went out.

* *

Al-Arish lay well south of Gaza, where the coast curved around to the west toward Egypt. On this narrow strip of land between the sea and the desert, several springs of good water bubbled up, and twenty generations of farmers had made canals, planted orchards and vineyards, strips of gardens. But the desert began within sight of the surf, so sharp a boundary between the farmland and the dryland that a man could stand with a foot in each place.

When Rikart rode in there were bright-painted boats pulled up on the beach under the date palms, and people gathered around there haggling over the fish. The wind had changed, blowing in from the Mediterranean, smelling of salt.

The Mamelukes had a tower on the far end of the town, a square block of yellow brick. When he rode up to it, he saw, beside the massive doorway, under a swarm of birds, a head stuck on a pike.

He reined in, recognizing the head, even with the eyes pecked out. It was Gilbert's.

His stomach tightened. He dismounted from his horse and went to the door, and the sentry came out to him.

"I want to see Baibers," he said. "Tell him Rikart Rannulfsson is here and I have news for him."

In no hurry, the Mameluke looked him over. He wore the black turban of the Bahriyya. He said, "Wait here," and went back through the gate. Rikart looked up at Gilbert again, remembering their last meeting. You should have listened to me, he thought. His fate: no one listened to him. The sentry came back.

"This way."

He went into the tower, and up a wooden stair and into a hall. The sentry left. He was alone. The room was bare pale yellow stone; the late afternoon sun came in through the high windows and reached up to the ceiling, and below was almost twilit. The prayer rugs of the Mamelukes were rolled up against the wall. Below the west-facing windows, along the wall, was a table, and he drifted toward it, curious. On it among several cowhide maps was a Mongol bow, unstrung. The bow was old, its leather wrapping worn dark and shiny. Beside it was a heavy arrow. The door opened, and he swung around, thinking to see Baibers.

The man who came in was not Baibers. He was short, for a Kipchak, but he had such a way about him that Rikart knew at once who he was, even without the medallion on his turban. Baibers followed him, and shut the door.

Rikart's back prickled up. He said, "Peace be with the Sultan of Egypt."

The short man stopped. His thick dark moustache hid his mouth. His eyes were cold and black and direct. He said, "You are the Frank called al-Shab'h." His voice had a kind of purr, like a cat's.

"Yes, lord."

Qutuz looked him over a moment, went to the table, and picked up the bow.

"Show me how to string this."

Rikart took the bow; Baibers held out a coiled string. Rikart said, "This is a Mameluke string, this won't hold." He looped one end of the string over the bottom syrah of the bow and snugged it tight, hooked the other loop around his left thumb, and laid the bow across the back of his leg. With his right hand, using all the force of his shoulder, he bent the bow forward over his thigh. He had not done this in a long time and the effort made him clench his teeth. Most Mongols could do this on horseback at a full gallop. Steadily the limbs of the bow curved in his grip. When it was flexed, he slipped the bowstring's loop from his thumb to the top syrah.

He stepped out of it and took hold of it by the grip. The bow felt lively in his hands, eager. He picked up the arrow. Without a thumbring he could not draw the bow deep or long, and he nocked the arrow, pulled halfway, and shot into the wooden door.

The crack of the string against the syrahs merged with the thud of the arrow on the door. Qutuz jerked, his eyes wide. Baibers went to the door and opened it. The arrow had sunk in to the fletching through the four inches of wood.

"Impressive," said the Sultan of Egypt. "You don't look that strong." He reached for the bow.

Before he could take hold of it the bow gave a loud thwang. All along the string, fibers popped out. The string spun, dwindled to a thread and abruptly broke, and the bow snapped straight again.

"I told you," Rikart said.

Qutuz took the bow from him. Baibers had come back up the room, the arrow in his hand. "You said you had news for me. Tell it now."

They were offering him no food or drink. There was no surety in this. The backs of Rikart's hands were tingling. His whole body was trying to warn him.

He said, "The Khakhan has died. The king of all the Mongols."

Qutuz was still looking over the bow; he seemed not to be listening. Baibers tossed the arrow on the table. "I don't see what this means for us."

"This is a gift," Rikart said. "Hulegu will have to go back to Karakorum, half the world away, to elect another Khakhan. That could take years."

Qutuz was sidling around behind him. The Sultan said, "Who will be the Khakhan next? Do you know?"

Rikart shifted a little, trying to keep them both in front of him. "I don't know. Very likely one of Tuli's bunch—the youngest son of the great khan. They have been killing off the other branches of the family for a while. Mongke was Tuli's son, and Hulegu, and there are several others." He met Qutuz's eyes. "This is the best chance we will have against them. Hulegu will take most of his army back with him, his best officers, maybe for years."

Baibers went over to the table, and looked down at a map. Qutuz said, "How many men would they leave behind? Where?"

"I don't know. I can find out." He leaned forward a little, trying to drive this. "When he has gone, march north. Challenge whoever he leaves behind. Push them out of al-Shams, back past the salt lake, up onto the steppe. We might even be able to recover Baghdad."

The cold dark eyes showed nothing. "But if I lead my whole army out of Egypt, and he gets by me—by whatever means—Egypt is helpless. Why should I not wait until he challenges me?"

"Because when that happens he will have his whole army again. And if he reaches the Delta—there is pasture for his horses, and he'll stay. Move now. When the Il-Khan's army has gone back past the Tigris. He won't turn back. The Khanate is what matters to him." Baibers was moving around behind him again. He said, "Think about this," and started toward the door.

Qutuz tossed the bow onto the table. "Where do you think you're going?"

"I'm leaving," Rikart said.

"Oh, no, you're not."

Qutuz was in front of him, Baibers behind him. His gut churned.

Baibers said, "You're going nowhere. You're a spy. You'll go straight to them." Rikart, not looking, heard the whisper of a knife leaving a sheath. "Better to be safe."

"If I were a spy for the Mongols would I be here?" He spoke to Qutuz. He thought of Gilbert's head, the blank empty eye sockets. Qutuz' face was expressionless, his eyes going from Rikart to Baibers just behind him and back to Rikart. Rikart said, "You still need me."

Baibers moved, and Rikart stepped quickly to the side, putting the two Mamelukes both in front of him again. Baibers had a knife in his hand, but he stood where he was, his arm at his side. Rikart's fingers twitched; he had a knife strapped to his forearm, and he lowered his hand and flexed his wrist and hidden by his sleeve the blade slid smoothly into his grip. If they came at him, he would go for Baibers.

Baibers said, "What if the squints sent him here to bring us out where they can reach us?"

Rikart said, "I should have left you in Damascus."

Baibers hesitated. Qutuz said, "Kill him, if you're going to."

Baibers said, in a flat voice, "He saved me in Damascus. But he's a spy. That's what he does, he sells what he knows."

"Have I asked you for any payment?" Rikart said.

Qutuz put out one hand toward Baibers. "Hold fast." He looked at Rikart. "You know them well? How do they fight? Do they use lances? Swords?"

Rikart let out his breath. Through the side of his eye he watched Baibers with the knife. But he saw Qutuz was considering this, and his blood quickened. Qutuz was listening to him. "I've never seen one any good with a sword. They usually carry a hand axe and a knife." Like the knife in his hand now, his fingers tight on the hilt. "Sometimes they use lances and they're better with those, they have hooks on the ends, they try to pull you off your horse. Mostly they surround you and shoot arrows at you."

Qutuz looked over at the bow on the table. "Are they good soldiers? Do they obey orders?"

"They're very disciplined, and they're used to this. They fight and ride and hunt all their lives. They know how to work together. The army is built on tens—ten men is an arban, one hundred a zuun, one thousand a mingghan, ten thousand a tumen. Even down to the level of the arban the leaders have a lot of authority to do what they want. If a man falls, his arban stays with him and brings him back, or they all die." Rikart glanced at Baibers and back to Qutuz. "They move really fast. Each man has several horses, which he brings along on lines, and they can switch horses at a gallop. The tumen commanders don't lead them into battle, they find a high ground and watch, so they can see everything. They signal with flags, horns, drums. They have some new kind of arrow they use to signal."

Qutuz said, "How do we beat them?"

"Nobody ever has."

Baibers said, "God will be with us."

Rikart said, "God didn't help the caliph."

Qutuz smiled at him again. "You should be encouraging us. Shouldn't you?"

Rikart shrugged. He thought he had given Qutuz all he needed to know.

"Bohemund is with them, the Prince of Antioch," the Sultan said. "The Armenian King. What about the Templars? The people in Acre? Do you know them?"

"I know the Templars. I don't have much hope for the Venetians."

Qutuz waved his hand at Baibers. "Put up your weapon. I see a use for him. God has a use for him. If we go north, we need to have some surety from the Christians in Acre that they won't attack us from the rear. We can't fight both the squints and the crossers at the same time. If we can get the knights with us—Can you do that?" His eyes came back to Rikart.

"I can try." Rikart let himself relax a little; unobtrusively he pushed the knife back up into its sheath. "At least I can get you a truce with them."

"God is great. Even the devil serves god." Qutuz looked at Baibers. "Let him go."

Rikart had the fleeting feeling they had been playing a game with him. They had let him handle the bow. He said, "God with us all, then," and he walked toward the door and went out.

His horse was still out by the gate, cropping the grass by the road, the reins dragging. He mounted and rode quickly away, heading north again. Soon, as he jogged his horse along the coast, he heard a voice behind him call his name.

He reined in, and Daud on his donkey galloped up to him.

"I told you to stay back in Gaza," Rikart said, but he smiled.

The boy's eyes widened. "What if you had needed help? Where are we going now?"

"To Acre. Not for long."

"Then?"

"Then, I think we're going to have a fight."

Cecelia Holland

# CHAPTER 8

## AIN JALUT

Nikola had Moseh up in front of him on the saddle; Dinah had stopped watching to make sure the little boy didn't fall off. She said, "I don't want to go. I said I would go when I thought you were going, too."

Ahead of them the broad plain crawled with moving people, as far as the horizon. The train of wagons rolled along beside them, slower than they were, packed high with the goods of the ordu. She let her reins loose on the pommel of her saddle; on its own her horse would walk along beside Nikola's.

He said, "It will only be for a little while. My father and his brother have all the power. We'll elect a new Khakhan, my uncle Kubulai, and then they'll come back here and pick this up again. My mother loves you, not just for my sake. She loves our baby. You'll do well there. It's good there, in Karakorum."

Dinah studied his face, his deep-set eyes, his poky little moustaches; under her gaze he began to smile, and he said, "I will miss you every day. You miss me, too. No finding someone else." He leaned toward her. They kissed the Mongol way first, their cheeks together, and then they kissed her way, lips on lips. He lifted Moseh up and held him out to her.

The boy screamed; in her arms, he reached back toward the horse. She tucked him down in front of her on the saddle, and he quieted at once. She handed him the reins. She was going to cry. Nikola took hold of her hand a moment, and his smile slipped; she saw, startled, that his eyes brimmed. Then he wheeled his horse and galloped away, back toward the west.

Moseh lifted up the reins and tried to swing Dinah's horse after him. "No, no," she said. She did what Nikola had taught her, tightened her legs around the horse, leaned the way she wanted it to go. "We're going somewhere else. Where your father came from." She did that all the time now, called Nikola his father, who was not, and yet, who was. She wiped her eyes. Moseh was watching her; he was more than two years old now, not a baby anymore.

She turned to look behind her. At first she could not pick him out among the loose swarm of horses and wagons coming after her, and her chest tightened with alarm. Then he came into view again, riding up a low rolling hillside, the only horseman going west. He disappeared again over the crest.

She turned to look east, where the passage of the army had churned up a haze of dust, a vast emptiness. Moseh pulled on her deel.

He said, "Ama, I take care of you." He leaned against her and put his arm round her.

"Oh, Moseh," she said. "Oh, Moseh," and hugged him, and cried.

\* \*

Kitboqa wheeled around, his jaw set. "What did you say?"

Nikola said, patiently, "Now that my father is gone we should send a force down to Damascus, to keep an eye on things down there."

The Turk strode across the room toward him. "And who would command this force? You?"

Nikola shrugged; the Turk's bad temper mildly amused him. "Who else?"

"I am in command! You do not make decisions."

Nikola was still a moment, wondering how far he could push this. He said, "If you can't see—"

"I asked the Il-Khan not to send you with me. But he is far off now. Do not be insolent with me. Get out of here. Go patrol the highway. Be back by moonrise, I'm holding a council."

"You're not—"

Kitboqa came straight up to him and shouted in his face, "You will obey me! I am in command here!"

Nikola turned on his heel and went out of the room. He remembered what Zuchi had told him once, that Kitboqa hated him. The urge came over him to go back and sink his knife into Kitboqa's chest. He could say the Turk jumped him. His body went hot, all over, but he kept on walking, down to the courtyard, to get his horse. At least now he could get out of this city.

\* \* \* \*

The wild goat burst out of the draw, its legs thrusting, and bolted straight up the slope. Nikola charged after it; he pumped his body, trying to squeeze more speed from his horse, but the goat was already pulling away from him.

On the slope above, Zuchi appeared, galloping across the goat's path, and the goat swerved back toward Nikola. Its chunky body was sand colored like the rocks. Its head high, it carried its long curved horns back over its withers. It flew along the broken ground and with each stride drew farther ahead of the Mongols. Zuchi was already far behind them. Nikola drove his horse at a dead run across a grassy stretch but the goat was almost to the ridgeline now.

He slammed his horse to a stop and raised his bow; for an instant he had a clear shot, but he did not loose the arrow. The goat vanished into the brush along the top of the hill. He lowered the bow, sighing.

Zuchi came up beside him. They were both dripping sweat, gasping for breath, and they looked at each other and laughed. They turned their horses around and rode back the way they had come.

Below them the pale slope, clumpy with brush and patches of grass, swept down toward the valley. Beyond a rumple of foothills the floor of the valley stretched flat away to north and south. Stands of trees covered it, long strips of plowed ground. Nikola could see a little clump of houses, the spire of a mosque. He drew rein, not wanting to go there. The people there hated him and the orderliness and fussiness of the land made him angry. The wild goats didn't go into the valley and neither should he.

Far off, on the road down the center of the valley, he saw a line of riders: a Mongol patrol. Kitboqa had them all out scouting, all the time.

The sun was sinking down toward the jagged mountain tops. They had to start back soon.

Zuchi held out a skin of airaq. "Did you bring anything to eat?"

"We can catch some of those little birds."

Nikola took a long drink of the sour milk. He was supposed to be back in Anjar by moonrise. If they had to hunt down something to eat and then cook it, they would likely spend the night out here. He liked that idea. He hated the idea of sitting on a bench in a stuffy room listening to Kitboqa talk about supply trains and who gave orders and who took them.

He knew that if his father had told him to be back in Anjar by moonrise, he would be there. He took another long pull of the airaq.

"No," he said. "Let's go into camp." He swung his horse around down the slope, angling to join the patrol coming along the road.

\* \*

Bella had a pair of Han scissors, the silver handles shaped like dragons; she was using them to cut Daud's hair. Rikart sprawled on the bed watching. Daud sat in front of Bella on a stool, his head bent, his pale nape appearing through the thick dark hair. Rikart had forgotten what love was, that outflow of passionate caring.

Bella said, "I have been thinking of going to Italy."

He gave her a quick look. "Do you have family left there?"

"Some cousins. They are well-born." She sighed. "But I have never been anywhere save Acre. And how would I live?"

"Marry somebody," he said. He smiled at her. "You'd have your choice."

"Should I stay? Am I making too much of this?"

He shrugged. The snip-snip of the scissors drew his eyes. He said, "Who knows what may happen? Venice is a fine rich city, I've heard. You would not be so out of place there."

"What about you? Will you go?"

"I have no place," he said.

The boy looked around at him, wide-eyed. Bella brushed the loose hair off his shoulders, put her hands on him, kissed his head. Rikart reached for his purse and got out a piece of silver. "Go. Be back by sundown."

Daud flashed a wide smile at him and went out of the room. Rikart dropped the purse on the floor, on top of the rest of his clothes.

"He's a good boy," she said.

She put the scissors down on the table by the bed. She wore only her shift, all her softness pressed against the sheer cloth. His body quickened.

"The best."

"I could take him with me. To Italy."

"You could ask." He knew what Daud would say.

"How did it go, yesterday, with the Templars?"

"The Pope is their overlord. He's forbidden them to do anything against the Mongols. He's still stuck on the idea that they're Christians."

"Aren't they?"

"Some of them honor a great shaman they call Christ. A shaman is somebody who travels back and forth between us and the spirit world, which doesn't sound like Christ to me. None of them cares anything about the Pope."

"Shall I send for breakfast?"

"Not yet," he said, and reached for her.

* *

Daud looked up at Bella, wide-eyed. "But I want to stay."

She leaned toward him, took his small dirty hands in hers. "This is not going to go well. You could die." She remembered what he had already endured. She imagined him in velvet pantaloons, with proper shoes. Clean. Safe. Loved.

He said, "Thank you, though." He did not sound grateful.

She said, "Listen to me, Daud." But she couldn't think of anything to say. He regarded her, wide-eyed, thoughtful.

"You just want Rikart to go with you," he said. He smiled, and left the room.

* * * *

The Grand Marshall of the Templers, Yvain de Foret, rode with Rikart and Daud down to the gate. Three other knights, came after them, and a groom leading a fourth horse. The sun was barely risen but already the air shimmered with the late summer heat. At the gate the guards came straight up to attention. Trains of camels waited to come in, a line of people carrying bales and baskets. In the city, bells began to ring. Yvain crossed himself.

They went out onto the road, past the crowd, and Yvain reined up and Rikart came up beside him.

"We are not stupid," Yvain said. "We see what this is. We will give the Sultan a truce, and free passage across our holdings. They can resupply. They must stay away from the city."

"That's enough," Rikart said.

"Good, because that's all. I brought you something." He gestured, and a groom brought up the led horse.

"Honor this,' he said, and gave Rikart the leadrope.

"I'll do what I can," Rikart said.

The Grand Marshall faced him. "The Order is doomed, whatever happens. The Mongols are already demanding we surrender Acre and pay tribute and of course the Venetians are fine with that, and when the khans rule here they will see us gone. Once we lose Acre, we'll be of no value to anybody, not even the Pope. If the Mamelukes win, they will turn on us next. We're burnt offerings." He held out his hand, and Rikart gripped it. "God wills it," the Marshall said. He wheeled and rode back to the city.

* *

In Anjar, Kitboqa had taken over the top level of the main gate tower. When Nikola came in, the Turk was standing by the window, looking out.

245

"Everywhere you go, those old stones," he said, and wheeled toward Nikola. His long face was set. "I have not forgotten your insolence. But now there's a problem, and I—" His face distorted a moment, his teeth clenched— "I want your counsel. There is an army coming out of Egypt."

Nikola lifted his head, excited. He went over to the blind wall, opposite the window, where Kitboqa had put up some maps drawn on hide.

"Show me."

The Turk growled at him. "I give the orders, remember, cub?"

Nikola slid his hands behind his back, not looking at the commander. Kitboqa was right: they had to get to a truce between them. He looked down at the maps. Two were of the land east of here but on one he recognized the western coastline, with Egypt at the bottom, and Antioch at the top. Anjar was nearer the top. Along the coastline were marks for the other cities, and Kitboqa came over and pointed to one.

"They are coming along the sea road, here. They've passed Gaza, where you were, and they're keeping along the coast."

"What's that next city?"

"I don't remember the name. It belongs to Acre, the big city here." He stabbed at the map with his forefinger. "All this along the sea here belongs to the people in Acre. The fools there are letting this slave army cross their territory."

Nikola ran his gaze over the map. His father had said they should be careful, having only a single tumen, and that mostly Turks. But looking at the map, Nikola thought he saw a chance.

"Go straight past them, then." He swept his hand down the map, from Anjar toward Egypt. "Take Cairo. Give them nowhere to come home to. Cut them off and cut them up."

"You scouted that stretch yourself and you said it's a desert."

Nikola shrugged. "Three days' ride from the end of the valley there, if we push it. We could carry water with us. Fodder for the horses." As he said this it seemed less possible. "It's a green land beyond there, I've heard."

"When we're done with this slave army we'll go after the fools in Acre," Kitboqa said. "Then Egypt will fall to us like a ripe fruit." He held out one hand, as if a plump orange might suddenly drop from nowhere. Nikola kept still. This sounded like something Kitboqa had heard someone else say. He looked back at the map, frowning.

Kitboqa said, "I want you to lead the vanguard. We'll go down the long valley here—" His hand swiped over the map— "and get around between the slaves and Egypt."

"Good," Nikola said, excited. "Good."

* *

The Mamelukes camped outside a village at the edge of the Jezreel; in the south the round summit of Jebel Faqqua stood against the sky, the mountain the Christians called Gilboa. After morning prayers Baibers went up on a little hill where he could see to the north. After a while Qutuz rode up beside him; for a while they did not speak, nor even look at each other, but stared into the north.

"No sign of them yet," Qutuz said, finally.

"You heard the scouts," Baibers said. Men had been riding in since dawn.

Qutuz grunted. He stood with the his horse's reins in his hands, running the leathers through his fingers. "The Ghost thinks they could be down here by the midafternoon. Everybody else says they're still up by the Sea of Minya. He's wrong."

Baibers was eating dates. He spat out a pit. The scouts had reported the Mongol army coming down along the foot of the Golan; every scout had said something different, as usual. Baibers believed the Frank, who knew the squints better than anybody.

Someone was riding up the hill toward them. Qutuz's bodyguards went over to stop this newcomer, spoke a moment, and let him come on. Baibers stood to see. This was a single man on a big horse. Behind him on the low ground was a little band of other horsemen, on the same heavyset horses—cataphracts, he thought, although they were not wearing their armor. The man riding up to them stopped and dismounted and bowed to him. Baibers made a gesture with his hand. Qutuz turned.

"Lord," the newcomer said, and knelt down and put his forehead to the ground. "May God exalt you, Sultan of Egypt."

"As I serve him, he will," Qutuz said. "Who are you?"

"My name does not matter, lord. I am the commander of the city guard of Nablus. We have come to join you to fight in God's cause."

Qutuz took a step toward him. "May God be with us. How many?"

"Twenty men, lord."

Qutuz stroked down his moustache. "Praise God."

Baibers said, "You are cataphracts. Are you not?"

"Yes, lord." The soldier got to his feet. "We have our armor on our pack horses."

Baibers snorted. "Yes. We all know what happened to the cataphracts at Aleppo."

The man from Nablus dropped his gaze. Qutuz walked up past Baibers, casting a quick dark look at him, and faced the cataphract. "You are welcome here. We shall fight soon."

Baibers looked back toward the north. Qutuz annoyed him. The Sultan pretended such devotion, he had the zebiba on his forehead, but he preened and strutted like a cock. Baibers wanted to get moving, and he strained his eyes, trying to see what was coming down toward them from the north, willing it within his reach.

Qutuz was saying, in his silky voice, "Perhaps you could join the Bah-riyya."

Baibers jerked his head back toward the cataphract. "No. I have to move fast." He sneered at the newcomer, a city soldier, a clanking lump, who would be mud under the Mongols' hoofs if he fought at all. Behind him, coming up the hill, was the Frankish knight Rikart. Qutuz's men, recognizing him, let him approach unhindered. The boy from Baghdad trailed him on his little grey donkey. Baibers' heart lifted. The child was a sign, a messenger; wherever he was, there was victory. He knew this as he knew the words of his prayers. Not to Qutuz, but to him.

The knight rode a heavy horse, wore mail, a white surcoat, a scarlet cross splayed over the chest. Baibers said, "Here comes another clunker." He spat again. But an old fear stirred, he remembered, once, these same red-crossed knights charging him, and how his horse went down under that weight. Only God had saved him. He had run like a hare. His mind flinched from the memory, like touching a bruise. His gaze fell briefly on the detachment of cataphracts waiting below the hill; some had gotten into the orchard there and were surreptitiously eating the fruit.

Qutuz was saying, "What shall we do with the Ghost?"

Baibers said nothing. He turned to look north again.

Qutuz was staring at him. He said, "You know this ground. We need to trap them where we can close in on them."

Baibers drew in a deep breath; he had been thinking about this but he had not expected to be able so easily to direct it. He pointed across the flat open farmlands of the Jezreel, toward the eastern hills.

"Do you see those hills? The springs of Goliath. You see how that there's a valley opening up between them? It's a low ground, steep slopes all around, and there's only one way in and out. I will draw them that way. You be ready."

Rikart had reached them; he swung down from his horse. On his breast the hated cross. His face expressionless, he looked from Qutuz to Baibers and back again.

"What do you want me to do?"

"You look like one of those clunkers," Baibers said. He glanced at Qutuz, who let him go on. "The cataphracts. Take command of them." He stepped forward, looking across the flat ground. "See that crossroads? Hold that."

The knight's face didn't change, but he gave Baibers a long stare. He turned to the boy beside him.

"You stay with Qutuz. He'll keep out of the fighting so he can command."

Qutuz said, "I will watch over him." His mouth kinked under the moustache. He knew what Baibers was doing.

The Frank said, "Stay lucky, little brother." He turned and rode away, down the hill, toward the cataphracts from Nablus. The boy waited behind with Baibers and Qutuz, although his eyes followed Rikart.

Qutuz said, "You need a horse. The donkey is too small." He signaled to someone behind him.

Daud licked his lips. He was shivering all over, suddenly, as if Rikart leaving had taken away some layer of warmth. He slid down from the donkey, and went to the tall, rangy horse they brought to him. The Mamelukes were all watching him, Qutuz among them smiling, Baibers grim. He took the reins and hopped up to get his foot into the stirrup and swung into the saddle. When he was seated his feet hung down high of the stirrups and the groom fixed them. He looked away, down the hill, where Rikart and the cataphracts were already only specks on the road; he knew them only by the glint of the sun on their armor. His stomach churned. He shut his eyes, and for the first time in a while he said a prayer.

\* \*

Baibers rode out toward the north with his two hundred men, leading them along the old highway that ran straight as a ribbon up the center of the valley. On either side were fields of ripening wheat, strips of orchard, clusters of huts white in the summer sun. Where the road crossed a canal they had to slow to cross the bridge, riding two by two. Only a trickle of water ran through the canal; this late in the summer, there had been no rain for months. There were no people, no goats or camels or donkeys, no one on the road.

In a deserted grove of olive trees near where the road came in from Umm al-Fahm, he left all but twenty of his men behind, and led those at a quick trot up the valley. The heat made the air soft. The great head of a sycamore tree seemed to float in the air like an island. Even the birds were quiet.

Ahead, in the haze, he made out something moving, not on the road.

Baibers' hair stood on end. He looked broadly around and saw nothing else. He brought his gaze back to what was out there and now he could make out several horses. He lifted his hand, and led his men forward toward those distant riders.

\* \*

Nikola was riding in the peak of the advance, leading his spare horses after him; his zuun was two bowshots behind him, spread out in a long line across the valley. He stayed off the road, which he thought was probably bad for the horses' feet. Coming to a canal he slowed and trotted along the edge of it, seeing how the sides went straight down to the thin brown trickle of water in the middle of the bed. Everything was lined with rock. The canal was too broad to jump and the sides too steep to ride down.

Ahead, an arched bridge crossed the canal, and he nudged the horse up to a lope toward it.

Then, beyond the canal, he saw men on the road, coming toward him.

He cast a long look to his other side, to the north, and saw, out there, the first dark moving edge of his zuun, the oncoming vanguard. He flung up one arm, not knowing if they would see him, and bolted toward the bridge, unslinging his bow as he went.

The bridge was a dozen strides long, a hump over the canal. Two or three white buildings stood at this end. On the far side, the riders coming toward him burst into a gallop toward the bridge. They wore helmets, blue coats. An arrow fluttered toward him, then several more, dropping short. He nocked an arrow and shot back.

In the pack of bodies one body fell. The others let off a furious volley, a dozen arrows that spread over the sky toward him. He was still beyond their range. He thought there were maybe two arban of them. He hurtled in among the buildings at the end of the bridge and reined in a moment, letting his horses breathe, and listening to the faint, growing pound of hooves. He unhooked his helmet from his saddlebow and put it on. Then he wheeled in past the last white wall and charged onto the bridge.

The oncoming fighters were just starting to cross from the other side, but the narrow bridge held them up. He got off two shots before they shot back. Something banged off his helmet and his horse staggered. The men clogging the bridge ahead of him lifted their bows.

Behind him the drumming of the hoofs swelled to a thunder. Flying over his head came such a swarm of arrows that the sky darkened. The blue-coated riders on the bridge flinched, wheeled and ran. Nikola held his horse fast. Around him the long line of the zuun swept up through the village and all along the canal, and more arrows harried the fleeing riders away.

Nikola rode across the bridge and swung down from his horse. On the far side three men lay on the road, arrows in their chests. One was alive, on his back, whispering something. Nikola killed him with his belt knife. He pulled out the arrows; two were his, with their blue bands. He put them in his arrow case. His horses had followed him across the bridge; the little bay he had been riding had a long deep gash along the meat of its shoulder. He threw his saddle on another horse and jogged back to his men.

By the foot of the bridge, under a huge broad-headed tree, was a water hoist, which filled a stone trough, and several men were watering their horses from it. Nikola let his horse drink.

His arban came up around him, and he led them off into the shade of the tree. Zuchi came up to him with a sack of airaq.

"Who was that?"

Nikola shrugged. "Maybe nobody. Maybe the first of this army from Egypt." He saw Kawyi nearby and beckoned him over. "Go back and tell Kitboqa Noyon that we made contact and to get moving." He drained the last of the airaq and went back to the trough, to fill the leather sack with water.

* * * *

Baibers had lost seven men, including the two now too hurt to fight, and he did not think they had taken down any of the Mongols.

In a meadow by the road he stopped and let his men rest. He sent a rider back south toward the olive grove where he had left the rest of the Bahriyya, to bring them on. The others sat in little groups around the meadow, passing waterskins and talking, and he went around from one to the next, talking to each one.

"Our brothers will feast tonight in paradise. God willing we may join them."

253

They were quiet, but they met his eyes, and he saw they were resolute. He himself was eaten with a worm of doubt. The speed of the attack still unnerved him. He had seen the oncoming Mongols but they had seemed still so far away, he had thought he could kill that one man and seize the bridge.

Then from an impossible distance, the storm of the arrows.

"They shoot farther than we do. But our horses are faster."

He ordered the two wounded to find their own way back south; he thought they would die before they got there. He stood beside an olive tree. The heat of the day shimmered in the distance. He tried to fit what he had just learned about this enemy into his battle plan—much faster than he had expected, a longer reach. Far down there, where the hills pinched closer around the valley, was Qutuz, with the rest of the army.

He went back to his horse. When they saw this his men at once got into their saddles. "God give us victory," Baibers said, and with a wave of his arm he led them forward again, to meet the oncoming Mongols.

* * * *

The cross roads where Baibers had posted Rikart and the cataphracts was out in the center of the valley floor. On either edge of the flat, tilled ground rose the steep loom of hills , dark with trees, at the far end the round summit of Gilboa like a plug in a  cask. Where the two roads met, half a dozen houses stood among garden patches, between some threads of side canals. Rikart went from house to house, leaning down from his saddle to bang on the doors and shout, "Get out! Get out!" in Arabic. He saw no living thing, not a goat or a chicken, and he thought these people had all gone days before.

The cataphracts had put on their armor. Even their horses were draped in the supple metal cloth. The sun glittered on their coats, their helmets.

They waited on the road, in even lines, as if they were parading, their lances pointing up.

The Nablus city guard. Probably the most fighting they had ever had was chasing cutpurses.

The commander came up to him, saluting with his hand, and tipped up the front of his helmet. "Command me, lord. I wait."

Rikart looked around the little village. This was totally exposed here. He knew Baibers had sent him here to get him killed. From the north edge of the village he could see far up the valley, the dust rising, a long pale stream in the air, stretching from horizon to horizon, as if the land itself lifted up.

He said, "We are not staying here. This is death here. Get your men ready to ride. Do you have water?"

"Yes, lord. We are equipped."

Rikart grunted. He twisted to look north again, over the plain. Somewhere out there was Baibers, bringing the Mongols down on them. Off to the south and west were the low dark hills that Baibers had pointed out to Qutuz. Rikart went back to the double line of cataphracts and rode up and down along the line.

He saw their eyes widen at the cross on his surcoat. He put his hand on that and said, "I am a Templar. You are Arabs. This makes no difference now. Follow me. Don't stop for anything. We're going over there, to Ain Jalut. Raise your shields up. Stay spread out. Don't make a big target. Keep moving."

He turned west; he held his shield on his left side, toward the north, and socketed the bottom of his lance into his stirrup. Up there the dust cloud was turning the sky yellow. They were grinding up the fields into raw dirt. He heard a distant shout. He thought he saw horsemen galloping away in the distance. He looked ahead, toward the hills, where the land crawled with moving bodies. Qutuz, getting his army up into the gap between the wooded hills. Rikart took a deep seat and lifted his horse into a gallop.

* *

The Mongols were streaming over a bridge across a canal. Baibers held his men at long range and rained arrows on them. He was getting a better count of this band and thought there were only a hundred or so of them; they trailed a lot of loose horses with them, so it looked like many more. The first eight or ten of them thundered across the bridge and held up on the road, protecting the men coming after them, laying down a steady fire toward the Mamelukes. Baibers drew his men back, still shooting, and the Mongols charged.

The Mamelukes held their ground a moment, trying to pick off the leaders, and then ran. Baibers held his horse to a trot, letting his men get on ahead of him, his gaze on the oncoming squints. He looked northerly, up the valley past this Mongol band, and saw dust rising along the horizon. That was the rest of their army; once he would have guessed them to be at least half a day away still but now he knew better. With arrows raining down around him he set off after his men.

"La il-allah—"

The shrill cry rang out, and his heart leapt. Up through the haze out of the south the rest of the Bahriyya were swarming, a mass of blue coats, yipping and screaming.

Ahead of him, the other men were already spinning around to join the charge. Baibers turned his horse.

The Mongols were coming at a dead gallop; the first wave of Mameluke arrows pelted them like hail, and now Baibers saw some of them fall. They peeled neatly away, half to the east and half to the west, and as they turned they shot backwards, over their horses' rumps.

Baibers reined his horse down. He saw how the two wings of the Mongols spread out to either side, trying to encircle him, and he swung his left arm over his head. Around him all the Bahriyya raised their arms, and wheeling on their horses on their hocks they raced away south again.

A jolt on the arm almost knocked Baibers off his horse. He clung to the saddle, gasping. Pain flooded him. In front of him a horse went down, throwing its rider hard, and Baibers' horse vaulted over the fallen one. One stride on, the Mameluke was trying to rise and Baibers' horse knocked him flat. They were crossing plowed fields. Bent over his saddle, dizzy with pain, he saw crushed wheat flying by beneath him, the only clear thing. He caught his breath, looked up. The swift Arab mares were pulling away from the Mongol horses. He settled down into his saddle; with his good hand he reached out to his arm and felt the arrow sticking there.

It had gone all the way through the muscle of his upper arm. He could not pull it out; he clamped his arm to his side, to hold it steady, and rode hard toward the hills.

* *

Rikart heard the cries and screams before he saw the Bahriyya racing up across the valley, a stream of blue in the yellow dust. He glanced behind him; the cataphracts were on his heels, not spread out as he had told them but in a bunch. He could not stop now to school them and he pushed his horse in a steady gallop toward the hills ahead. The Bahriyya were shooting back the way they had come and now out of the haze there poured a great snake-like line of riders.

Rikart pounded through a field full of green melons. Swinging up his shield he hunched his head down into his shoulders behind it. The tang of the crushed fruit reached his nose. A canal was running along on his right, angling through the fields, and he prayed it did not cut him off. The end of the Mongol line was swinging around to get behind him. Reaching the canal he galloped along the bank, through a fringe of fig trees. The cataphracts were still clumped together behind him, and from beyond the trees came a flurry of arrows.

Rikart wondered who was shooting at him. The trees blocked most of the arrows, but ahead, the grove ended, and he raced out onto flat open ground. Off on his left, a long bowshot away, a line of horsemen galloped along parallel with him. Out of the hazy yellow churn came another flight of arrows.

Behind him somebody yelled. He twisted to see a cataphract on the ground, two more stopping to help him. He spurred his horse on. The Mongols were closing on him. On the other side the canal penned him in. Ahead the white squares of a dozen houses stood along both sides of the watercourse. An arrow smacked into his shield. He raced into the narrow path between the houses and the canal. He could not see Baibers anymore, or even the valley in the hills; the slope loomed ahead of him, the stony hillside studded with trees. The canal led straight along the foot of it. Another arrow punched his shield. His horse was flagging. He held it straight, not toward the opening into the valley, but up the side of the hill itself.

In an outcrop of stones he drew rein and let the horse blow, and looked back. The cataphracts were trudging up the slope after him, their horses dragging, and the men buckled in their saddles like metal sacks. He swung around, standing in his stirrups, to look north, and saw that out on the flat land, the Mongols had stopped. They made a dark mass in the dust. A hundred, maybe, he thought, just the vanguard, and now they had seen Qutuz in the valley and thought he was trapped and they could wait for the rest of the army to catch up.

He stepped down out of his saddle, let the reins hang, and went around his horse, looking for wounds. The horse was sound enough. It dripped sweat, and its sides were still heaving, but it was holding its head up. He slapped its neck, grateful.

The armored men rode up around him, and one leapt down from his horse and tramped toward him, yanked off his helmet, and spat. A young man, his face beardless under the grime. He said, "We left my brother back there. You let my brother die."

Rikart said, "We all came here to die. Didn't we?" He counted them; there were only sixteen. The commander was gone. He faced the young man again. "Go, if you want." He took the reins and on foot led his horse across the stony tree-studded slope, following the canal. He did not bother to look back at the city guard of Nablus. Ahead, the slope broke into a little draw, and in it was the spring that fed the canal. He went down there to water his horse. While he was loosening the girths on his saddle and slipping the bit, the cataphracts came up beside him, one by one.

He left them to tend their horses and went off a little way on foot, away from the Muslims, and in the thin cover of a stand of trees he stood and stretched out his arms. He expected nothing, only to stand there, as usual, in silence, but as he stood there, a deep sense of peace fell over him. He felt the weight of his life lifting off him. His body was light as an angel's. He lowered his arms, cool. For the first time in his life, he felt God all around him.

When he went back to the cataphracts he saw that they had gotten their backs up again; they stood there glaring at him. The young man stamped up to him.

"What did you go? What right do you have to command us?"

"I've fought Mongols," Rikart said. "Have you?"

The young man stared at him but said nothing. Behind his scowl his eyes glistened with fear. Another of them said, "What can we do? They're archers. We can't get near them. They'll just shoot us down. We're lost."

"You're right," Rikart said. "We need to close in on them. Follow me. Don't stop for anything, keep a sharp watch out."

They looked back at him, gaunt-faced, and did not move.

"What good will that do?"

"If you don't want to come you can leave." Rikart went to his horse and tightened up his saddle girths. The cataphracts stood there, uncertain, looking from one to another. Rikart reined his horse around up the slope, and in a straggling line, they followed him up across the hill.

\* \*

Nikola in the vanguard slowed to a walk. They couldn't catch up with the slaves, who were anyway getting into the hills now, and he expected a lot more of them waited there in the cover of the trees. He spat dirt out of his mouth. He had seen that tilled ground gave up a lot of dust and his tongue tasted bitter. The vanguard was pulling up around him, and a lot of them set quickly to changing horses. He liked this horse he was riding, which was strong and eager and loved to run, and he stayed in his saddle. Behind him, the rest of the army rode in a broad reach across the valley, flat and open.

His arban came up beside him, sharing airaq; they passed a sack of cheese and some dried horsemeat around. The sun was near the peak of the sky and under his coat Nikola's silk shirt was stuck to his body with sweat. He wiped his face on his sleeve. He thought by nightfall this would be over and they would camp in the cool of the trees. He glanced north again, eager.

\* \* \* \*

Qutuz with a hundred of his men climbed the northern hill, to where a ledge of rock capped the slope; he brought Daud with him. From here they looked down on the whole of the low ground running like a trough through the hills, where the army waited. Daud shaded his eyes from the sun. It was past noon.

Qutuz pointed toward the slope below them. "There is Baibers. He is hurt." The Sultan stood in his stirrups, looking north, and muttered under his breath. Daud raised his eyes, seeing the oncoming Mongol army, a swarming cloud of moving bodies across the whole broad open ground, coming steadily toward them.

Baibers rode up, slid out of the saddle and sank to the ground. One of Qutuz's bodyguards rushed to help him, but Baibers pushed that man away and stood, his face green. He steadied himself. Turning to the man he had just thrust off, he said, "Help me."

He held out his arm; an arrow pierced it. Daud shuddered. The other Mameluke broke off the arrow head and pulled the shaft out of the wound. Baibers stood without flinching, his mouth a narrow line. The other man opened his blue coat and tore a strip from his shirt, and he wrapped Baibers' arm in it. Blood soaked the cloth. Still in the saddle, Qutuz looked down on this, his eyes narrow, but he nodded, half-smiling.

Baibers came up between him and Daud. Qutuz gave him a flask of water and he drank, and Qutuz with his head gestured toward the oncoming army.

"You said there were fewer of them than there are of us. There are many more."

Baibers said, "They aren't as many of them as it looks. They're bringing along a lot of loose horses." He turned to Daud. "God has preserved me." His eyes stabbed at Daud like arrow points. Daud looked away, off across the valley, where they had sent Rikart. He wondered if he would ever see Rikart again.

Qutuz said, in his velvety voice, "Perhaps you should go to the rear, since you're wounded."

Baibers jerked all over, head to foot, and glared back at him. "I will rejoin my men," he said. "When the moment comes, seize it." He turned to his horse and sprang up into the saddle. Gathering his reins, he gave Qutuz another furious stare. "Do not fail this." He rode away.

Qutuz laughed under his breath. His dark eyes met Daud's, and he tilted his head, smiling, as if they shared a joke. Daud swallowed, his stomach churning. He looked away out over the plain, toward the boiling dust cloud of the Mongol army. Qutuz turned and spoke to the man on his far side, who carried a flag on a pole, and that man rode up a little higher on the hill and began to swing the pole around.

An armorer came over to Daud, carrying a shield and a bow. Daud held back, but Qutuz caught his eye and nodded.

"You may need this. Take it."

The armorer held up the shield, a great heavy dish of wood and metal; Daud needed both hands to hold it, and he slid his left arm through the leather loops on the back and held onto the saddlebow with his left hand to keep the shield up against his shoulder. That meant he could not use the bow, but he didn't need to, being up on this hill. He hung the bow and the case of arrows on the right side of his saddle.

Rikart had told Qutuz to watch over him, and the Sultan was doing that, keeping Daud close by, stirrup to stirrup. His hand fell on Daud's shoulder. "See how they are coming at us. They'll try to get around the end of our line, encircle us—that's what the Ghost said they would do. But the hills here will keep them in front of us, see?" He pointed. "They will have to come at us, and that will bring them within our reach."

Daud saw what he meant; the line of the Mamelukes ran across the valley's mouth from slope to slope. Qutuz's hand rested on his shoulder still. Qutuz said, "See how Baibers is leading his men up. He is a master at this. His men follow him anywhere." He smoothed down his moustaches with his fingers. "The squints are still hours away, I think, though."

The enormous mass of men coming south had slowed down. Daud licked his lips. In the haze of distance the oncoming army seemed a single river that churned and eddied, every piece moving separately and yet all part of one motion, flowing across the flat ground toward them. They seemed to eat up the ground as they came. Qutuz was frowning at them.

"Maybe sooner than that." He gave a little shake of his head, and turned, and looked out over his own army.

Daud said nothing. One of the two flagmen brought the Sultan a flask, and a round of bread; Qutuz took the flask and waved the bread toward Daud. The servant held it up to him, a flat loaf, its crust brown and crisp, and he was suddenly ravenously hungry; he tore off a piece and stuffed it into his mouth.

* * * *

Nikola lounged in his saddle, half-asleep in the baking sun; around him his arban told jokes and fiddled with their bows and stared bored into the distance. A horn blew, and he sat up. Kitboqa was riding at a gallop along the front of the Mongol line, his flag bearers streaming after him. Nikola gathered up his reins. He gave a quick look from left to right, seeing his arban pull even with him, and the rest of the army stretching off beyond and behind him. A hot bolt of excitement passed through him. He faced forward, where the slaves were packed into their valley, a single solid target.

Out there Kitboqa was going up with his flags and messengers on a low rise. The flags began to wave. Nikola could see riders on the hill above the slave army, in among the trees there. Maybe more fighters moving in. Do this fast, he thought. The horns blew again, and he looked toward Kitboqa, but the ground was too low and he could not read the flags. But the horns were blowing. His body burned. Up there at the end of the enemy army, he saw the blue coats he had been chasing all day. Good enough, he thought. And charged.

\* \* \* \*

Daud let out a yell. From the hilltop he could see all across the low ground. Down there the great swarm of the Mongols was hurtling forward, closing the gap between them and the Mamelukes. Qutuz, under his breath, was muttering orders nobody else could hear— "Steady! Steady, now—shoot!" Arrows in a wave rose out of the Mameluke line and pounded the Mongols, who wheeled, all together, and shot back.

Daud clutched his saddlebows. His mouth was dry and his heart pounded. He saw how the center of the Mameluke line swayed and buckled, and the Mongols in their undulating mass swarmed toward them. Screams rose like threads of sound. At the far end of the line, the blue coats of the Bahriyya were shifting toward the center, which stiffened, and stood fast, and then, the Mongols were surging away again, all one great massive animal, back onto the flat ground.

In the space they left behind, the air filmy with dust, bodies sprawled and thrashed. A man staggered up and ran a few steps and collapsed again. A horse galloped aimlessly along the line. The long mass of the Mamelukes churned with people moving up and back. They were carrying off bodies. Daud shaded his eyes. Someone caught the loose horse and threw a body over the saddle and led it away. The blue coats seemed fewer. They didn't reach the foot of the far hill anymore. He shivered all over, although the sun beat down on him. His mind was stuck, he could think no level thought. And now the Mongols were charging again.

\* \* \* \*

Baibers' horse danced under him; he was in the front line of the Bah-riyya, his men all around him, like a wall. He whipped another arrow onto the bowstring and shot into the dark swarm hurtling toward him. Before he could nock another, their arrows pelted down on him. His horse reared up. He kicked his stirrups loose, gripped his bow and two arrows, and as the mare went down he leapt to the ground. The horse thrashed in the dirt and he shrank back away from her, and the horse on his other side suddenly bolted, riderless. All around him his men raised their bows again. He shot. He was standing alone, suddenly. He looked around and saw bodies on the ground. The man nearest him on his left fell.

His horse had stopped beating the air with her hoofs and lay still. Arrows stuck up out of her shoulder, her neck. He lunged into the shelter of her body. His arrow case was on the saddle and he groped for it. Across the mare's back he saw the oncoming Mongols like a dark wave. The arrows burst through the dust like a thousand moving points. Dirt sprayed his hand. They were on him, they were on him. He huddled against the dead mare as horses bounded over him. Under him the ground trembled. Dirt in his mouth, in his eyes. The thunder of the hoofs was like a great storm passing overhead. God did not send me here to die. The crash and pound of the charge faded. They had gone by. He lifted his head, and saw around him a carpeting of blue coats. Looking the other way, he saw the Mongols, back on the plain, regrouping.

He lurched to his feet. A stray horse galloped past. The rest of the Mameluke army still stood on the flat ground before him and he staggered toward them. Ahead of him another man was trying to rise. Baibers got him by the arm and hauled him to his feet, and together they hobbled back to their own lines.

Out there, the Mongols were charging again. But now he saw what how to do this. He cast a quick glance toward Qutuz, on the hill, hoping he would see it too. God follow me, he thought, and looked around him for a horse.

* *

Rikart's horse had gone lame. On foot, the lance over his shoulder, he led it to the crest of the hill and stopped. He did not look over his shoulder at the city guard of Nablus. He knew many of them had given up, back there on the stony slope, and fallen away.

He ran his hands over the horse; it stood with its left foreleg stretched out, only the toe of the hoof touching the ground. Its head drooped. When he bent to lift the horse's hoof up it groaned, protesting. He cupped the battered hoof in his palms and pressed his thumbs against the heel and the horse shuddered.

The boy who had been jabbering at Rikart all day started in again.

"The Mongols are Christians, aren't they. You're a crosskisser. You're working for them."

Rikart set the hoof back on the ground. His body felt like a unreal case around him; he went forward to where the hill turned down again.

He could hear the fighting now, far down there through the screen of the trees, the surging rumble of the horses, the screaming, but he could see little. Dashes of motion, of color. The dust hung in the air, and above that, swaying in great circles through the sky, were the vultures. He ached with all his being to be down there, as if the best part of him were already there.

He went back to his horse for the water jug, and faced them, clumped together on the ground before their horses, grim-faced. There were only six of them now. He tipped the lance against his saddle and drank from the jug.

"Why should we follow you any farther? You're a traitor. You're a curse."

"Go, then," Rikart said. "Leave me your horse."

The boy shot to his feet. "I'll see you die first. I'll see you dead for what you've done to my brother." He put his hand to the hilt of his sword.

Rikart stood away from his horse, his hands at his sides. "Give me the horse, or I'll take it. I don't want to hurt you." He wanted to seize the boy in his hands and tear him to pieces. Everything in him yearned toward the battle, a tidal pull.

The boy drew his sword out. By the way he held it Rikart knew he had never fought with it. Rikart made no move toward a weapon; he would not need a weapon. The boy took a step forward, jabbing at him with the sword, and Rikart took a step to one side.

One of the others reached out and grabbed the boy by the sleeve. "Ayyub, give him the horse."

The boy threw his head back, red-faced. "What! Ali==He's a traitor— he's a filthy cross-kisser!"

"He's about to kill you, idiot." The man who had spoken got to his feet. "Give him the horse. You can walk back to Nablus." He went to his own mount and gathered the reins. Silently the other men followed him. Rikart started toward the armored horse beside Ayyub; he watched Ayyub's eyes, not the sword the boy still waved menacingly in front of him. Ayyub stood his ground, but his gaze faltered, and at the last moment he backed up. Rikart took his horse by the bridle and led it forward and vaulted into the saddle.

The man who had spoken for him rode up stirrup to stirrup with him. "Lead us. We've come this far."

Rikart saluted him. Turning the cataphract's horse, he rode past his own, and picked the lance up, and rode over the brow of the hill.

Ahead, a roar of voices rose, a thunder of hoofs. Through the trees, he saw horsemen rushing into the low ground. He nudged the horse on, pushing on down the slope, and the battle like a wave of heat rose up to meet him.

* *

Daud looked around him; there were many more men gathered here than before. Qutuz was riding back and forth among them, talking. Daud braced his hands on his saddle and looked out toward the plain.

The hair rose all over his head. The Mongols were swooping on again. They weren't attacking the center of the line now. They were crowding toward the end, toward the last few blue coats of the Bahriyya, pouring toward the gap between them and the distant hillside. Daud swallowed, and clutched his reins; he was shaking all over. Down there the Bahriyya disappeared under the hoofs of the Mongols, and the Mongols swarmed into the gap they left, and the arrows stitched the air.

Qutuz gave a hoarse cry, and pulled his long saber out of his sash.

"Follow me," he cried; he swung around to sweep a look behind him, at the gathered Mamelukes. "Now will we conquer, in God's name!" He turned forward and his voice roared like a lion.

"My Islam!" He raised the saber over his head and launched his horse straight down the slope before them. "My Islam!"

Daud's horse was moving even before Daud kicked it on. He shrugged the shield up on his arm and followed Qutuz, and all the Mamelukes came after.

Within three strides they were hurtling down the hill at full gallop toward the fighting. Daud drew even with Qutuz, one of a wave of men, all screaming. He realized he was screaming. Through the boiling yellow dust he saw Qutuz's sword stretched up like a banner staff and he pressed close to that. He could not get his bow out of the case. They reached the flat ground and pounded on, striking into the rear of the Mongol army, and from the sky ahead of them there came a deluge. Daud huddled behind the shield. Arrows pelted on the shield like hail. Qutuz galloped up ahead of him, and on the Sultan's heels, he plunged forward, standing in his stirrups, the reins loose in his hands. The horse's body thrust and bounded under him. All around him men were screaming, not words, only shrieks like banners of sounds above the pounding of hoofs. Ahead, he saw a dark shifting mass—the enemy army. Another tide of arrows beat down on him. Qutuz was turning, moving left, toward the enemy. Something stabbed in Daud's arm. Ahead of him, suddenly, the sword disappeared.

He sat back, startled, slowing his horse, and through the dust saw Qutuz's horse thrashing on the ground. Qutuz rose up from the dirt there in front of him. Daud reined toward him, and stretched one arm out, and the Sultan gripped his forearm and vaulted up behind him. Daud's horse staggered a moment. Caught its balance again. Qutuz was roaring in Daud's ear. The horse swept on, its head stretched out, its ears flat. Daud hid behind the shield. All around him the dust moved and shook, full of galloping horses like phantoms. Qutuz was shouting again. Waving the sword overhead. He reached around Daud for the reins, and bent the horse leftward again. Daud held tight with his legs. The horse switched leads, stumbled, caught itself. He lost his stirrups and came up out of the saddle and the man behind him held him down again. They were slowing. Ahead of them the tree-covered hill rose up, gilded in the sunlight. On the first little rise Qutuz reined in and they stopped.

The Sultan bellowed, triumphant. "God is great! Thanks and praises to God!"

Daud looked behind him; the mass of the Mameluke army stretched away in a long curve behind him. He could not see where the Mongols were. A wave of arrows rose from the Mamelukes, aimed into the trough between the hills. Daud shrank down behind the shield. His sleeve was bloody. An arrow had bitten through his shield and the long iron head was tearing at his arm.

"On," Qutuz was bellowing, with wild swoops of his arms. "On! God rides with us! On!" Mamelukes streamed by him at a dead gallop into the low ground.

Then he saw that the Mamelukes were all shooting ahead of them, into the valley, so that was where the Mongols were. Trapped. Daud shivered. He thought of Baghdad. Of the roof collapsing in Baghdad. One of Qutuz's flagmen rode up toward him, clutching the other flagman up against his horse; reaching the Sultan he let go, and the other man slumped to the ground and coughed blood. Daud's stomach heaved. He shut his eyes, which only made it worse.

* * * *

Nikola wheeled his horse, but there was nowhere to go. Around him the green hills loomed up and the Mamelukes were shooting at him from all sides. He had made a mistake. Trampling over the last of the blue coats, he had let the rest of the Mamelukes get behind him, and now he and most of the Mongols were caught in the narrow low ground.

A plunging horse slammed into him and his horse half-reared. The men around him milled, confused. Arrows showered down on him. Zuchi rode up beside him, shouting something Nikola could not hear. Back the way they had come, the Mamelukes were surging across the open ground, penning them in tighter.

That stretched the slave army's line. There were far fewer of them than before and between the end of their line and the hillside was a way out. Nikola plunged toward it. Get through there, into the open, regroup, and attack again. He flung his arm up, summoning any man who could see him, and galloped toward the open ground. Zuchi rode ahead of him. They hurtled through sheets of arrows. His horse stumbled and slammed down hard, and Nikola leapt off. When he landed his leg buckled and he went to his knees. He looked down and to his surprise saw an arrow in his thigh. Zuchi had turned, was riding back toward him, his mouth open, shouting words lost in the screaming and the pounding of hoofs. Nikola staggered to his feet, Zuchi three strides away, and then an arrow struck Zuchi in the throat and another in the chest and he slid down into the dust.

Nikola caught his horse by the bridle and  dragged himself into the saddle. He had kept hold of his bow, and he had one arrow left and he nocked it. He wheeled around, raising his arm again, and charged again toward the gap in the Mameluke line.

The slaves swung toward him, but he was a stride ahead of them. The open plain lay before him. He bolted toward it.

Then from the woods there burst a pack of heavy armored men. The sun shimmered on their metal chests, their metal-shrouded horses. Nikola drew his bow. A man in a white tunic, a red cross splayed on his chest, hurtled toward him behind a lance. He shot straight into that cross, but the lance took him through the chest and he was gone.

\* \*

The vultures were circling, lower with each pass. Night was coming on and the heat of the day was fading. The smell of blood hung in the air like a foul mist.

Qutuz led the way along the low ground; the bodies lay so thick here he had to let his horse pick a slow way through them. Baibers came up beside him, filthy, slack with exhaustion, his face fierce with triumph.

"A great victory. God has given us a great victory."

Qutuz's chest swelled. He knew this was so. His blood was on fire, his whole body hot. Exalted. He glanced at the boy riding beside him, and saw him pale as a girl.

Yet he had saved him. Maybe saved them all. Baibers was right, the child came from God.

Most of his men had drawn back onto the plain, but some few were moving out among the fallen Mongols, rifling through their clothes, killing any who still lived. As the Sultan approached, they straightened, all around the field, and gave a cheer; they waved their arms, and pushed toward him, shouting his name and whooping.

He gave a wide look around, wondering how many men he had lost. God would welcome them, he thought. For this God would lift them up into Paradise. He leaned from his saddle, reaching his hand out to these men God had touched.

"Qutuz!" they were screaming. They walked along beside him, cheering and leaning toward him, their hands stretched out. "Qutuz!"

"Glory to God," he cried back. "God is great!"

Up ahead was a band of loose horses, Arab mares and the shaggy short-legged Mongol horses, herding together. Startled, he saw among them a great horse, caparisoned from head to tail in metal. He remembered the cataphracts Baibers had sent out across the valley.

Then the boy cried out.

He leapt down from his horse, ran forward, and threw himself on a body on the ground. Beside Qutuz, Baibers said, in Kipchak, "God's breath." The dead man there was the Frankish knight they called the Ghost.

He lay sprawled on his face in a puddle of blood; his back was a welter of blood. The boy was sobbing over him, calling his name.

Qutuz said, "Isn't that the knight you sent in some opposite direction?" He wiped his hand over his face. The look on Baibers' face amused him. "How did he come to be here?"

Baibers said, "He is in the hands of God now. He served God, who will forgive him his sins."

Qutuz laughed. "I'm sure the seventy virgins won't be lost on him." He rode forward, and bending down from his saddle drew the boy up to his feet.

"He is dead, boy. We will bury him—" They would have to bury them all, somehow. "You are one of us now. Do him honor with your life in God's service."

The boy never looked at him. Shrugged him off. Qutuz watched him walk slowly away across the battlefield, small among the dead. A sudden shudder went through the Sultan of Egypt. His gaze wandered over the field of the dead, taking in again how great a victory this was.

God's victory. Not his. God only used him. He felt something huge shifting around him, some monstrous reordering of the world. The boy was already out of sight in the confusion. Qutuz's skin crawled. He wondered what he had actually done here, what would come of this. He looked around him again, at all the dead men, and his gaze came to Baibers, staring back at him, unblinking.

\* \* \* \*

The ghost rises. He has died before, although he never remembers. He returns up from the wreak of the dead, above the holy, blood-soaked land, doomed to its endless war. No one ever wins here. This place is never still. This is the heart of the world, always churning. Trapped in this eddy, the ghost flies again to Baghdad, to try once more to save Reb Moseh.

# NOTE

Since earliest history the Middle East had been the heart of the world, where three continents came together and the great trade routes all met. Through the trading cities of the Mediterranean coast, silk and gold, ivory and spices traveled from all over the world into Europe. If the Mongols had won the battle of Ain Jalut, they would have kept those routes open: trade was their wealth. But they lost.

On the way back to Egypt from Ain Jalut, Baibers murdered Qutuz and made himself Sultan. He devoted the rest of his life to rooting out the Christians, and he leveled the cities of the Levant. The Venetians kept open a trading post in Constantinople, but the trade into Europe began to dwindle.

75 years after Ain Jalut, through the Venetian port on the Black Sea came one more great product: the Black Death, which killed half of Christendom. But the thirst remained among Europeans for the riches of the East. By the time the Turks took Constantinople in 1453, the Europeans were already looking for other ways to gain those luxuries. Barred from the Middle East, they sailed around Africa, and established the sea routes, and they sailed west to reach the east, and made the world one. And the Heart of the World became a backwater.

Made in the USA
Las Vegas, NV
17 December 2020

13893059R10153